The Wild Adventures of Doc Savage

Please visit www.adventuresinbronze.com for
more information on titles you may have missed.

PYTHON ISLE
THE FORGOTTEN REALM
THE DESERT DEMONS
HORROR IN GOLD
THE INFERNAL BUDDHA
DEATH'S DARK DOMAIN
SKULL ISLAND
THE MIRACLE MENACE
THE ICE GENIUS
THE WAR MAKERS

(Don't miss another original Doc Savage adventure coming soon.)

PHANTOM LAGOON

A DOC SAVAGE ADVENTURE

BY WILL MURRAY & LESTER DENT
WRITING AS KENNETH ROBESON

COVER BY JOE DeVITO

ALTUS PRESS • 2013

First Edition — December 2013

DESIGNED BY
Matthew Moring/Altus Press

SPECIAL THANKS TO
*James Bama, Jerry Birenz, Nicholas Cain, Condé Nast,
Jeff Deischer, Dafydd Neal Dyar, Chuck Juzek, Dave McDonnell,
Matthew Moring, Ray Riethmeier, Howard Wright,
The State Historical Society of Missouri, and last but not least,
the Heirs of Norma Dent—James Valbracht, John Valbracht,
Wayne Valbracht, Shirley Dungan and Doris Leimkuehler.*

COVER ILLUSTRATION COMMISSIONED BY
Terry Allen

Like us on Facebook: "The Wild Adventures of Doc Savage"

Printed in the United States of America

Set in Caslon.

For Walter M. Baumhofer, the first
artist to paint the Man of Bronze—

He set a standard for excellence his successors
still strive to achieve eighty years later....

Phantom Lagoon

Table of Contents

Chapter I

GIRL OFF AN ISLE

A **WISE MAN** once observed that trouble has walked around in skirts since the beginning of things.

This particular wise man did not proclaim such a thing in so many words, but every man knows it to be true. Particularly seamen understand this, just as they know to batten down their hatches and furl sail when the wind strengthens and becomes strange.

It was around noon in the Caribbean when the liner *Amberjack* happened upon the little wart of a cay with the troublesome girl on it.

The *Amberjack* was one of those dazzlingly white ships that ply the Caribbean Sea looking like a floating castle built of polished seashells. Her passengers were invariably tourists. In the expensive brochures that were used to entice the public to part with their hard-earned money in return for a five-day passage from New York City to Port of Spain, Trinidad, with port stops in Haiti, Barbados, Havana and Port Charles, romance was hinted. Sometimes, it was found.

The *Amberjack* was on her return leg when she passed the isle. It was a clear day. A few lost-lamb clouds plodded across the too-blue sky. There was a breeze that smelled of salt and sand. The placid Caribbean Sea was a cerulean hue that might have been associated with the Afterlife.

The cay was a low stretch of white sand off to port, crowned with a few shaggy-headed palm trees. Sultry breezes shook their leafy skulls like Hula dancers calling sailors ashore.

In the crow's nest, the lookout suddenly shouted, "Cap'n, ahoy! A distress signal on that island!"

The lookout couldn't see the girl, and so was not in a position to reflect on the recorded opinions of wise men in regards to skirted trouble.

The liner captain ordered engines stopped, and a small regulation dory was put off. Its outboard motor toiled noisily as it headed for the isle to investigate the distress signal.

"Probably some Carib native playing a prank," muttered the First Mate, who understood that the laws of the sea required that the signal be looked into. It was a stretch of the Caribbean that saw no fishing boats, few pleasure craft and only a passing liner now and again.

As the dory drew near the isle, it could be seen that in addition to the drooping coconut palms, there was a little coral honeycombing the cay. But not much.

A figure stood on the white beach waiting for them. The figure was indistinct under the brassy sun, but it seemed to have its hands planted purposefully on its hips. It also stood next to the distress signal—a ragged skirt flapping atop a pole and planted in the white sand.

That was where the skirt came into the picture.

The skirt-pennant made the First Mate sit up at attention. He had the requisite sailor's interest in the opposite sex. He adjusted his black tie.

As the dory beat closer, the indistinct figure lost its indistinctness.

"Split my keel!" the First Mate exploded. "It's a dame!"

The others sailors grew interested then.

THEY ran the dory onto the white sands, cutting the engine in the last few yards of turquoise water so the propeller would not have to fight the granular stuff.

The sliding keel made a brief grating sound, stopped. They piled out and dragged it the last several feet onto dry land, where it promptly leaned over like a drunken boatswain. The dory crew were themselves looking a little unsteady as they approached the one they had come to rescue.

It was a girl. No doubt about it. Clad only in a kerchief bra and a pair of ragged shorts. She was a blonde—tall, with some excellent curves of a kind not usually seen in tall girls. She had a thin nose and a rather grim mouth. Standing there with her mouth and her arms folded impatiently, she was enwrapped in an attitude that suggested anything but what she appeared to be—a marooned beachcomber.

"About time you mugs showed up," she said tartly.

This comment took them off-guard. As far as they knew, they were not expected.

Yet it was obvious that she was alone on the cay. The hump of sand and jungle was that small. There appeared to be no sign of a boat, wrecked or otherwise.

"How long have you been here?" the First Mate wondered, noticing her sunburned and peeling features.

"Two weeks."

"Anyone else with you?"

"No."

"Lady," exclaimed the First Mate, "you mean to say that you have been living on this dab of an island—all alone?"

The blonde girl at once showed she was inclined to answer no questions. "Listen, stupid!" she snapped. "If you're gonna rescue me, then rescue me—and don't ask fool questions."

The *Amberjack* crew swapped befuddled looks. Probably half of them had at one time or another fantasized about rescuing a castaway as fetching as this one.

This was not how they envisioned the reality of it. Their faces soon grew long with disappointment. They wore them that way even as they helped the girl into the dory and all during the trip back to the liner.

WHEN the blonde castaway was safely aboard the liner, her attitude did not noticeably improve.

"How I got on that blasted island," she informed the Captain almost before he could put to her a complete question, "is my own business. And I'll settle it myself—don't think I won't!"

"You might at least give your name," the nonplussed Captain said.

The blonde put her hands on her hips, stuck her pert chin in the air, and snapped, "Listen! That's my business! Now will one of these white-coated stiffs show me to my cabin, or do I pick one for myself?"

The First Mate showed the willful young woman to an empty cabin on a lower deck, upon which she promptly slammed the door on his face and locked herself in.

"If there is anything we can get you, Miss—" the First Mate began to say.

The girl's tart voice came through the door. "Three things. Food. Privacy. And something to read."

A well-rounded meal and a stack of newspapers arrived within twenty minutes, on separate trays. The steward was instructed to leave them outside the cabin door and after he had departed, the trays were claimed. The ship's skipper provided these amenities for sound business reasons. He knew the kind of publicity that would greet the *Amberjack* once it docked in Manhattan. In fact, he radioed ahead to the home office so that this would be arranged for.

Nothing more was heard from the cabin for the rest of the day. The incident had to be reported to the maritime authorities, of course. Inquiries as to the castaway's identity crossed via ship-to-shore radio in both directions. The upshot was, no one seemed to have lost a tall, shapely blonde with a thin nose and even thinner patience.

It was a deep mystery, and naturally it was the talk of the *Amberjack* passengers and crew as she steamed north to the United States.

The liner published its own newspaper, a modest thing not much larger than a Broadway program guide. The next morning's edition was headlined:

BLONDE MYSTERY GAL RESCUED
OFF TROPIC ISLAND

REFUSES TO EXPLAIN HOW SHE GOT THERE

The story below was remarkably bare of facts.

A copy was delivered to the erstwhile castaway's cabin as a courtesy, and she had not had it more than two minutes when she came storming out of her cabin, leaving her breakfast eggs and toast untouched.

She was now clad in a rather sporty ensemble that had been contributed by a sympathetic passenger, and made a fetching sight as she bowled down the promenade deck, chin lifted with an air of leave-me-alone. Heads turned, naturally. A few passengers called after her. She ignored them pointedly, found the captain's office and burst in with all the quietude of a blonde typhoon.

"What's the meaning of this?" she demanded of the Captain, flinging the paper at his immaculate uniform front. "Can't a gal have any privacy on this tub?"

The Captain ignored the outburst and said in a reasonable voice, "We have had inquiries, miss. No one seems to know who you are."

"Listen! I've told you that's my business! And I aim to keep it that way!"

The skipper looked pained. "Could you at least give us something to call you?"

The blonde fixed him with a baleful blue eye. "If I give you a name, will you leave me out of your silly shipboard rag?"

"I can arrange that, yes," the Captain allowed.

"Call me Henrietta."

The Captain looked disappointed. "No last name?"

"That wasn't in our agreement," the blonde snapped. "Next time get it in writing." And with that, the salty castaway calling herself Henrietta stormed off.

She got several paces, halted, and snapped sunburned fingers sharply.

"Dammit! I meant to ask where and when this tub will put into port."

Her sun-inflamed face twisted and softened. "I know. I'll just mingle with the *hoi-polloi.*" And with that, Henrietta made a very determined beeline for the nearest unoccupied deck chair.

This drew attention.

"Are you the gal off the island?" a smiling Joe College type in a sleeveless varsity sweater asked in passing.

"What if I am?" snapped Henrietta, lip curling.

"Ah, I was just making conversation."

"Come back when you've grown into your long pants, sonny boy," the girl said acidly.

Abashed, the college boy betook himself away.

A very snappily dressed gentleman tried to board the blonde windjammer next.

"Hello, babe!" he called cheerily.

"G'wan! Scram!" growled the brazen blonde.

The would-be swain sought more agreeable companionship.

Others attempted to engage Henrietta in conversation, but to no avail. She put them all off. Even the sportiest guys on the ship couldn't pick her up. She ignored them all.

There was a magazine on a table beside the deck chair and she snapped it up, burying her thin nose in it. Idly, she paged through the periodical, looking up every so often.

Whenever a passing male caught her eye, she abruptly lifted the magazine by way of discouragement. They invariably moved on.

Passing women brought a different reaction. Henrietta attempted to catch their eye. Contrarily, they hurried along.

"My reputation must have preceded me," she muttered to herself.

Finally, a woman possessing more nerve—or perhaps a larger than usual curiosity bump—than the others came and claimed an empty lounge chair across the promenade deck.

Henrietta lowered her magazine and asked, "Where is this ark bound, anyway?"

"Manhattan. Did no one tell you?"

"Forgot to ask." And Henrietta buried her head in the magazine as a pointed inducement to be left to her sulking.

At one point, she began muttering under her breath, "I gotta pay them mugs back—but how?"

The nearby woman looked interested. "Eh?"

"Nothing."

Henrietta had not been reading very far when she came upon an article that was entitled:

"MODERN GALAHAD SLAYS DRAGONS OF TODAY
WITH BRAIN AND BRAWN"

Sunburned brows puckering, Henrietta narrowed her eyes and read along.

Abruptly, she threw the magazine up in the air and yelled, "Yippee! I've got it! Clark Savage is the man who can help me!"

"Got what?" asked the other woman.

"Nothing. Never mind."

"Did I just hear you mention Doc Savage?"

"Who is Doc Savage?" asked Henrietta with what appeared to be genuine puzzlement.

"You don't look old enough to have been stuck on that island quite that long, dearie."

"Same to you, I'm sure," Henrietta said huffily. "So who is he?"

"Merely the marvel man of the century," Henrietta was told.

"A big shot, eh?"

"That is a vulgar way of putting it," the other returned with more than a trace of frost.

Taking the magazine, Henrietta got up and went in search of an officer. By sheer luck, she happened to cross the path of the First Mate who had rescued her.

"Are Clark Savage, Jr., and Doc Savage one and the same person?" she asked without either salutation or preamble.

"Yes," admitted the First Mate. "I believe so."

"Where can he be contacted?" asked Henrietta.

The First Mate laughed. "Don't tell me you've got trouble for Doc Savage to crack! Savage makes a business of other people's troubles, you know."

"Where can he be contacted?" Henrietta repeated stiffly.

The First Mate lost his laugh as if he dropped it and the article had shattered underfoot.

"We dock in New York in a few hours. You can look him up when we put in. Doc Savage operates out of that city."

"Point me to the radio room," ordered the blonde bombshell.

The First Mate offered to show her the way, but Henrietta put him off with a curt, "I can navigate without assistance, thank you."

The First Mate gave succinct instructions to the radio room, and went off to nurse his wounded male pride.

HENRIETTA marched into the radio room, snatched up a blank and began writing.

"Send this and make it snappy," she said, slapping the yellow flimsy onto the countertop. "Collect."

The radio operator glanced at the message and saw the name of Doc Savage. He whistled in surprise.

"That Savage is quite a guy from what I hear," said the radio operator expansively. He had a fresh, innocent face and Henrietta decided she could motivate him faster with hand-wringing than scorn.

"Can you send the message right away?" Henrietta asked anxiously.

"No reason why not," said the operator. "Funny thing. This Doc Savage is a man known all over the world as the guy to go to if you've got big trouble. When I was in Africa on my last ship, I heard talk of Doc Savage. Believe it or not, the guy is as well known there as he is over here. He's sure got a reputation. Know him personally?"

"Only by repute," said Henrietta.

"I saw Doc Savage's picture once," the operator volunteered. "He is a giant of a man, his skin bronzed by the sun."

"You don't say."

"It was in an electrical engineering trade journal. Doc had discovered something new about the nature of atomic forces."

"This fellow suffers no flies to alight on his collar, now does he?" Henrietta said dryly.

"Doc Savage," the radio operator said with grave sincerity, "will probably be remembered two or three thousand years from today."

"You," she shot back, "just remember to send my radiogram!"

With that, the brassy blonde flounced out of the radio shack.

Chapter II

LANDFALL

THE ADVENT OF of the pleasure liner *Amberjack* was the occasion of great excitement along New York City's steamship docks. Long before Gotham tugs nudged their blunt tire-fendered snouts alongside the gleaming ivory gem of the Atlantic, reporters began showing up in anticipation of her arrival.

The reason was evident in the bulldog editions the reporters and camera boys clutched, still warm from the heat of the presses.

Proclaimed one:

MAROONED BLONDE DUE IN GOTHAM

Wondered a second sheet:

WHO IS MYSTERY CASTAWAY?

Screamed another:

CASTAWAY GAL REFUSES TO TALK!

The assembled representatives of the press were in hopes of changing that last headline. They jostled rubbernecking Manhattanites who jumped up on tiptoe with each blast from the nearing tugs.

It was a pleasant Autumn day in November. Not as pleasant as the Caribbean had been on the previous night, but for New York, it was as splendid as the city got.

The crowd grew, swelled as, at about the point the sheer numbers of the assembled threatened to push those on the outer edges of the South Street Seaport wharves into the dingy waters of the East River, the liner hove into view.

That was the cue for the police—who were out in force—to take up their nightsticks and begin to push the crowds back so the dock workers could prepare to receive the giant ship.

She was speedily made fast, the *Amberjack's* horn gave a final blast of relief and the gangplank was set in place.

The Captain himself escorted the blonde girl—who was still clad in her rather loud and revealing sport ensemble—to the top of the gangway and unhooked the chain so that she could disembark.

"There she is!" shouted one reporter.

"That's the gal they found on the island!" barked another.

Instantly, flash bulbs popped, were ejected and new bulbs inserted to be ignited and discarded as fast as the cameras could be worked. Newsreel cameras ground busily.

"That's her!" the crowd began shouting.

"Boy," said one scribe. "I wouldn't mind being marooned with something like *that!*"

"Hey, sis!" shouted a photographer. "I'm from the *Daily Comet*. How about a li'l picture?"

The blistered blonde covered up her face to prevent her picture being taken and started down the gangplank.

"We want an interview!" yelled a reporter.

"How about a statement for the press?"

The girl did not pause when she reached the foot of the gangplank. She was hard-boiled and in a hurry.

"Scram!" she snapped. "All you newspaper mugs!"

"Come on, lady—say something. This is the press."

"Go peddle your papers!" Henrietta flung back.

The excited newshawks jostled closer. There was not much choice involved in the matter. The surrounding crowds, eager to catch a glimpse of the mysterious castaway, were pressing in. A catastrophe impended.

No doubt a tragedy would have taken place had not the police intervened. Whistles shrilled. A wall of blue, festooned with brass buttons, surrounded the girl. When it surged, she moved with the push.

Thus was the blonde girl escorted to the first in a line of waiting taxis idling nearby.

"Thanks," she bit out as a copper opened the passenger door for her convenience.

"Think nothing of it," the cop replied, touching his cap politely. "What did you say your name was, miss?"

"I didn't," sniffed the blonde, slamming the door.

To the taxi driver, she said, "Take me to Doc Savage's hangout. And make it snappy."

This was overheard by the officers of the law. When the cab departed in haste, they declined to follow, as was their plan. If the mystery blonde had business with Doc Savage, it was no business of theirs. For Doc Savage held an honorary commission with the Manhattan police, and they were under strict orders to defer to the bronze man in matters such as this.

As they trudged back to the crowd with the firm intent of breaking it up, one officer was heard to mutter, "What I wouldn't give to be Doc Savage for just one day. Imagine! Having a fetching thing like that come all the way from the Caribbean to ask for my help."

"She might have been fetching, but she had herself a sharp enough tongue," another bluecoat observed candidly.

A MAN who had been crouching inside a waterfront warehouse door, waited for the cab to get out of sight. He was a tall, thin-faced individual wearing an expensive tan hat with a snap brim, tan shoes and kid gloves of excellent quality. The rest of him was obscured in a rust-colored overcoat. His face was also obscured—by a handkerchief. The handkerchief—he was holding it to his face—was a big loose thing of pearl-gray silk, and it prevented much being discerned about his features.

The well-dressed man spun suddenly and ran back into the warehouse, to a dark corner where another man lurked at a knot hole that overlooked the pier at which the *Amberjack* lay docked.

"It was that she-hornet!" he barked.

The man at the knot hole spun. His face was a dim shape in the poor light. He remained in the shadows, as would one accustomed to doing so by force of habit. All that could be discerned of him was his shirt. It was a rich chocolate brown. "You sure of that, Pippel?"

"Positive."

"What the hell is she doin' here?"

"Must've got rescued," growled Pippel, letting the handkerchief fall from his face.

"But why would she come to New York?"

Pippel said, "Only one answer to that. She's wise! The question is: what are we gonna do about it?"

"Only one answer to that, too," said the one at the knot hole grimly.

"You're probably right. You stay here. I'm gonna follow the girl."

Pippel ran on to a side door of the warehouse, slipped outdoors, and piled into a small green sedan. The car pitched over ruts and took the turn into the street on two wheels.

There is quite a fleet of taxi cabs prowling the island of Manhattan, each with its own distinctive livery. The cab hired by the blonde castaway happened to be one of the more rare types. It sported a ghastly two-toned blue paint job, and this was easily found and overhauled.

"Let's see where she goes," the man called Pippel muttered under his breath.

IN the two-toned taxi, the blonde, peering out the back window warily, said, "Step on it, driver!"

"Lady," said the driver, "they got a speed limit in this town!"

Then came a stream of sulfurous words from the otherwise delectable lips of the blonde so blistering that the driver bore down on the gas pedal as if in hope of outrunning them.

The taxi made good time. The driver barely had opportunity to peer into his mirror to examine his unusual passenger. A stoplight afforded him his first opportunity.

The girl had her head turned completely around and her sun-blistered nose all but pressed against the rear window.

"See that green sedan?" she said suddenly.

"Yeah."

"He's tailing me."

"Must be press. Them guys stick like glue."

"Lose him."

"What about Doc Savage?"

"What I have to tell Doc Savage is between him and me," snapped the blonde. "And I don't need any nosy reporter butting in. Get me?"

The driver did. When the light changed, he began cutting in and out of traffic and got to work on losing the green sedan.

Finally, by detouring to Brooklyn, he did.

"How's that for service?" the driver beamed into the rear-vision mirror.

"If you're expecting a big tip, don't," the blonde said tartly.

The taxi driver's long face fell. "Why not?" he demanded, rather bluntly.

"I just came off a desert isle, buster. I ain't even got a seashell in my pocket."

"Does that mean you can't pay the fare?" the jehu asked unhappily.

"I am," the blonde retorted, "down to my last clam."

This admission did not sit well with the cab driver. He promptly pulled over, got out and flung open the rear door. He cocked an angry thumb over his uniform shoulder.

"Out," he snapped.

The blonde folded her sunburned arms.

"Make me," she said in a defiant voice.

"Believe me, blondie, I will," the cabby averred. "And I have just enough experience with fare beaters like you to make it stick."

"If you knew who I was," the blonde said, "you wouldn't talk to me that way."

The cabby was insistent. "I don't care if you're Amelia Earhart come back from the Great Unknown. Out!"

The blonde made stubborn faces. The cabby stood his ground.

Finally, the grim girl stepped out of the cab, seized the taximan by the point of his nose and gave it a painful twist.

It wasn't exactly judo, but it had the same effect. The cabby let out a pained howl and found himself staring at assorted stars and colored comets. He went down.

Came the *clunk* of a car door shutting, followed by another.

When the cabby regained normal vision, he was watching his hack depart the vicinity.

The green sedan pulled up not long afterward. A man leaned out of the driver's window and asked, "You look like a guy who's been gotten the best of by a blonde."

"You can say that again, brother. First she tries to beat me out of the fare. Then she steals my hack."

"Where was she headed?"

"Back to the city. If you're after her, how about a ride?"

The man in the green sedan might have heard the request. On the other hand, he might not have. In any case, he took off in the general direction of the Brooklyn Bridge.

EVIDENTLY, Pippel knew this section of Brooklyn, for he presumed the girl would, after a suitable interval to ensure that she had shaken all pursuit, head for the famous bridge across the East River. He took a short-cut, drove in a crow-flight line through cramped streets with gullied pavements. Repeatedly his lips moved soundlessly as he calculated whether he was going to be able to head the girl off. When he reached the bridge, he was looking pleased with himself. He had made it.

Parking in a side street at the Brooklyn end of the bridge, he waited and shortly the girl's sedan appeared in the traffic.

Pippel then pulled out into the stream of vehicles and followed her. The girl slammed across the bridge, took a screeching turn at the first opportunity and arrowed toward the downtown skyscraper section.

Pippel trailed her. Two or three times he swore at the girl ahead, and the rest of the time he was scowling and preoccupied.

"Damn her!" he snarled more than once. His oaths had a vicious canine quality about them.

The young woman stopped her car before one of the tallest buildings in the city. The building was a towering monolith of steel and brick. Pippel gave a violent start and popped his eyes at the structure. His hands choked the steering wheel.

"Whew!" he gasped. "She's going to—to—" He got starkly pale.

The girl sprang out of the car and ran toward the entrance of the skyscraper.

She was hailed by a policeman.

"Sorry, Miss," the cop called, "but you can't park there."

If the girl heard, she gave no sign; she kept on running.

The cop was evidently in a bad temper, because he dashed after the girl and caught her. The cop took hold of her elbow.

"Hey," the cop growled, "you can't park—" He gulped when he saw the terror on the girl's face. "Glory be! What's wrong with you?"

"I—er—" The girl swallowed two or three times, and got control of herself. "Nothing," she insisted in a flinty voice. "I'm just—just in a hurry."

The cop peered at the girl. "You look like the wrath of Old

Nick was after you. What's wrong with you, lass?"

The girl swallowed. She looked to be on the verge of venting some of her cargo of sulfur, but thought better of antagonizing an arm of the law.

"I'm—just—late—picking up a fare," she explained grimly. "Get me?"

Evidently, the cop had no patience with women who showed up late for anything, because he snorted derisively.

"Lady," he said, "late or not, you can't park your car where you've got it now."

The blonde throttled her abrasive personality, became wheedling.

"Please—just for a few minutes," she pleaded.

"Sure, I know. The few minutes will be the whole darn mornin'!" The cop jerked his thumb at her car. "Get it outta here!"

The girl stamped an irate foot, then tapped back and flounced into her taxi, and wrenched the little jitney out into traffic.

Enough arm waving had accompanied this incident to make what had happened clear to Pippel, who had double-parked in a spot where he could observe. He watched the girl leave.

Then Pippel wheeled his machine into a side street, pulled up beside a parked taxi, and jumped out. He accosted the taxi driver.

"Look, hackman." Pippel showed a five-dollar bill. "Park my car for me, will you? I haven't got time. Business appointment. Hell of a hurry."

The taxi driver looked at the five-dollar bill and nodded.

"O.K.," he said. "But how'll you know where I parked your car?"

Pippel pointed at a sign which stood on the sidewalk. It was a black and white sign on a metal frame, and said, *Taxi Stand*.

"Take a pencil and write on that where you parked the car," he said. "And leave the keys in the machine."

"O.K." The taxi driver jumped into Pippel's machine and drove off to park it.

Pippel ran to a cigar store, dived into a telephone booth, and the dial mechanism whizzed while he was getting his number.

He recognized the voice which answered.

"Listen!" he exploded. *"The damn girl went to Doc Savage!"*

This apparently failed to register at the other end.

"What?" the voice asked.

"Doc Savage! Damn the girl—she's going to Doc Savage! A cop wouldn't let her park in front of the building, and that gives us a few minutes to get organized."

"Why so worried?" the voice interrupted.

"She's going to Doc Savage!"

"And so what?"

"Listen, you fool, haven't you heard of Doc Savage?"

The other admitted, "I remember a story in the newspapers about a Doc Savage who had invented something called an electro-scalpel, for a new painless kind of surgery. But why should we go into a cold sweat because the girl ran to some medico?"

Pippel looked as if he wanted to bite pieces out of the black telephone mouthpiece.

"I didn't think you knew much about Savage, you dummy! The guy's a doctor the way the President of the United States is a politician. What I mean, that ain't the half of it. He's some kind of professional trouble-buster."

"What do you mean?"

"It's his main line of work. Solving other people's troubles. He works without pay. Does it for the thrill of it, I hear. I know it sounds crazy, but when the girl spills what she knows, it's gonna be too bad."

"What makes you so sure she knows anything?"

"Look, sucker, why else would she be going to Doc Savage? Get over here quick as you can. That girl is gonna have trouble finding a place to park. I got a little time, but mighty little!"

"What are you going to do?"

"What we should have done to start with. Get rid of her."

"And what about Doc Savage?"

"If she talks to Doc Savage first, I'll have to get rid of him, too."

"Ain't that pretty drastic?" the telephone voice blurted out.

"We can't have any stink stirred up," Pippel growled. "Hell, we're just ready to start everything. We can't have anybody getting suspicious. This is too big."

"This is bigger than big," the other muttered. "This is the future of the world that's gonna change, if things go right."

"They," growled Pippel, "are going to go right no matter who ends up sleeping in pine boxes."

Chapter III
THE EXPLODING LADY

THE BLISTERED BLONDE calling herself Henrietta had driven about five blocks before she found a place to park. She parked, then sprang out of her machine and looked around for a taxi. She was in a hurry. But this was a side street in the garment district and there was nothing in sight but trucks. She had to walk back to Doc Savage's skyscraper headquarters.

As she approached it, Henrietta studied the building. It was the tallest spire in the forest of masonry skyscrapers that constituted the city. By reputation, it was the tallest such structure ever built. Tourists came from all over the world just to stand in its modernistic lobby. Despite herself, Henrietta was impressed.

She barged in, showed no interest in the office directory, going instead directly to the sleepy-looking proprietor of a lobby cigar stand. Once again, her manner abruptly changed. She was again snippy.

"Wake up, buster. Where can I find Doc Savage?"

The proprietor seemed to take no offense to the unexpected familiarity.

"Screening room is on the twentieth floor."

"Screening room?"

"That's where people who want to see Doc Savage are weeded out from those Doc doesn't want to see."

"He'll want to see me."

"That'll be up to the screeners."

20

The blonde leaned over the glass counter. "Is there a quicker way?" She batted her crystal blue eyes.

"Doc Savage has the eighty-sixth floor to himself. Private elevator around the corner. But people who stick their snoots up there without being invited are usually disinvited kinda firmly."

"I'll take my chances."

The blonde stormed around the corner.

A private elevator, she realized, would cost plenty of dough. She expected something ostentatious. To her moderate surprise, Henrietta located a lift which was dignified and restrained.

The cage surprised her when it arrived. There was no uniformed starter. Just a button marked Eighty-sixth Floor. Boarding confidently, she stabbed it.

The cage door closed. The elevator shot upward. The ride began smoothly. After a dozen floors, the blonde fell to her knees and began feeling like an inebriated elephant was balancing on her shoulders.

When the doors opened again, she was astonished to discover she had reached the eighty-sixth floor.

The combination of the breathtaking ride and the speed with which it had been completed seemed to take some of the gustiness out of her mainsail. Picking herself off the floor, she tentatively stepped out into the plain corridor on rubbery feet.

At the end of a corridor she found the door. It was painted bronze. On the front was modestly lettered:

Clark Savage, Jr.

"At last!"

Composing herself, Henrietta assaulted the panel with her knuckles.

The door fell open right away and she found herself face to face with a striking individual with the general air of a snowy eagle.

"Who might you be, gramps?" she demanded.

"Ham Brooks," the eagle replied.

Her eyes narrowed. Henrietta's first impression had been that he was an overdressed fop, and she revised that opinion. Indeed, the white-haired Ham would have been considered, in any city but New York, a fop because of the striped afternoon trousers, tea vest and spats.

He held in one well-manicured hand a tasteful black cane.

"Call me Henrietta," she said. "I'm the gal who sent the collect telegram."

"You are not expected," Ham Brooks said. "And we do not accept collect telegrams from persons we do not know. Normally, unexpected visitors are received on the twentieth floor."

"This is too important for ceremony, glad rags."

This saucy comment seemed to get Ham Brooks' attention, because he stepped back, allowing Henrietta to enter.

"You must be the legal eagle who pals around with Doc," she observed tartly.

Ham looked injured. "I am Brigadier General Theodore Marley Brooks, one of Doc Savage's associates."

A remarkaby squeaky voice broke in: "Don't let him kid you. He's only Doc's personal chauffeur."

Henrietta found herself standing in a reception room. The spires of Manhattan were visible through the tall windows. There was a desk—really a massive table decorated with inlays—a gigantic floor safe of significant age, and through an open door was what looked like a library filled with tomes and dominated by a globe of the world that was no less than twelve feet around.

The owner of the voice ambled in from the library. He was a squat, apish fellow possessing an incredibly homely but pleasant face. He had the kind of face that dogs wag their tails at and kids follow. There didn't seem to be room for more than a spoonful of brains in his bullet of a head, but Henrietta knew this impression was deceptive.

"You have to be Monk Mayfair, the industrial chemist," she said.

Monk beamed. He obviously enjoyed being recognized by attractive females.

"In the flesh."

"In the fur, you mean," sneered Ham. "You might want to keep your distance, miss. He sometimes suffers from fleas."

"Yeah, blondie," growled Monk, suddenly rolling up both sleeves to reveal amazingly red-furred forearms. "Keep back. His mouth is liable to fly in any direction once I knock his block off."

The odd duo traded fierce expressions that suggested impending slaughter.

Henrietta half expected war to break out. In fact, it looked imminent when Ham Brooks lifted his dark cane and raised it threateningly. It was revealed to be a sword cane. Monk blocked rusty fists and the pair appraised one another like two bull moose contemplating a vigorous round of butting heads and horns.

"If this doesn't beat all," she said acidly.

"What's that?" asked Monk, not taking his small eyes off his opponent.

"A man-monkey versus a man in a monkey suit."

Ham snapped out of his fighting stance. "Here now, what is your business with Doc Savage?"

"I understand he owns a submarine," the blonde said loftily. "I want to hire it and a crew. No questions asked."

"By whom?" asked Ham, puzzled.

"I said no questions asked!" the blonde snapped back.

"You just answered this fashion plate's question," chuckled Monk. "And we're not exactly in the sub-renting business."

"Where is this sub?" Henrietta suddenly demanded.

"Sure you don't wanna tell me what you want it for first?" asked Monk.

"I don't explain myself to just any ape," Henrietta snapped.

Monk looked pained. As a matter of fact, it had been his

experience in the past that he had very good luck with feminin-ity, and the prettier they were the better his luck, as a rule. His complete homeliness seemed to fascinate them, or something.

Henrietta, seeing that she was getting nowhere, promptly changed tactics. "I demand to see Doc Savage!" she yelled.

"Doc is presently conducting a scientific experiment of some consequence," related Ham in an important tone.

"Yeah, he left orders sayin' he can't be disturbed," Monk chimed in.

"You mean you won't let me in to see him?" Henrietta snapped.

"Listen, lady," Monk said. "Doc is busy in the laboratory. You gotta tell us what it is you want, or you don't get in. And don't yell at me!"

"I'll do more than yell at you!"

Monk Mayfair's bullet skull boasted a furring of rusty red hair. Henrietta took told of two tufts of this and commenced screaming at the top of her healthy lungs. "I've got to see Doc Savage, and I'll see him if I have to tear you apart!"

Her long fingernails raked his homely physiognomy. This so startled the homely chemist, he backed away, muttering, "What hit me?"

Ham Brooks stepped in then, and attempted to settle the blonde into a soft chair. She turned around and barked his elegant shin with the toe of one sharp shoe.

Howling, Ham grabbed up his shin and hopped in place. He managed to retain his polished cane during this procedure. It made a very comical picture.

Stepping in, the fire-eating blonde took hold of the dapper lawyer's cravat and gave it a forceful yank. Still hopping, Ham made a grab for the dangling adornment. He lost his cane.

Henrietta snatched it up, and gave it a twist, saying, "I read about this frog-sticker of yours." The cane came apart, revealing a long thin blade of excellent steel, with which she proceeded to slash gaping tears in Ham's faultless attire. The dapper one went into paroxysms of horror. He attempted to dance out of the way of the flashing blade, was chased into a corner.

This struck the homely chemist as hilarious. He quickly forgot his own injury and began shouting encouragement to the blonde. "See if you can spear his tie without cuttin' his throat."

Tossing aside the useless portion of the cane, Henrietta backed the beset barrister into a corner and began flaying the knot of his silk tie.

"How do you like them apples, you fancy Dan?" Henrietta hissed.

Ham howled, "Monk, you anthropoid! Don't just stand there—restrain this madwoman!"

Monk doubled over with mirth. He was enjoying himself immensely.

"After you shred his tie," he encouraged, "see if you can harvest his cufflinks. The diamonds are supposed to be real."

AT that moment, Doc Savage entered the room. No sound attended his arrival, no shadow preceded him to warn of his silent approach, but instantly the atmosphere in the room changed. It was as if a dynamo had started up, filling the air with the crackle of electricity and the promise of exciting things.

Henrietta felt some of that electricity. She turned. Her crystal blue eyes fell on the imposing figure of Doc Savage. They widened. Her grim mouth lost its elastic band quality.

"Oh, doctor!" she exclaimed.

Doc was a bronzed giant of a man, but there was nothing beefy about his build. His neck sinews, the tendons in the backs of his long-fingered hands, looked as supple as bundles of violin strings. There was a flowing ease about his movements that indicated great agility and Herculean strength.

Doc's features were regular, and he had remarkable penetrating flake-gold eyes. His hair was bronze, slightly darker than the hue of his skin, and a disturbed lock of it hung down on his forehead. His big bronze body was encased in a white laboratory smock. The contrast between the smock and his deeply bronzed skin was arresting.

"See?" muttered Monk in disgust. "Now you've disturbed Doc in the middle of his work."

"What seems to be the trouble here?" Doc asked in a noticeably well-modulated tone of voice.

"This dish-faced ape told me I couldn't see you," Henrietta complained, flinging aside the sword cane.

The bronze giant noticed the worse-for-wear Monk and Ham. "What on earth happened to you two?" he inquired.

"I'd try explainin'," the homely chemist muttered, "but it's too embarrassin'."

Ham said nothing. He was contemplating his ruined attire as if it were burned and peeling hide.

Doc took in the blonde's severely sunburned skin, her loud and revealing outfit, which ran to polka-dots.

"What can I do for you?" he asked.

Henrietta composed herself and her voice.

"Honestly, Mr. Savage, you have quite the reputation," she breathed. "I read all about you in a magazine." She batted her striking eyes. "I think you're just the guy I need to help me."

The bronze man retained his poker face. Obviously, he was not susceptible to flattery.

"This is new," Henrietta murmured to herself. "A man who is impervious to feminine charms."

Henrietta experienced her first inkling that Doc Savage, the Man of Bronze, was something more than an ordinary man.

Doc Savage belonged to a class of mortals who demonstrated that if a man set his sights upon a goal and devoted intensive efforts in the pursuit of that goal, astounding results might be achieved.

In this case, Doc had been set upon the path to greatness by his parents, who entrusted him into the care of a succession of scientists and other renowned experts, with the firm and unwavering purpose of transforming the lad into a scientific superman.

All knowledge, from science and medicine, to how to ride a horse and sail a sloop, as well as the rougher arts of combat, wilderness survival and speaking foreign languages, had been made available to him. And Doc had mastered them all, becoming in adulthood a greater expert in these respective disciplines that those who had tutored him.

All of this strenuous activity had been channeled to a single noble purpose. Doc Savage had been trained for the far-ranging career he was following—righting wrongs which ordinary forces of law and order could not combat. This altruistic career—for Doc took no pay—sometimes took him to the distant and dangerous corners of the globe.

"Trouble, Incorporated" might have been the name of the concern which Doc Savage headed. But it had no name, other than his own, for everyone knew that if you had troubles too large to handle, Doc Savage was the man to see.

Hence, the arrival of Henrietta and her presumed problem was not a unique thing.

Doc Savage appraised the blonde with his compelling flake-gold eyes. No emotion registered on his metallic lineaments.

"Aren't you the girl they found marooned on a tropic island?" he wondered.

"Yeah, I'm the gal off the island," Henrietta returned, "and don't starting asking me my name or how I got here!"

"Said her name was Henrietta," said Monk, feeling of his face and hair.

The girl stepped up to the bronze man and made fists at her sides. "I've got a proposition for you, big boy," she said.

"Proposition?"

"Call it a job. And I'll pay you plenty to do it—but no questions asked, see?"

Doc began removing his smock. It presently became obvious that he possessed the muscular development of a gladiator. He stood taller than he had at first seemed, which was the result of the unusual symmetry of his wonderfully well-developed physique.

"I think you have us wrong, lady," Monk interjected.

Henrietta spun on the apish chemist.

"You stay out of this, King Kong!" Whirling back to Doc, she said, "Listen, I read about you in a magazine. You're professional trouble hunters, ain'tcha?"

"In a way," Doc admitted. "But we are not for hire."

"Whatcha mean—not for hire?"

Doc, showing more patience than the occasion demanded, replied, "We mix in things that interest us—and where we can do some good. We don't care to be hired, and we certainly don't go into anything unless we know what it is."

Henrietta's face grew indignant. Her voice reclaimed some of its previous volume.

"Well, you're going to work for me, like it or not! And don't think—"

Doc Savage broke in. It was a testament to the restrained power of his voice that it was heard over Henrietta's screeching.

"We are not interested, Miss. Monk—show her to the door."

"With pleasure," Monk declared. Ambling up, he batted Henrietta's flailing hands away and tucked her under one hairy arm. The blonde firecracker kicked wildly, pounding helplessly on the hairy chemist's chest.

As the apish Monk carried her from the reception room, Henrietta howled a parting threat, "You mugs! You'll see! You don't know who you're fooling with! *I'm Hornetta Hale!*"

MONK MAYFAIR bore the struggling, kicking blonde to their special elevator, summoned the cage with the thumb-press of a button, and when it arrived casually asked, "This the lift you took?"

"Yeah, you big monkey. It practically disjointed my skeleton on the way up."

Monk chuckled good-naturedly. "Well, you might want to curl up in a ball on account of the ride down is even more bone-jarrin'."

The doors opened and the hairy chemist deposited the blonde into the waiting cage. He sent it on its way.

As the doors closed, the blonde hellion called out, "You'll hear from my lawyer! I'll sue your pants off for this, don't think I won't."

Grinning broadly, Monk started back for the reception room. Ham suddenly burst out, saying, "Come on, you baboon!" He pointed imperatively to the door with his recovered sword cane.

"What's up, now?"

"Trouble down in the screening room."

So fast did the elevator run that by the time the pair reached it, the cage was again free, having deposited Hornetta Hale in the lobby.

They reached the twentieth floor screening room and found two men there. At sight of them, Monk and Ham went instantly on guard. One was tall and thin and held a pearl-gray handkerchief before his face. A rust-colored overcoat enveloped his rangy form, and the brim of his hat was pulled down low. The other was short and blond and had a nondescript air about him.

"Can we help you gentlemen?" Ham asked coolly.

"Yeah," said the shorter of the two. "We're looking for a woman."

"Really?"

Monk asked, "A blonde? Kind of sassy?"

"Yeah. That's her. Where is she?"

"I ain't seen hide nor hair. I was just testin' you. We get a lot of cranks here."

"We have to screen visitors very carefully," added Ham in a suave tone.

The pair didn't know whether to explode or not. They stood

on their feet with a general air of race horses awaiting the starter's pistol.

"What makes you think you'd find your nameless blonde here?" Ham asked pointedly.

"Just a hunch. You see, she's my kid sister. Goes by the name of Hornetta. She fell out of a tree a few months ago and it knocked her cock-eyed, if you know what I mean."

"Cock-eyed, eh?" said Ham.

"Yeah. Hornetta's a little off. She's been talking about coming here to see Doc Savage for weeks. We think she—well, her head is so full of wild stories we're not sure what she was going to tell him. Anyway, she up and ran away and this is naturally the first place we thought to look."

"Ain't seen her," Monk repeated. The apish chemist then addressed the man in the rust-hued overcoat who kept his handkerchief before his face at all times.

"What about you," he asked. "Cat got your tongue?"

"Hab a code," the man said thickly.

"Yeah, it sounds like you got yourself a whopper of a cold," Monk agreed.

Ham inserted, "Would you gentlemen care to identify your-selves?"

"We would not," said the nondescript one. "This is a family matter. Confidential, you understand?"

"Perfectly," drawled Ham.

Monk and Ham regarded the duo, patience written on their faces. The odd pair seemed reluctant to leave.

Finally, the short one said, "Well, if you're sure our sister never showed up...."

"Absolutely positive," returned Ham crisply.

"In that case, we'll be on our way."

"Sorry we can't help," said Monk.

"Good luck with your search," added Ham, stepping aside to allow them to pass.

The two men then departed in sullen silence. At no point did the tall one allow his features to be viewed clearly. After the door had closed, Monk asked of Ham, "Whatcha make of their story, shyster?"

The dapper lawyer shrugged. "It sounded like a story."

"But it could be true," Monk suggested contrarily.

"It might," allowed Ham.

THEY consulted Doc Savage in his eighty-sixth floor laboratory.

The bronze man took in all they had to say in absorbed silence. Then he announced, "It would have been better had you trailed those two rather than stopped to consult with me."

The remark was not offered as criticism. Merely as an observation. No tone of recrimination touched Doc's well-modulated tones. Still, Monk and Ham looked instantly crestfallen. Ham twisted his elegant cane in both hands until his knuckles turned white.

"Should we give chase?" he asked.

The bronze man shook his head. "My experiment is too important for me to abandon it without sound reason. The girl did not appear to be in trouble, if her appeal can be believed."

"Gotcha, Doc," said Monk. "We'll skip it."

"If this matter is important, we will hear of Hornetta Hale again," Doc said, then turned his attention back to the experiment he was conducting.

Seeing that their leader was immersed in his work, Monk and Ham silently withdrew to the library.

"For my part," sniffed Ham Brooks, looking at the ruin that was his garments, "I would just as soon forget that woman ever darkened our door."

"Same here," muttered Monk in rare agreement with his arch-nemesis.

Chapter IV

THE JAM

THE NAME OF of Hornetta Hale was not an easy one to forget.

True, that was not her real name. A newspaper journalist had hung the appellation on her back in the days when she dominated the headlines. That had been several years ago. She was not exactly forgotten these days. Adventuresses of Hornetta Hale's stripe are hardly ever forgotten. But her luster had dimmed since the short-lived era during which she and her smart racing job of a seaplane had buzzed the world.

She had been Henrietta Hale then. Which was supposed to make her pretty extraordinary. She had done so much that sometimes she felt old at twenty-nine—people generally believed she was older than that, yet she looked younger. She was a stunningly pretty girl, just a little regal. Most men were scared of her, the average male preferring to wear the chest hair in his family. After an average male heard about the time the Tugeri headhunters of the Dutch East Indies besieged Hornetta Hale for six days, he was apt to crawl away.

It had been profitable, this freelance adventuring for pay. It had been a calculated and planned business. The idea had occurred to her after she got what she considered a lucky break, and became the leading débutante of the season. They called it No. 1 Glamour Girl now. Ordinarily the attendant fame lasted for a few weeks; maybe it lasted longer if you were good newspaper copy and appealing camera fodder.

Henrietta had made herself a job. The job was the nation's adventure girl. She was not American First Family; she wasn't even Park Avenue. She was only a tall blonde gal whose folks had come from Oklahoma with some oil money, most of which they'd lost. It was a good background. The public ate it up.

With the war in Europe in full cry, the exploring racket was slipping; it was a dying horse. But Henrietta Hale in her heyday made good copy and good camera fodder, so she made the old nag gallop. She flew to Australia, via the South Sea Islands, and got stranded on an uninhabited island. She had no food. So she ate plankton. They're the little sea organisms on which whales live. Depend on Hornetta Hale to come up with the unusual. For the papers had taken to calling her that by that time.

She had earned the nickname by buzzing one of the European passenger dirigibles as it had docked at Lakehurst, New Jersey, flying her tiny personal plane, dubbed the *Hornet*. In an effort to upstage the event, and grab headlines for herself, she had flown rings around the slow-moving airship. When the European government had lodged a formal complaint against the reckless aviatrix, Henrietta Hale gave a radio interview, during the course of which she expressed a choice opinion of that country's war-mongering dictator.

The dictator was not pleased. He promised that if Henrietta Hale ever crash-landed in his country, she would be stood up before a brick wall and shot as a spy.

After that, she was Hornetta Hale. She did her best to live up to the nickname. Her speech became salty and her sharp tongue infamous. The American public couldn't get enough of her exploits. This went on for years.

Eventually, she simmered down and was heard of less and less. The spreading war in Europe was accorded much of the blame. People who had enjoyed the dangerous life of Hornetta Hale vicariously through the rotogravure newspaper sections were now preoccupied with real danger. She was, in a word, *passé*.

HORNETTA HALE was still on the minds of Doc Savage and Monk Mayfair as they tooled one of the bronze man's sedans along a country road in upstate New York. Doc was at the wheel.

The sedan was typical of the type of machines Doc Savage preferred. It was subdued, unobtrusive. The paint job was not flashy. The motor, however, was an eight-cylinder dynamo capable of speeds in excess of one hundred and eighty miles an hour. The steel body was bullet-proofed, as were the windows. Tires were composed of sponge rubber; they could not be flattened by nail or bullet.

There were other aspects of the sedan that were also remarkable. The hydraulic brakes were of the bronze man's invention, as were the airplane-style shock absorbers.

It was these latter innovations that Doc Savage was testing at present. For this was the sedan's maiden run.

"Oh boy!" said Monk happily. "Some day for a drive in the country. Ain't that right, Habeas?"

The apish chemist scratched the head of a peculiar dwarf pig that was sitting on his lap. This was Habeas Corpus, who possessed a body that was undersized and huge ears that were oversized.

Roused by his master's touch, Habeas climbed up and leaned his long inquisitive snout out the passenger window. Slipstream filled his ears like sails, making them spread like wings. The ungainly shoat seemed to be enjoying himself immensely.

"The machine seems to be performing as expected," noted Doc as he whipped through winding country switchbacks.

"Say, Doc, you hear any more out of that Hornetta Hale?"

"Nothing after we put the young lady out of our office the other day," the bronze man replied as he took a sharp turn at hair-lifting speed. No expression of concern crossed his metallic features. Doc rarely showed emotion. It had been schooled out of him at an early age.

"What do you suppose she wanted?"

"Given her past as a wild woman," the bronze man said, "probably publicity, or something equally foolhardy."

"Mebbe so," the apish chemist returned. "But she ain't been heard from since she came off that Caribbean isle. What do you suppose that was all about?"

"Hornetta Hale," said Doc Savage, "has a knack for becoming stranded, marooned, or otherwise landing in the center of attention."

"She sure was a publicity hog in her day," Monk agreed, giving Habeas' back a vigorous scratching. "Maybe she done it to herself to grab off some headlines. I still wonder who those two guys were."

"Hornetta Hale was rumored to have gone broke after her last escapade," Doc Savage offered.

Monk grinned. "Maybe it was bill collectors who stuck her on that sandpile."

The sedan had been barreling along at a surprising clip, given the twisting road. A professional race car driver would have sworn that no man-and-car combination could have held the road at the speeds at which the bronze man navigated the turnpike. Yet Doc Savage drove with an ease of handling that verged on the superhuman.

That skill was no more in evidence than when the sedan slid around a hairpin turn and, abruptly, there was a truck van blocking the road. The rear was open, the doors flung wide, and a steel ramp had been lowered.

There was no going around it, and precious little room in which to stop. Monk Mayfair grabbed the door frame with both hairy hands and squeezed his piggish eyes shut. Habeas, more intelligent than most dogs, scooted for the floorboards.

Doc pressed the brake pedal with a smooth, sure tap of his oxford-shod foot.

Slewing not at all, the roaster slid to a stop, its front bumper jutting just over the bottom of the waiting ramp.

"You may look now, Monk," Doc suggested quietly.

By this time, the hairy chemist had clapped his hirsute hands over his homely face. He dropped them. His jaw sagged cavernously.

Staring into the yawning mouth of the van interior, Monk muttered, "I sure don't like the looks of this…."

Monk Mayfair had little chance to digest the view. For zooming up behind them came barreling a sturdy milk delivery truck. It struck their rear bumper. With a clash and clang of steel, the sedan was knocked half way up the ramp.

"What the blue blazes!" Monk howled.

The milk truck roared into reverse, stopped, then came at them again. This time it pushed the subdued machine fully into the van interior.

It was that slick. The milk truck spun back, and out popped a peppery blonde. She rushed up to the rear of the van, and with surprising speed, pulled a pin that caused the ramp to drop free.

That was sufficient to prevent to sedan from backing out safely.

There were two swinging doors affixed to the van body. The blonde threw one, then the other shut. Then she bolted them tight, adding a sturdy brass padlock for good measure. That took care of any last chance for escape.

Climbing in the van's cab, she gunned the motor to life. The van roared off, its captured cargo jouncing in back on immobilized tires.

"Wouldn't work for me!" Hornetta Hale cried gleefully. "Hah! I'll *make*'em do it!"

THE van lumbered along for perhaps a quarter hour. Behind the wheel, Hornetta Hale was talking to herself.

"I knew that big bronze bohunk was overrated the minute I laid eyes on him," she sniffed. "Sure, he has a reputation. Probably hired himself a good press agent."

Presently, the van approached a grade. The blonde firecracker proved that she could have made a fair living as a teamster. She double-clutched up the hill, reached the top and slid down the summit, foot off the gas, allowing gravity to pull her machine along.

"Doc Savage, my fancy foot!" she bit out.

During the climb, the truck gave a mighty jounce just before reaching the hilltop. The jounce was accompanied by a commotion such as might be produced by a pig being fed alive into a meat grinder. A compressed procession of piggy squeals, grunts and other porcine sounds filled the van interior, then abruptly ceased.

"What the hopping hell was that!" exclaimed Hornetta Hale, sounding a little like a teamster now. She peered out the side mirror, but saw nothing. For she had begun her slide down the grade, and became busy keeping the van on the road. The graded dirt road behind her was no longer in view.

When the road smoothed out, she fed the engine gas and the van continued its progress. The piggy cacophony continued intermittently, finally settling down.

Before long, Hornetta pulled onto a side road that ran through unkempt weeds until it reached a clearing where an old barn stood slowly falling into ruin.

For some reason—simple homespun thrift probably—farmers have a tradition of letting old disused barns succumb to the elements rather than paying to demolish the structures.

This one was in the early stages of decomposition. The weatherboard sides had been stripped of all vestiges of paint by time and rain and wind. The roof presented a profile like a broken-backed carcass. Obviously, a beam had caved. The sides were solid barnboard, however. And when Hornetta Hale stopped the van and got out to run the door open, it still operated, although its big hinges squeaked in protest.

Dusk was falling now. Hornetta drove the van into the barn and darkness swallowed the big machine. Then, jacking a bullet into the chamber of an automatic she reclaimed from the front seat, she stormed around to the van and addressed the closed doors.

"Listen, you mugs! I have a gun and I ain't afraid to use it." To prove her point, she fired a single slug into the barn roof. Old hay and sawdust filtered down from above. "If either of you overrated clowns try to jump me, it will just be too damn bad, see?"

No response came from the padlocked van body.

Hornetta pressed on. "Now I'm going to open up these doors and we're going to have us a good old-fashioned pow-wow. No tricks, either of you. Or else. Get me?"

Still no reply came from within.

"No tricks," Hornetta repeated, "or it'll be *pow!* And then *wow!* I know how to turn loose bullets, and I know where to shoot a man. Right in the belly where it hurts most."

Her bravado was met with even more silence.

Hornetta seemed to hesitate. Her blue eyes narrowed suspiciously.

Finally, she gathered herself and, unlocking the big padlock, threw open the doors.

In the dimness of the barn, the interior of the van was a box of gloom. Still, one could see into it. There was sufficient light for that.

What Hornetta Hale saw—or rather did *not* see—was enough to cause her stubborn jaw to hang open. Her flinty eyes struck sparks. The words that came tumbling out of her mouth would have done credit to a mule skinner.

For the interior of the van into which she had forcibly introduced a two-ton sedan was utterly and undeniably empty!

"I don't believe it!" Hornetta snapped. "I do *not* believe it!"

Incomprehension seemed to seize her voice, her expression and her mind. She stood as if stupefied. Then, succumbing to an irate anger that brought hot color mounting to her cheeks, Hornetta yanked a flashlight from a pocket and shone it inside.

The beam disclosed nothing but the quilt-hung sides of the interior.

It was impossible! Hornetta knew that mere minutes before, she had locked the sedan within. She had felt its weight and drag as she piloted the van to this destination. True, the last portion of the trip felt lighter, but…a sedan cannot be made to melt away into thin air, she knew. And yet one seemingly had!

Hornetta Hale reached for a handhold, levering herself up and into the back, determined to investigate every inch of the van's boxy body. Her mind was running to tricks with mirrors when she distinctly heard the powerful roar of a machine outside.

Jumping down, she went to investigate.

If astonishment had ridden her pretty if hard features before, it roosted there for good now.

For up the dusty road came a familiar subdued sedan. At the wheel was the homely face of Monk Mayfair. He was grinning from ear to ear. The grin looked a mile wide. Beside him, in the passenger seat, was a pig. It stood up on its hind legs, forepaws resting on the dashboard. It seemed almost as if the pig were grinning, too.

The sedan pulled up and braked.

Hornetta Hale simply exploded. "How the holy heck did you get loose!"

The pig opened its mouth more widely. And seemed to speak.

"A magician never reveals his tricks, honeybunch."

"A pig and his ventriloquist!" Hornetta retorted. "Where is the big bronze guy?"

From behind, came the surprising answer. "You are not the first to attempt to capture us by that same artifice," said a quietly confident voice that Hornetta recognized just before strong bronze fingers seized her neck and performed movements that caused the world to release its grip on her.

Monk jumped out of the auto, beaming.

"She never heard a thing, thanks to Habeas."

Doc Savage nodded. "The shoat's chorus prevented Miss Hale from hearing the sedan slide out the van doors during that last climb."

"New shocks worked like a charm on landin'," Monk agreed. "Easy enough to run so close behind her that she never knew we were on her trail until that last turn. Our silenced motor couldn't be heard under the roar of that truck. The hard part was pickin' the padlock on the door bar with the truck moving along at a good clip."

"Do not forget that while we were trailing her so closely, you had to clamber onto the hood in order to reclose the van doors, so she would not suspect a thing," reminded Doc.

"It was nothin'." The hairy chemist eyed the troublesome Hornetta lying on the ground. "Guess we go to work on her, huh?"

"Miss Hale," said Doc Savage grimly, "has quite an awakening ahead of her."

Chapter V

TALL TALE

HORNETTA HALE WOKE up in what she first thought was a zoo.

She was in a cage. She realized that almost at once. The cage was of good size. It had to be, in order to contain both Hornetta and the monkey.

Now Hornetta Hale had done her share of exploring. She had been chased by baboons, set upon by orangutans and once a howler monkey had run her up a tree. The monkey that squatted at the other side of the cage resembled no species of anthropoid she had ever seen or heard of.

In some respects, it rather resembled a miniature version of Monk the chemist. It possessed the same gimlet eyes in a broad face. Even the color of its fur—a rusty red—brought to mind the apish chemist.

"What are *you* doing here?" she asked thickly. Then her head began clearing. She changed the question.

"What am I doing *in* here with *you!*" she exploded.

Hornetta looked around. It was not dark exactly. There was some light. It seemed to be coming through a haze, or something.

"Hello. Is anyone home?"

Silence.

The monkey approached. It wore a curious expression.

Looking about for a weapon, Hornetta found nothing. So she took off her shoe and, grasping it by the toe, threatened to brain the monkey with the heel.

"Stay away from me!" she warned.

The monkey ambled closer.

Hornetta threw the shoe. It bounced off the monkey's skull. The monkey grabbed the top of his hairy head, emitted a sharp squeak of pain and then scrambled after the shoe.

It is said that monkeys possess the fundamental trait of imitation. This one proved it. He grasped the shoe by its toe and promptly and expertly bounced it off Hornetta's forehead.

Hornetta retaliated by letting the monkey have it with her other shoe.

The monkey snatched up the other shoe and, in retaliation, swiftly let fly.

The two shoes bounced around the cage interior for more than five frenzied minutes until both combatants lost the energy and enthusiasm for combat.

"How did I ever get into this mess?" Hornetta moaned.

The monkey looked equally pained, but said nothing.

After a period, the lights came up and a voice said calmly, "We are interested in your story, Miss Hale."

Hornetta scrambled to her feet.

She saw Doc Savage standing nearby. He stood in a vast room, as large as—it seemed at first glance—the concourse of Grand Central Station. White tiles covered the walls, as if she were in a hospital.

"You!"

"The tables appear to be turned."

"Get me out of this cage!"

"In due time," said Doc Savage unhurriedly. "First, I would like to know what was behind these shenanigans of yours."

"I told you last week. I want to hire you!"

"For what purpose?"

"That's my business," snapped Hornetta.

"You showed interest in my personal submarine. Why was that?"

Hornetta pulled herself up as if about to launch a verbal pitchforking.

Abruptly, she subsided.

"If I tell you, will you let me out?" she pleaded.

"If you promise no more hijinks."

"Deal."

"Go ahead, then," said Doc.

"You know I am an explorer."

"After an unorthodox fashion," allowed Doc.

"I earned a living at it for a while. But this time I have a way of amassing a young fortune."

"I am listening."

"Did you ever hear of a Chinese warlord named Lei Chi?"

"I have not," admitted Doc.

"Lei Chi wanted to smuggle some gold out of China before the Japs came in and looted everything. He came up with a nifty idea. Boats usually have keels formed of lead, to insure stability. This wily old warlord melted down all his gold and poured it into the keel of this ship, the *Hussy*."

Hornetta paused, apparently for dramatic effect. "The *Hussy* sank in the Caribbean," she added breathlessly. "I think I know where it is. If I can find it, then raise it, there's ten million dollars in pure gold in the keel. We'll be rich!"

Doc Savage said nothing.

"What's the matter, big boy? Immune to gold?"

Doc continued to be silent. In fact, the bronze man was already quite wealthy. Moreover, he had access to more gold than anyone could want or need. But he said nothing of that.

Instead, he asked, "What were you doing on that cay?"

"I was scouting the waters off Bimini. My plane went down. I managed to swim to that isle. I was stuck there for weeks and weeks. Good thing for the conch."

"What conch?"

"The ones I caught and ate," replied Hornetta off-handedly. "They're tough, but if you pound them enough with a rock, you can eat them. Even if they are kinda like chewing on a tough snail. After this, it will be a long time before I ever eat anything but cow again."

Doc Savage regarded the sunburnt Hornetta Hale in silence for a long time. His eerie flake-gold eyes seemed to be measuring her. Hornetta suddenly felt as if she were some species of wild animal instead of a formerly famous aviatrix and explorer.

"I have done a little research on your recent activities," he said quietly.

"Yeah. What of it?"

"Two weeks ago, Arthur Bottorff hired you to fly down to South America to do aerial surveys for the Magellan and Amazon Oil Corporation. You flew out of Teterboro Airport and were never heard from again."

Hornetta grimaced. "Why, that was just a story I floated so no one would suspect the truth. Any treasure hunter can claim the *Hussy*, according to the law of the seas."

Doc Savage said steadily, "I spoke with Arthur Bottorff by telephone. He confirmed that he hired you, but that you have been missing since that day."

Hornetta Hale fell silent. Her eyes narrowed craftily. She seemed to be thinking.

"I won't tell you he's in it with me," she said at last. "But I won't tell you he's not. This is my discovery. And I ain't sharing. But I'll cut you in if you'll let me have your sub for a week or two. I'll return it undamaged." She touched her chest. "Cross my crafty heart."

"Not a chance."

"Why not?"

"I told you. We are not for hire. Especially to prevaricators."

"To—what?" Hornetta sputtered.

Doc Savage walked away.

"Wait!" Hornetta implored. "You said you'd let me out of this monkey cage."

Doc turned, eyes metallic. "On the condition that you tell the truth. Who were the two men who came looking for you after your visit here last week?"

"What two men?"

Doc Savage described the two quickly and effectively.

Hornetta Hale made a rather grim mouth. "That was a close shave," she murmured after recovering her powers of speech.

"Who were they?"

"Devils. Crooks. Treasure hounds. If I don't get out of here and start down to the Caribbean, it will be too late. It's less than a week until—" She stopped, cut off her words.

"Until when?" asked Doc Savage.

"Nothing. I just figured they won't let any mosses sprout on their ambitions, that's all."

Doc Savage stepped up and unlocked the cage.

"That means you believe me?"

"No," said Doc, not mincing words.

Carefully but firmly, he guided Hornetta Hale into the library where Monk and Ham were exchanging insults.

"You frog-faced ape!" Ham howled.

"You should talk, you unsaddled clothes horse!" countered Monk.

Hornetta inserted one of her own.

"I just met your baby brother," she told Monk snappily.

Ham Brooks grabbed his midriff and roared out his laughter.

"I threw a shoe at him and he threw one back," Hornetta added. "We had quite the battle. Too bad he lost."

Ham's roaring laughter choked off. "Chemistry! What has happened to him?"

"He is fine," Doc reassured him. "Merely an exchange of spleen."

Ham dashed into the lab and came back with the tiny ape in his arms.

"Don't tell me he belongs to you," Hornetta snapped.

"My pet," said Ham defensively.

"My pain," growled Monk, eyeing the tiny replica of himself with ill-disguised scorn. The ape stuck out its pink tongue at the hairy chemist. Monk lifted a chair threateningly, and the unclassified anthropoid executed a backflip and disappeared under a table.

Doc addressed his aides. "Did you hear her story?"

"Every syllable," sniffed dapper Ham. "And I don't believe a word of it."

"Ditto," added Monk.

Doc piloted Hornetta into an overstuffed chair. He simply laid one bronze hand on her peeling shoulder and urged her over and down. Hornetta sat as if she had no power of resistance.

"You're stronger than you look," she grimaced, "and you look plenty strong."

"We will ask you to repeat your story," said the bronze man.

Hornetta did. This time the *Hussy* was owned by a Greek who needed to get his gold out of Ethiopia. There were other embellishments. None noteworthy.

"You are not even trying to lie convincingly," Doc told her.

Hornetta made a face. "I'm a little shook up, if you don't mind. It's been an ordeal. Now am I under arrest, or can I be on my merry way?"

"You are neither."

But when Hornetta stood up to go, Monk Mayfair gave her a casual shove and back she went into the cushions.

Her snapping eyes shed blue sparks. "Now look here, I—"

A red light began flashing on a wall. All heads turned toward it.

"Trouble!" Ham howled.

Monk grinned. "It's about time."

"What do you mean—about time?" demanded Hornetta. "What are you—a glutton for punishment?"

Doc Savage said, "When we drove you back here, we picked up shadowers."

"Yeah?"

"They were the same two who were inquiring after you last week."

"Is that so?" Hornetta asked thinly. Her sunburned face seemed to pale half a shade. But it remained ruddy.

"We thought if we let them get a good look at you being brought back to our headquarters, they would try something," Doc explained. "Now they have."

"That's quite a banana bunch of coincidences," Hornetta said slowly.

"Not really," returned Doc Savage, "After your visit, I did some research on you. Operatives in my employ discovered your seaplane adrift in the Caribbean, many miles from the cay upon which you were marooned. Far too many for you to have put down and ended up on that remote isle. You will be interested to know that it was flown back to Teeterboro Airport, and is in airworthy condition."

An intrigued light came into Hornetta's blue eyes.

"My interest was naturally aroused by these circumstances," continued Doc. "Since you seemed so set upon hiring us, and your pursuers equally determined to locate you, I thought a quiet drive in the country might draw one or the other of you out. Instead, it drew both."

Battering sounds came from without.

Hornetta cocked an eye at Doc. "If there's shooting to be done, how about handing me my fair share of bullets?" she said fiercely.

"Not a chance," returned Doc.

"Yeah," chimed in Monk. "No tellin' who you'd perforate once you got started."

"A pal you are!" Hornetta flared, looking about wildly. "Is there a back way out of his mausoleum?"

Before anyone could reply, a thunderous explosion sounded from the reception room area.

The connecting door jumped off its hinges and catapulted across the library jamb, knocking over a ponderous bookshelf, which struck another and created the effect of fantastic falling dominos. Glass shattered unmusically.

"*Ye-e-o-w!*" Monk howled and began firing into the cloud of evil black smoke that rolled in like a boiling fog bank of doom.

Chapter VI

DEVIL GRAB DEVIL

PANDEMONIUM BROKE LOOSE in the magnificent library of Doc Savage. It sounded like a succession of earthquakes rolling across the spacious room. More bookcases toppled. The ceiling cracked in three places.

Monk and Ham were firing blind into the oncoming smoke. They wielded intricate machine pistols which produced a deafening thunder. That was just the commencement of the vigorous proceedings.

Quickly, they reached into their coats and drew on compact gas masks. Doc Savage did the same.

From another pocket, Doc also pulled a flat silver object, which he flipped open in the manner of a cigarette case. Inside, carefully nested in cotton, were tiny clear globules.

Doc began pitching these into the oncoming smoke. Glass tinkled.

"Retreat!" rapped the bronze man.

They retreated from the paneled library, which resembled a jumbled profusion of giant fallen dominos, closing the substantial door as a barricade. The great globe of the earth which dominated the room had become dislodged from its bronze mounting and rolled off into a corner of the room like a titanic blue and green marble.

Hornetta Hale came along, but not by choice. Doc Savage picked her up bodily and slung her over one shoulder. He dropped her onto a stool and swung to a wall. Depressing a stud caused a woodgrain panel to hoist up.

Exposed was a large glass plate—an experimental television device. It displayed the interior of the laboratory with its glittering forest of test tubes and glass piping, and other complicated scientific apparatus.

Men were emerging from the smoke. They, too, wore gas masks. These were of the type that made men resemble goggle-eyed elephants.

Seeing this, Doc's hands flew to a switch. In the other room large exhaust fans began whirring.

The choking smoke was rapidly drawn into ceiling vents and the laboratory began to clear. The invaders seemed surprised by this.

Doc Savage scrutinized them momentarily, his flake-gold eyes intent.

They wore ordinary coats and ties. That was where the outward semblance of the ordinary ceased. Some carried spike-snouted pistols of a foreign manufacture. Quite a number wore unusual shirts of a dark hue.

From Doc's surprise-parted lips, emerged a peculiar sound. A trilling, so low it was at first a vague thing, but then escalating into a tuneless melody that permeated the room like a curiously searching banshee. This was the sound of Doc Savage— a mental quirk that was his substitute for expressing emotion.

The sound piped up, then died, leaving in its aftermath a lingering note that told that the bronze man was intrigued.

For Doc Savage recognized that these were the latest military pistols of a foreign government. They were not likely to be in the hands of ordinary American thugs. Not at all.

Others brandished rifles. These were military-type rifles, also of the latest manufacture.

The raiders—six caught their number—moved with the cold precision of a well-oiled engine. Military precision.

"These babies look mighty serious," Monk snorted.

Ham exclaimed, "By Jove! If they are soldiers of fortune, they have good backgrounds for it."

The raiders rushed to the laboratory door. It was strong. They proved it by unleashing a storm of steel-jacketed slugs against the portal. It held.

Five of the men retreated.

Doc tapped a key. The angle of the televised image shifted.

Evidently, several concealed cameras were positioned throughout the big library, and Doc could transfer between viewpoints at the flick of a switch.

Doc spotted the man kneeling at the door. He was working with something there. Wires showed.

"Bomb!" warned Doc.

No sooner had he said it, than the man retreated to the reception room. A flick of another switch showed clearly that they were rushing out into the corridor, and as far away from Doc's offices as humanly possible.

Doc Savage realized then the magnitude of the danger they faced.

"Escape!" he rapped out, his voice metallic and urgent.

Doc had trained his men well. That one word was all they required.

They raced for a far wall. Doc grabbed Hornetta and once again ignominiously slung her over his shoulder.

Hornetta had no comprehension of what next transpired. She was dimly aware that a large section of outer wall somehow opened. She was dumped into something resembling a capsule, such as department stores send through their pneumatic tubes, only this one was of gigantic size.

Unnerving sounds—hissings and clanks—preceded the wildest ride of her life. The capsule dropped. All dropped with it, man and monkey, girl and pig. It was as if the bottom of the world had dropped out from beneath them.

Unexpectedly, the capsule changed course, corkscrewing madly.

It ran horizontally for what seemed an eternity, but was only hurtling seconds. Then it kicked upward and came to a skull-jarring stop.

All sprawled there amid padded quilted cushions for long seconds.

Doc Savage was the first to rouse to activity. He threw open a double set of hatches and began helping everyone out.

"Boy," enthused Monk, windmilling his long, hairy arms. "That gets my blood pumpin' every time!"

Ham climbed out and, predictably, fell to fussing with his clothes.

Hornetta found herself in a concrete blockhouse of some kind. She looked around. Behind her was a cavernous warehouse of some sort.

Lights were dim. Hornetta tried to make out the interior. She perceived great solid shapes cobwebbed in gloom. A spidery crane was the only thing that she could discern.

Gradually, light came on so as not to hurt the unaccustomed eye.

Hornetta was staring at a veritable fleet of modern aerial conveyances. A great four-motored amphibian was visible. Others included smaller planes and a gyroplane that looked a good ten years ahead of anything she had ever seen, or flown.

Hornetta was a connoisseur of aircraft and she had to resist an unladylike urge to whistle at the speedlines of the various craft.

There were also several boats ranging from a small speedboat to a sleek cabin cruiser docked in a water-filled basin. All were ultra-modern beauties. But then her gaze fell upon the submarine. It lay in a drydock trough. It was a razorback hog of steel, unlovely, and to all appearances unseaworthy. But she started toward it eagerly.

"How much to hire by the day?" she breathed.

No one answered her. They were too busy dogging the double hatches of what was a pneumatic car.

"I said, 'How much?'" she repeated.

Doc Savage was in the act of throwing shut the outer hatch when a gush of foul black smoke struck him in the face.

"Blazes!" Monk gulped. "Blazes!"

DOC SAVAGE raced to a televisor plate. He manipulated several controls. Distant cameras were relaying closed-circuit images from the eighty-sixth floor of their headquarters.

But no images came. The frosted glass screen remained dark. Doc checked the circuits. All were in working order.

"This can mean only one thing," he said gravely.

"What's that?" Hornetta asked.

"Our headquarters has been destroyed."

The eyes of all three men turned in Hornetta Hale's direction. They were not pleased eyes to behold. Even the calm flake-gold orbs of Doc Savage contained a harsh metallic light.

Hornetta Hale thought fast.

"O.K.," she said slowly and distinctly. "That hooey about a racing boat with gold in her keel instead of lead. That wasn't true."

"We know," said Doc.

"It's bigger than that," Hornetta admitted.

"That much is obvious," said Ham dryly.

"Yeah," added Monk. "Them guys who just wrecked our headquarters aren't garden variety thugs. They're serious."

"It's bigger than you think," said Hornetta. "It's bigger than you can imagine."

"Imagine it for us," prompted Ham Brooks, wringing his cane.

"This thing is so big, it might change the course of history!" snapped Hornetta Hale with such force of conviction that all doubts about her veracity instantly evaporated.

Doc Savage requested, "The complete details, please."

Hornetta hesitated. What she would have said was never known. The acerbic blonde wavered on the verge of confessing whatever tale she might have been willfully withholding.

But all thought of that fled when the door on the land side of the warehouse caved in.

A truck came rushing in. To the bumper was affixed a construct like the prow of a ship, made of two curved pieces of steel welded into a wedge. It was a plough or battering ram such as those the Department of Justice men affixed to their trucks in the hectic days of Prohibition.

Doc Savage rapped out, "Seek cover!"

Doc and his men scattered. They gave Hornetta the option of finding her own shelter. She did. Predictably, she ran for the submersible.

Men were dropping off the truck. They had submachine guns. Not Tommy guns, either. But modern military weapons.

They began unleashing lead like torrents of rain.

Gun thunder echoed. Bullets flew madly in all directions. There was a lot of gray gunsmoke, which began obscuring everything.

Monk and Ham unlimbered their compact supermachine pistols and began returning fire. The sound of giant bull fiddles filled the great space.

Doc normally went about unarmed. But he was not without resources. From his pockets, he extracted large steel grenades. Flipping firing levers, he began tossing them.

They produced violent noise concussion and smoke. The smoke was tinged with a malevolent ochre. That made the attackers think of mustard gas and they ceased all shooting to don gas masks of the type used in the First World War.

That gave Monk and Ham time and opportunity to use their machine pistols to good advantage. The tiny weapons moaned, hosing "mercy" bullets, hollow capsules which did not kill, but produced swift unconsciousness after breaking the skin of victims, thereby introducing a potent drug into surface blood vessels.

Attackers began dropping out.

Seeing the tide turn, Monk and Ham moved in, clapping

fresh ammunition drums into their superfirers, Doc called out a sharp warning for caution. The bronze man had noticed something the others had not.

Too late. Some of the fallen raiders jumped to their feet and opened up on the hapless duo with vicious intent.

Monk and Ham broke in opposite directions, and beat one another to shelter. They hunkered down behind a spidery crane.

Doc raised his voice. "They are wearing some type of body armor!"

A man called out, "You think we don't know about those trick bullets you guys use. We have on mailed union suits that will turn them babies."

Monk howled. Ham groaned.

Throughout the warehouse—it was really a combination hangar and boathouse—Doc Savage had secreted many hidden controls. He found one such station and threw a lever.

At the far end of the hangar, which faced the Hudson River side of Manhattan, great roller doors swung open, admitting brilliant outdoor light.

This caused momentary consternation amid the attackers. They were still mixed in black smoke, but now the sudden light was throwing them into confusion.

Doc rapped out guttural orders in Mayan, the ancient language he and his assistants shared in common, and employed for secret communications.

They raced for a plane. Doc had directed them toward one in particular—a seaplane nearest the river.

They clambered aboard, closed the door.

"Where's that gal, Hornetta?" Monk wanted to know.

Doc said, "In the sub. Safe. She dogged the main hatch after her."

"We leavin' her behind?"

"That remains to be seen," Doc Savage said grimly. The bronze man knocked the engine into life.

Propeller slipstream began beating back, throwing the coiling poisonous-looking black smoke around. This added to the confusion of their attackers.

Releasing the brake, Doc jazzed the throttles. The plane started down the sloping concrete apron which dropped into the river.

Bullets began arriving. Snarling, they clipped the duralumin empennage and snapped at the tail.

Doc got the plane into the water. It wallowed. He threw the throttle all the way, and the speedy plane gave a lurch.

Gunmen surged onto the apron. Dropping to their stomachs, they took up stances that showed superb training and began shooting with methodical rapidity.

These men—whatever else they were—were marksmen. Hardly a bullet went awry.

The window glass on Doc Savage's planes were as tough as modern science can manufacture tempered glass. That made them bulletproof—within reason.

An unreasonable quantity of lead began punishing the stuff. Glass was chopped out of the side windows. The windscreen cracked, then fell open. The tail became perforated, and started to come apart under the relentless hammer of storming steel. It was as if unseen sledges were at work.

Doc realized very quickly that attempting flight was hopeless.

A sudden whiff of aviation fuel gave the first warning of what was coming next.

"They got the tank!" Ham screeched.

"We're sunk!" groaned Monk.

Doc Savage was pushing the speed ship as hard as he could. The hull pontoon was hammering across the river, trying to get on step.

The thundering aircraft never made it.

The relentless gunfire took its toll. Observers along the Jersey shore got the best sight. The plane was bouncing along the water without any preliminary flash or fire. It simply exploded.

A ball of red fire shot upward. Black smoke billowed up after it.

The detonation was not loud, compared to the pyrotechnics which accompanied it. But when it all subsided, there were flares and flame on the water and blackened debris began showering down, to show that nothing remained of Doc Savage's plane.

A grisly silence followed.

Chapter VII

HORNETTA STINGS

AN EERIE INTERVAL of quiet followed the destruction of Doc Savage's racing seaplane.

The last shards of wreckage finally fell on the heaving Hudson, to plunk beneath the waterline. A patch of oil burned for a time, then died down to faint, licking flames. Smoke continued to coil upward.

On the riverward side of the Hidalgo Trading Company warehouse, the attackers on the sloping concrete apron kept their eyes and their gun sights trained upon the water.

Their leader strode up. He was a fair-haired individual with anthracite-black eyes that might have been all pupil, and raw, sunburnt features.

"Any sign of *der bronzemann?*" he asked in his guttural native language.

"*Nein.*"

"If there is, treat him as a duck hunter treats a roosting fowl."

The men kept their eyes on the water. But no heads bobbed to the surface.

The leader trained field glasses of expert workmanship on the smoky patch of burning oil.

"*Der Mann aus Metall* is finished," he said. "*Kaput.*"

The others began picking themselves up off the concrete. They formed a rigid row as if at field inspection.

Fire engines wailed in the distance. They were drawing near.

"What about the meddling *fraulein,* Kolb?" asked one of the assembling men.

"We did not see her."

Kolb demanded, "What do you mean—did not see her? Was she on the airplane or not?"

"We do not know."

"She must have been. Search the entire place!"

"But—there is no time. Those are sirens."

Making harsh faces, the black-eyed Kolb ground his teeth in exasperation.

"Torch this place. Blow it up. If the girl is still here, let it become her tomb."

"Jawohl."

They set about tipping over various fuel drums gathered from a storage area.

Some were rolled to the corners of the warehouse. Others were set in the center, among the aircraft hangared there.

The group retreated to the landward side of the building.

They began puncturing drums with well-placed rifle slugs. The stink of high-test gasoline filled the vast interior.

Oil-soaked waste rags were ignited, and open tins of kerosene tossed in.

Gouts of flames exploded. They made racing tongues of fire along the concrete flooring. Fire met fire. Combustible mixtures encountered other combustible mixtures.

The Hidalgo Trading Company was completely ablaze by the time the three machines fled the vicinity.

The fire engines arrived too late. Water hoses were unreeled and firemen fell to work at attempting to quench the spreading flames. But all to no avail.

Within an hour, all that remained of the Hidalgo Trading Company was a smoking brick shell that breathed malodorous, noxious smoke.

NIGHT had fallen by the time the exhausted firemen had collected their hoses and stowed away their equipment.

The warehouse was a total loss. Almost nothing of Doc Savage's fleet had survived the ferocious conflagration.

Deep into the night, something could be heard in the ruin of a building.

A charred timber shifted. Another. A clattering of dry wood came. The rank odor of burnt wood assailed the nostrils. Had there been any nostrils to assail, that is.

In the dry dock of the boathouse section of the building, a hatch came open in stages. More timbers settled. That was what had caused the clattering.

On the razorback submersible, a hatch clanged all the way open. Coughing and hacking, a lithe form emerged.

"Damn that man!" choked Hornetta Hale.

What man she consigned to eternal fires remained unknown, however.

Hornetta concentrated on getting out of the still-smoking ruin without inhaling any more pungent odors.

The submarine had been an unpleasant place to endure a conflagration, and Hornetta looked as if she had spent the day in a steam bath, but she had survived the ordeal.

Casting a mournful glance back at the drydocked and immobile underseas craft, Hornetta slipped out of the blackened shell that had been the Hidalgo Trading Company boathouse-hangar.

A nighthawk taxi driver was loafing along the waterfront in search of a fare. Hornetta Hale stopped him by the most expedient method. She ran into the beams of his headlamps and waved her arms energetically.

The driver braked smartly, and craned his head out of the window.

"What's the big deal, lady? Trying to end it all?"

"Mind your beeswax," said Hornetta Hale, coming aboard.

She clapped the door shut. "Fade out of here and make it snappy!"

The driver grinned. "Where's the fire?"

She gestured behind her and forward. "Back there. And up ahead, too."

"Huh?"

"Skip it," sniffed Hornetta. Her eyes were red and swollen. It might have resulted from exposure to the smoky ruin. But it might have been repressed emotion.

"Where to, sugar?" the driver asked at last.

"Do they have flophouses for ladies in distress?" Hornetta asked disconsolately.

"I know just the place," said the cabby.

IT wasn't exactly a flophouse. But it wasn't the Ritz, either. The sign over the entrance read:

HOME FOR WANDERING WOMEN

Hornetta paid the driver and entered. Where she obtained the funds would have earned her a night in jail. She had picked a man's pocket on the street after he had whistled at her.

"I need a room for the night," she told the matronly desk clerk.

"Spat with hubby?" asked the matron.

"Not as big a spat as what's coming," Hornetta said fiercely.

"Excuse me?"

"Never mind. Just give me my room key."

"You don't have to be snippy about it, Mrs.—"

"Mudd."

"Huh?"

"Mary Mudd. That's my name. Mudd, with two d's."

Hornetta Hale took two flights of stairs, put the key in the lock with every intention of taking a much-needed bath and sleeping as long as necessary.

She got as far as opening the door to her room and half way across the threshold. Then she gave an uncharacteristic start.

Three men awaited her inside. They looked at her with unmistakably stern intent.

Hornetta Hale attempted to backpedal out of the room. She simply hadn't the moxie left for any more pointless flight.

A hairy hand grabbed the other side of the door knob and gave a yank.

Hornetta, clutching the opposite knob, was pulled in with the door. She was unceremoniously precipitated onto the threadbare rug, landing on her polka-dotted backside.

A thin blade of some sort touched her throat. It was long and vicious looking, the tip discolored with what Hornetta Hale mistook for dried blood.

"I am tempted to run you through," a thin voice sniffed.

"And I ought to break you in half," another male voice threatened.

But nothing of either sort happened.

Instead, Doc Savage reached down and took Hornetta by one flailing arm.

He lifted her to her feet by main strength and planted her in a wooden chair.

"How— What—?" she sputtered.

Monk squinted his small eyes at her. "That taxi driver belonged to us," he explained. "As a matter of fact, we set him prowling for you, along with other drivers."

"Indeed," seconded Ham. "He had instructions to take you here if you did not give another address."

"Yeah. And if you did, we would have collected you *there*."

"Either way," finished Ham, "you were bound to become our prisoner."

Hornetta looked flummoxed. Biting one pale lip, she turned her angry gaze up at Doc Savage, who through it all had said nothing.

"Stop looking at me like that, tall, dark and metallic. You make me nervous."

"If you had been honest with us from the start," the bronze man said simply, "a great deal of trouble might have been averted."

"That's nothing."

"Eh?"

"I said that's nothing."

"Explain yourself," prompted Doc.

"Compared to what's coming, I mean."

"Exactly what *is* coming?" Ham asked in his best barrister manner.

"I told you it was big," Hornetta reminded.

"You did."

"Bigger than big."

"Get to the point," snapped Ham.

"It's so big," said Hornetta Hale, "it could mean the end of the United States of America."

Doc Savage's uncanny trilling abruptly filled the room. It had a quality of astonished skepticism. The bronze giant stifled it with difficulty.

"Continue," invited Ham.

Hornetta Hale folded her sunburned arms stubbornly. "That's it. That's all I have to say."

"We have methods for making you talk," suggested Ham Brooks.

"Use 'em! See if I care. Pull out my fingernails. Singe my toes. Pluck me like a chicken. I ain't talking."

"Leave her to me, Doc," boasted Monk. "I'll make her crackle like a hen."

"You?" sneered the blonde. "That'll be the day! You're just sore because I got the better of you."

Ham opened his lean, mobile mouth to speak, whereupon Hornetta flayed the dapper lawyer with her exquisitely sharp tongue. "As for you, fancy britches, I can see that you're all in a lather because I wouldn't give you a tumble."

Ham turned purple and was reduced to sputtering inarticulately.

Doc Savage said steadily, "What is the point of all this stubborn silence? This is a serious matter. You are in very deep."

Hornetta snorted. "Deep as Davy Jones' locker, I'll tell a man!"

"Then come clean, sister," growled Monk.

Hornetta promptly changed the subject. "Listen, I got out of that brick kiln alive because I hid in your sub. It looked mighty seaworthy. What do you say?"

"Not without explanations," said Doc.

Hornetta suddenly thought of something. "Say, how did you three get away?"

"Our plane exploded," explained Ham.

"Yeah," said Monk. "But we weren't in it. We dropped out an emergency hatch on the opposite side, where we couldn't be seen."

"I heard all the little explosions before I heard the bigger one," Hornetta stated.

"That was our plane," admitted Ham Brooks.

"We just sat down on the riverbed until the coast was clear," added Monk.

"You and the local catfish, huh?"

"We have our methods," said Doc, cryptically.

"I'll bet you do," Hornetta said dismissively.

Hornetta continued her stubborn stance. She returned to the subject of her present obsession.

"What about that deal? Your sub for a ration of truth?"

"Only a ration?"

"I'm rationing out my truth these days. If you want your share, all of you have to string along with me."

Hairy Monk looked at the bronze man. "Doc?"

"Yes, Monk?"

"You got any of that new truth serum on you?"

Doc Savage made a show of going through his pockets. "I might just have some."

"'Cause I think that's the only way we're gonna get this leaky faucet to start gushing."

"Agreed," said Doc, extracting a case from one pocket. Opening it revealed a thin vial of colorless liquid and a hypodermic needle nestled in a bed of maroon velvet.

Doc directed quietly, "Monk, hold her arm."

"With pleasure, Doc. I always like to watch you go to work on 'em. Especially tough sisters like this one. They all think they have nerves of iron, but once that truth juice gets to work on them, they start spilling all their secrets like confession is going to come back into style."

Doc Savage charged the needle. He came over and took one of Hornetta's sinewy forearms. He pressed the needle point to the raw skin.

Hornetta's eyes grew wide. "You—you can't do this! It's illegal. Isn't it?"

Monk grinned widely. "Doc is a surgeon. Don't you know that? If the truth juice don't work, he's got a machine to X-ray your brain."

Hornetta's eyes protruded from their sockets. A starkness took hold of her shapely form. "All right, all right, you—win!"

"No tricks," warned Doc.

"Cross my heart and hope to strike gold," vowed Hornetta Hale.

Doc set the needle on a table as if to keep it handy should Hornetta reverse her decision.

Hornetta composed herself and began speaking.

"You remember when that German passenger dirigible went blooie a few years back?"

"Yes, of course," said Doc.

"And when the *Lusitania* sank?"

"Yes."

"And the assassin's shot that touched off the powder keg that was the last World War?"

"I do," admitted Doc Savage.

"Well, this will make all three of them look like barnyard accidents."

"How so?" asked Ham, eyes glowing with interest.

"Well boys, gather around and I'll tell you."

Instantly, Ham Brooks leaned in. A mistake.

Hornetta took a swipe at his sword cane, caught it, and claimed possession.

Bouncing out of her chair, she swiped the syringe off the table. It shattered.

Then she took aim at the center of Ham Brooks' elegant cravat and lunged in with the supple blade, saying, "Gonna inject me, were you? Well, try a taste of your own medicine!"

The blade probably only pinked Ham Brooks' throat. But that was enough.

The concoction on its tip was a chemical compound that brought swift unconsciousness.

Hornetta yanked out the long blade, and swept after Monk Mayfair, crying, "Next!"

Monk was no sissy. But years of being threatened by that keen rapier at the hands of the ever-dapper Ham gave him a studied respect for its incapacitating effects.

Howling, Monk bobbed back. The blade swished several times, slicing open his shirt front and revealing a red mattress of chest hair.

Doc Savage was moving now. While Hornetta sparred with Monk, he slipped up from behind, seizing her by the neck.

Hornetta had learned fighting skills somewhere. She kicked backward and barked Doc's shins, first one, then the other.

Doc lost his grip momentarily. That was all Hornetta needed. Spinning, she slashed and sliced wildly.

Hastily, Doc Savage retreated.

Luck was against him. One heel hooked a fringe of the threadbare rug, upset him. Doc got tangled up in a coat tree, had to arrest it with both hands before the heavy object could crash to the floor and create a commotion.

Hornetta flung up a window and made for the fire escape.

She stared down, paused, listened intently. Then, whipping off one shoe and throwing it to the sidewalk, Hornetta raced up toward the roof.

She was looking down over the stone parapet when Doc and Monk hit the sidewalk, discovered the dropped shoe, and raced in opposite directions in search of her.

After a while, they returned, dejected and empty-handed.

The last Hornetta Hale saw of them, they were carrying the unconscious Ham Brooks out to a waiting sedan. It whined off.

"That," said Hornetta Hale, peering over the parapet, "brings this evening to a satisfactory conclusion!"

She passed the night on the roof, and slept like a lamb. Which she was most assuredly not.

Chapter VIII

THE ARISTOCRATIC ASSASSIN

THE TIME WAS one week later.

It had been an uneventful week, all told.

After explaining to the authorities that they did not yet know who had undertaken to demolish his skyscraper headquarters and his riverfront hangar, Doc Savage had disappeared.

Doc's men were not, as a matter of fact, unduly alarmed, because it was Doc Savage's habit to disappear at times without a word of explanation. Sometimes he was gone for months, completely shut off from the world, in a far-off spot which he called his Fortress of Solitude, where he went to study and experiment. Even his five assistants did not know the exact location of this Fortress of Solitude, although they knew it was somewhere within the Arctic Circle. They were reasonably certain that Doc had not gone there. But the bronze man had many enemies, and it was always possible that someone had slipped something over.

The authorities had been skeptical. But Doc held a high honorary commission with not only the local police, but with the Department of Justice as well. He was taken at his word, even if there was some doubt on the matter.

Monk Mayfair had been left in charge of the rehabilitation of the eighty-sixth floor suite of offices. Ham Brooks was attending to legal matters having to do with that. The bronze man had a permanent lease on the building, but did not own it. The owners were irate. This was not the first time destruction had visited the eighty-sixth floor.* It was Ham's job to smooth down ruffled feathers.

Meanwhile, Monk supervised reconstruction. The reception room was relatively intact. The library was a wreck and the great laboratory was no more. Virtually everything would have to be replaced.

In the reception room, Monk was busy making telephone calls.

"Sure wish Renny and the others were here to help with all this."

Renny was Colonel John Renwick, a civil engineer of international repute. Together with Long Tom Roberts and Johnny Littlejohn, they comprised the rest of Doc's tiny band. All three were in different parts of the world pursuing their respective professions.

Since there was a lull in the investigation, Monk thought it unnecessary to summon them home. The man they most needed, Renny, was in Australia, supervising the construction of a new-style cantilever bridge. The big-fisted engineer had promised to return to the States as soon as practical in order to oversee the restoration of the Hidalgo Trading Company building, but there was no telling how long that might be.

By midafternoon of the seventh day after the raid on Doc Savage headquarters, a buzzer sounded.

Monk looked down on the big inlaid table that functioned as a desk. On a panel, a view of the corridor leading to the bronze door showed. A cautious soul, Monk liked to give visitors the once-over before receiving them.

"Oh boy, Pat!" Monk said happily.

Depressing a stud permitted the door to open.

In flounced pretty Patricia Savage, Doc's cousin and only living relative. She was smartly-attired in the latest Fifth Avenue autumn frock. Her skin partook of Doc Savage's russet coloring, but lacked the metallic aspect. Her eyes were a frank and inviting gold.

---

* White Eyes.

A wealth of bronze hair crowned the vision that was Pat. At sight of the homely chemist, she bestowed her most inviting smile.

"Hello, Monk. How goes the war?"

"Makin' progress, Pat. Doc ain't here."

Pat looked around her. "Where is he then?"

"No clue," said Monk. "But you know Doc."

Pat frowned. "I sure do. If he caught me here, he might bend me over his knee for a paddling and send me home."

"Aww, Doc just wants to keep you out of trouble, is all."

"Trouble," said Pat Savage, "is my main meat. Any word on that Hornetta wench?"

"Nope. I got a posse of some of Doc's private detectives out lookin' for her."

Pat dropped into a comfortable chair. "Well, maybe I'll just stick around here and see if anything pops."

"Suit yourself," said Monk, picking up a desk telephone from a bank of instruments. Inserting a furry finger into the rotary dial, he gave it a series of brisk spins.

Pat picked up a magazine, and attempted to peruse it. It proved to be a particularly erudite scientific journal and the bronze-haired girl found it impenetrable. She eventually gave it up as a bad job.

Noticing a neat stack of newspapers on the big desk, Pat reached for one.

"Nix!" snapped Monk. "I'm savin' those for when Doc gets back. The press has been beatin' up on him pretty bad since all this trouble hit town."

"I know," said Pat. "I read the news rags, too."

The newspapers did themselves proud.

SAVAGE FINALLY DOWNED

That was the way one sheet had it.

BAD MEN SHOOT BRONZE MAN

A tabloid said:

SAVAGE NOT SO SAVAGE!

"Maybe you should hide these instead," sniffed Pat.

"Doc owns a few of these sheets," countered the hairy chemist. "I think he might want to give some of them editors a good talkin' to."

Pat crinkled her pretty nose. "The way my cousin acts sometimes, he will probably give them all raises for being so darned honest," she said wearily.

NOT long after, the buzzer whined again. Consulting the television device, Monk looked interested.

A man stood in the outer hall. He was doing a strange thing—he was carefully twisting a metal cap off the lower end of a Malacca cane which he carried. When he had the cap off, he pocketed it, then hung the cane over an arm.

The man looked prosperous, faintly Continental, as if he had just gotten off a trans-Atlantic ocean liner. Striking though, was the way his skin appeared raw and blistered. Even in black and white, this was noticeable.

Peering over the homely chemist's shoulder, Pat Savage remarked cheerfully, "You don't look pleased to see company."

"I don't like the look of that cane," muttered Monk.

Pat arched one pencilled eyebrow. "You're just allergic to them after all the times Ham tried to brain you with his walking stick."

Monk scowled. "Take another look."

Pat did. "I see now. The cap is missing from the end."

"He just took it off."

"Why do you suppose he did that?" wondered Pat, brow creasing.

"Gun or gas in the cane, maybe."

"Recognize him?" asked Pat.

"Naw," said Monk. "But after all that's happened, I ain't takin' any chances. Step closer and roost on this rubber mat."

There was a rubber mat on the floor behind the long desk.

Pat complied.

The visitor with the large red hands and cane entered with his hat in hand. It was the type of hat called a Tyrolean. A stiff brush was tucked into the band on one side.

"Good day to you," he hailed, waving his hat. His voice sounded immensely pleased, like a voyager who had traveled far and had reached his long-awaited destination.

"We're busy." Monk returned shortly. "Whatcha want?"

"I seek the gallant known as Doc Savage."

"He ain't here," said Monk. "I'm his assistant, Monk. State your business."

The aristocratic man stood there on the decorative rug, cane gripped casually in both hands. He bent a supercilious eye on Monk Mayfair.

"I have important information for Doctor Savage, and only for him," he announced. "It is imperative that I consult with him."

Monk growled, "We don't know where Doc is, or when he will be back. And if you try to use whatever kind of weapon you've got in that cane, it'll be just too bad."

The visitor looked nonplussed in a casual way. He was, they saw, the cool and nervy type.

"My information," the man said without agitation, "concerns one Hornetta Hale."

Monk began, "If you would bust loose with some info—"

"Watch it, Monk!" Pat suddenly warned.

The visitor was tilting his cane up at Monk. The tip pointed at the notch between the hairy chemist's tiny eyes.

Monk tapped a small pedal on the floor.

Results were instantaneous.

The visitor shrieked unmanfully, dropped his came, and tied

himself in a knot. Moaning, he tried to pick up the cane. When his fingertips came near the brass handle, blue sparks leaped toward him. This produced another howl of anguish.

Scuttling like a crab, the man attempted to crawl out of the reception room, moaning and shrieking.

Monk depressed the floor pedal again. He leaped out from behind the massive desk and across the electrified rug, which was woven of fine wire which could not be distinguished from the other fibers unless a magnifying glass was used. The current had merely given the man an uncomfortable shock.

The visitor had quick wits. No sooner had the juice stopped contorting his paralyzed body than he yanked a small two-shot derringer from somewhere and gave Monk Mayfair both barrels in the stomach.

The caliber of weapon was undoubtedly heavier than the typical .22 derringer round. Monk was thrown backward with great force. That was enough for the man to reach the elevator, although he stumbled once and had to pick himself up.

The door responded instantly. That was fortunate for the man and unfortunate for the others. For Pat Savage had come flying out, a ludicrously large six-shooter in one tanned fist. She had extracted it from her commodious handbag.

Pat aimed and managed to send one .44 slug ripping through the closing doors. After that, the cage was sinking.

"Darn it!" she complained. She raced for the super-speed express elevator, with the intention of using it to beat the man to the lobby. Pressing the button, she discovered the cage was parked at the lobby level. Her eager expression sank to the marble floor.

"Drat!" fumed Pat.

Monk picked himself up with difficulty and grabbed a telephone. "Building electrician!" he shouted. When the connection came, he said, "Shut off the juice to the visitor's lift!"

"Will do, sir."

Then a bang came over the phone wire, followed by two more

bangs, a shout, and curse in the electrician's voice.

"Hell's bells!" the electrician snarled a moment later. "There's a guy with a gun in there watching the switchboard. He's masked. Wait a minute! He just lit out of here like his pants were on fire!"

Hanging up, Monk called the lobby and absorbed the unwelcome news that their courtly assailant had exited the building.

He ran out to join Pat at the special lift, growling, "They had it all figgered out. And that makes two of them, at least."

"Your trick rug didn't go so hot, huh?" Pat asked.

"Maybe," admitted Monk, rubbing his stomach gingerly. "But my bulletproof vest sure saved my bacon."

Halting, Monk stooped and picked up the cane which the Continental visitor had dropped. The examination he gave it was low and careful.

The cane barrel—hollowed out—yielded an ingenious mechanism consisting of a cylinder of compressed air, a valve which could be turned on by twisting the head of the cane, so that compressed air would feed into a tiny sprayer chamber. Monk noted the presence of a bilious liquid in the chamber, where it could be shot from the cane end.

"Sulfuric acid," he said thoughtfully. "It would have done a swell job of blinding me. You, too."

"Then maybe I was wrong about the rug," Pat admitted sheepishly. "It saved your eyesight, or Doc's, had he been around."

Monk finally got his breathing organized. "Come on, Pat. Maybe we can still get a line on 'em!"

Down at the switchboard, the girl described two men, one masked by a handkerchief tied around his lower face, the other was the would-be assassin.

Both had fierce sunburns. The girl gave a good description of them. So did the doorman. A taxicab had taken them away. Oddly, Monk accepted this datum without disappointment.

"What do lobster-red hands mean?" Monk asked Pat when

he was back in the office. "Remember, it's almost winter here. Sunburn ain't likely."

Pat considered. "Dishwashing?" she ventured.

"No good."

"Chemical burns?"

Monk shook his head. "Naw. I've been plenty burned by chemicals. It wasn't that."

"The tropics, then," hazarded Pat.

"That's an idea," muttered Monk. "It might mean they had enough dough to go south. Only a scorching sun would peel a man that way."

Within the hour, a desk phone buzzed. Monk scooped it up.

"Yeah? Great! Thanks." The apish chemist replaced the instrument. "We got a line on them."

"How?"

"Doc has this guy working for him, one of the graduates of our 'college.' He's usually stationed in the cab stand outside the building, for things like this. The two hired him and they went out to Long Island. The cabby just gave me the dang address." *

"Swell! What are we waitin' on?"

Monk made simian faces. They were comical in the extreme.

"I'll ring Ham in on this," he decided, reaching for the telephone.

"The more the merrier," Pat said brightly.

"Nix! Doc'll chew me out if I let you tag along," protested Monk.

Pat pouted prettily. "Doc doesn't have to know."

---

* *Doc Savage did not believe in prisons and incarceration. He understood that most prisons were actually breeding grounds for further criminality. So Doc created a secret institution in the wilderness of upstate New York, where criminals who fell under his power are subjected to a unique course of renovation. First, all memory of their criminal pasts are erased surgically. Then they are reeducated to despise crime in all forms. Finally, they are given new identities and taught a useful trade to prepare them for their second chance in life. Many of the "graduates" of Doc's secret "college" are employed by the bronze man himself, and quite a number have been trained as operatives of a private detective agency Doc had built up over the years.*

"If you get injured, or worse, it'll be my neck," Monk pointed out.

He had the telephone receiver in hand again and said, "Shyster, meet us here at headquarters." Monk gave an address. Pat, being no slouch, made a mental note of it.

"We can get there faster in my racing plane," hinted Pat after the apish chemist hung up.

Interest registered on Monk's simian features. "How many does it seat?"

"Two."

"Swell. Ham and I will borrow it."

"In that case," Pat countered snippily, "forget it. I'll meet you there, and may the best man win."

"Aww, Pat," said Monk.

But pretty Pat Savage was already out the door.

Chapter IX

THE SOUTH AMERICA TREND

PAT SAVAGE KEPT her racing plane stored at the seaplane base on the East River side of Manhattan island, at East Twenty-third Street. It was a two-place job, a glaring scarlet with black trim, boasting an engine that was overpowered for an aircraft of its class.

The establishment had an ingenious method of putting planes in the water. Pat had only to start her trim little craft, taxi onto a concrete turntable, and wait while the mechanism was engaged.

The turntable ramp was set at an angle so that one side dipped into the river. Pat's plane was slowly rotated until the amphibian's pontoon hull was delivered into the water.

Advancing the throttle, Pat slid off like a duck entering a pond, taxied some distance, and the smart little ship got on step. After some bumping along, the scarlet amphibian took to the air, and overflew the breathtaking ironwork structure that was the Queensboro Bridge.

Soon, she was winging toward the far tip of Long Island, near Montauk Point lighthouse.

Finding an address from the air was practically impossible, but with the aid of a handy road map, Pat was able to locate the spot. Barnes Road wound along to the shore and Pat imagined that putting down at the far end was the best place to begin her investigation.

She was mildly surprised to see a brick boathouse at the water's edge, with a seaplane docked inside, its snout visible, prop gleaming in the sun. This part of Long Island is inhabited by the well-to-do, so perhaps it was not so unusual.

Pat eschewed the hangar, however, beaching her ship in a sleepy cove. Tossing out a sea anchor, she picked her way carefully along jetty rocks until she reached solid ground. The area was sparse of homes, so Pat was not challenged by local folk.

The bronze-haired girl hiked to the place where Barnes Road terminated.

This time surprise seized her with greater force. For the number she sought—three hundred and thirty-four—was that of a brick mansion that plainly belonged to the seaplane hangar. Or vice versa, actually.

"Looks like I beat the boys, for once," she chortled as she reconnoitered the place.

That was not all she beat, it developed.

A long phaeton came sliding up. It eased onto a winding white gravel driveway and lurched to a stop.

Out of it stepped the Continental visitor of the day, his Tyrolean hat jauntily askew. Evidently, he had the presence of mind to carry it from the scene of his late embarrassment.

With him was a man wearing a rust-colored overcoat that Pat did not place. She had not been informed of the description of the earlier raiders on Doc Savage's skyscraper establishment.

"Mr. Trick Cane himself," Pat muttered. She unlimbered her six-shooter, which was charged with the same mercy bullets Doc Savage had invented. She rarely flung lead indiscriminately, although Pat was not shy about doing so if the occasion called for it.

As the pair entered the house, Pat slipped up, using topiary shrubbery for shelter. It allowed her to get within peeping-tom distance of a broad bay window.

Men were inside. Several of them. They were competent looking men with intelligent faces. There was a woman, too. She was seated in a high-backed stuffed armchair. Pat did not place her, and the angle did not allow her to identify the femme as the missing Hornetta Hale—if indeed it was she.

On the theory that a woman discovered in the company of such men as the Continental assassin and the others was as likely a kidnap victim as not, Pat resolved to liberate her at the earliest opportunity.

Creeping around to the front door, Pat used a hairpin on the lock. One of her less ladylike skills was lock-picking. Doc Savage had taught her a few tricks of the trade, knowing of Pat's propensity for getting herself into trouble. It was supposed that the bronze man had grown tired of rescuing his scrappy cousin from peril, and decided to equip her with a few necessary skills.

The lock quickly surrendered. Pat slid in, gun in hand, and eased through a well-appointed entryway. This led to a parlor dominated by a long sofa and matching armchairs upholstered in mohair. Along one wall, a grandfather clock ticked the minutes away.

VOICES were emanating from another room—evidently a library of some sort. Pat could catch glimpses of walnut book cases filled with expensive tomes that appeared from the perfect condition of their spines to be decorative rather than purchased for perusal.

A man was saying, "Now that this woman has been prevented from seeing Doc Savage, and *der bronzemann* has been neutralized, we have no time to waste."

That was the Continental fellow. No mistaking that suave voice. Pat recognized it at once.

"Everything now depends upon returning to the lagoon to accomplish what has begun," he continued.

"*Ja,*" another agreed. "Should we fly?"

"Too risky. We will go by boat. Liners are leaving for South America daily. We will blend in with the passengers. If we encounter difficulty, it may become necessary to commandeer the boat, but let us hope that such unpleasantness may be avoided."

"That will take time," a man pointed out.

"We have time. Our objective will not arrive at the secret location for another two days. We have planned a long time for this—many months. And now events are coming to a head."

They spoke reasonable English. But their pronunciation was not American. Pat recognized that they were the accents of one of the European warring powers that had stirred up so much trouble until finally war had broken out in Europe.

"Then it is time to book passage, *mein Herr Graf.*"

"Attend to it, Pippel. *Schnell.*"

The one named Pippel clicked his heels—if Pat recognized the sound correctly—and came out in search of a telephone.

Pat took up a crouching position behind one of the overstuffed chairs of expensive workmanship. Her bronze-haired head was cocked, eager to capture more information.

The whizzing of a dial mechanism came, followed by a rapid exchange.

"Yes. I wish to book passage on the next steamer for Nassau in the Bahamas. Yes? The *Caribbulla?* It will suffice. Leaving tonight? That is acceptable. Yes, there are five in the party. Book under the name of…" the man seemed to hesitate. "Jon Schmidt. That is right, Schmidt. Thank you."

Hanging up, Pippel returned to the library, saying, "It is all arranged."

"Not quite," Pat murmured. Coming out of her crouch, she stepped lightly toward the open library door, hogleg in hand.

Her intention was to get the drop on the group, cowgirl style.

Her intentions were good. The results were not.

Pat stepped boldly in, and started to say "Reach!" She swallowed the word, half-spoken.

For the six men were ready for her. They had spike-snouted foreign pistols out and all six were pointed at Pat and her frontier Colt.

Mentally, Pat did the arithmetic. Six guns against a six-shooter. She had one bullet for each man. They had, probably, nine slugs in each magazine.

Pat Savage did the only sensible thing.

"I surrender," she said weakly.

The Count pointed to Pat with a new cane. "Please to drop the pistol on the rug, *fraulein.*"

Pat obliged. She set it down carefully rather than drop it. The weapon had belonged to her father and to his father before him. It was a family heirloom she did not wish to damage.

When she was done, a blonde-haired woman walked up, appraised her comprehensively, and asked, "Miss Savage?"

"Miss Hale?"

"She knows too much," snapped the blonde, and promptly cracked Pat Savage over the head with a porcelain vase which shattered amid her luxurious bronze hair.

Pat crumpled to the nappy rug and lay still.

The Count—he was clearly the leader of the foreign band—began issuing harsh orders.

"Berling. Kolb. Vollensack. Be so good as to place her in the trunk of the autocar."

"Shall I kill her first?" asked one.

"No. Not necessary. We will make other arrangements."

"Perhaps we should take her up in the plane and dump her in the Sound?" another man suggested.

The Count's serious mien brightened. "An excellent idea. Change of orders. Take her to the seaplane hangar. We will all take a nice airplane ride and Miss Savage will go for a rather unhealthy swim. *Nein?*"

This seemed to be an attempt at humor on the part of the leader, but no one laughed. They were too truculent of face for laughter. In fact, they looked very grim indeed as they bundled the insensate bronze girl in a bedsheet and lifted her by the simple expedient of taking hold of both twisted ends.

In a grim silent line, the group wended their way down to

the seaplane hangar. The undergrowth was not well-tended here. There were weeds, late fall wildflowers. Cattails predominated. Recent abundant rains had caused them to grow to phenomenal height.

From across a clearing, a voice called harshly, metallically, "Lay 'em down, you yeggs! You're in a spot!"

Chapter X

THE PUGILIST

MONK MAYFAIR AND Ham Brooks chose that exact moment to pull up in Doc Savage's new sedan.

They had made fair time leaving the city, but to travel the entire length of Long Island was a chore. Even running with a concealed siren caterwauling, it had taken over an hour to arrive at their destination.

Prudently, they had parked several blocks before their destination and were approaching by foot.

They arrived in time to spot the procession of men working their way down to the oceanside boathouse which doubled as a seaplane hangar.

That was when the disembodied voice had crashed, "Lay 'em down you yeggs! You're in a spot!"

There was no sign of the author of the harsh warning.

The Continental leader began snarling, "Down, you men!"

The others flattened with military efficiency. They did not even drop their sheeted burden, but fell atop it. One hunkered behind Pat Savage's concealed form, fully prepared to use the unconscious girl as a shield.

The leader was calling to his men. "Someone is over by the hangar. Acts like he has a pistol. He yelled—"

"Stay down!" invited the voice from across the clearing. "I've done enough kiddin'."

The voice resembled that of a brawler of the waterfront variety.

The leader took deliberate aim at the voice, which seemed to be coming from the cattails. The swiftness with which he did that showed that he had been thinking of it. He fired. Gunsound whacked, echoed and reëchoed.

"Lay to with some sense!" rapped the voice that might have belonged to a dockwalloper.

Monk and Ham decided that falling flat was a smart decision, too. They got down on their stomachs, produced their mercy pistols. Unlatching their safeties, they began crawling forward.

"Whatcha think is up?" Monk muttered.

"Quiet, you ape," snapped Ham. "We'll find out soon enough."

Gunfire was erupting from the men. They began scything weeds with smart precision.

Return fire was non-existent.

The Count's men paused, then they climbed to their feet and began advancing in an organized skirmish line. They fired sporadically as they advanced.

Monk lunged forward in the middle of the cannonading. His rusty fist whistled and dropped a man. He booted another in the middle, with an eye to results rather than ethics, and folded the fellow like a jackknife. Then he jumped on Pippel's back with both feet, kept jumping, as if he were hopping on a trampoline.

Ham swept in, employing his sword cane. He plinked a man in the shoulder. The other, to his astonishment, wheeled and uncorked three shots, knocking the sputtering lawyer into a drainage ditch.

Bellowing, Monk seized the shooter by the back of the neck and began bouncing him in place. Various objects—keys, a wallet and extra money and coins—began falling out of his pocket. The pistol in his grip came loose, showing that it had a "broomhandle" grip.

When Monk stopped slamming him, the man corkscrewed in such a fashion his knees seemed to knock together as he fell on his face.

Scowling, Monk Mayfair looked around for another victim.

"That is quite enough violence," a precise voice said coldly.

Monk's piggy eyes fell on the speaker. He was the Continental leader. In one hand was a Mills bomb. He held it in such a way as to suggest he was unafraid to use it.

"If I and my comrades are not permitted to leave," he said coldly, "then I shall be forced to blast us all into eternity."

Monk saw that the man was deadly serious.

"That would be like committin' suicide," Monk pointed out.

"No," clipped the man. "It *would* be suicide. Such I am perfectly prepared to commit. Now stand aside. Your friend as well."

For Ham Brooks was clambering out of the drainage ditch, apparently uninjured. Only his chainmesh undervest saved him from serious injury, if not death. He flicked leaves off his fastidious person.

"I'll be damned," exploded the barrister. "What's behind this mad behavior?"

"We'll danged soon find out," grumbled Monk, keeping his superfirer trained on the Count. He was calculating the odds of putting the man out with a blast of mercy bullets before he could pull the pin on his hand grenade.

Then an entirely strange voice broke into the discussion.

"You'll find it's something unpleasant unless you stand very still."

Monk's neck was nothing to speak of. He had to turn his entire apish torso to look behind him, at the opposite side of the road.

A huge figure had lifted out of the weeds and was braced on widespread legs. It was an individual who looked like a prizefighter. He had a nickeled revolver which was small in his scarred, lumpy fist.

Monk started to swing his machine pistol around. The nickeled revolver lipped flame and noise. Monk ducked wildly.

"I'm levelin' about it," said the big man. "You two guys come loose from them guns or you'll be picking lead out of yourselves."

Monk considered that, then let fall his gun. Ham did the same. The pig, Habeas, sat down dog fashion and watched the proceedings with beady-eyed interest.

The pugilistic one gestured at Monk and Ham; then he pointed up the road. It ran west, toward the setting sun.

"You'd better take Horace Greeley's advice," he said. "And do it fast."

"Huh?" Homely Monk seemed not to understand.

"Pick 'em up and lay 'em down," growled the other. "Get on your bicycles. Raise a dust."

Scowling, Monk began to run. Ham trailed him. They looked back. The prizefighter snarled loudly and lifted his gun. The two men ran faster, ceased looking back.

The pugilist looked at the hog, Habeas Corpus, and said, "Scat!"

The shoat ran after the two men.

THE MAN who looked like a prizefighter laughed grimly. He was a human hulk. Facially, he resembled the caricature which cartoonists drew to depict Old Man Prohibition a decade back. Pounding fists in the past had thickened his eyes and brows. His nose had a too-perfect shape which suggested that it had been made over by a plastic surgeon. Thin gray lines of old scars were plentiful on his face and a thick net webbed his solid hands. He wore old khaki clothes of a disreputable type.

"Come on, you guys!" he rapped at the Count and his companions.

"Who are you, if I may inquire?" drawled the Continental fellow, pocketing his grenade.

"Starr. Gloomy Starr."

The man fit his description. He was a tall tower of muscle with a face that rather resembled an unhappy dray horse.

"I heard the ruckus and figured I'd join in," offered Gloomy.

"To what purpose, Mr. Starr?"

"I hear shootin' and it's like a call to action. I'm for hire, I might add."

"We appreciate your assistance," said the leader coolly, "but we do not need your help." He snapped his fingers once, sharply.

Two men went to drag out the sheeted form of Pat Savage.

The pugilistic one showed sudden interest. "What have we here?" he murmured. "A body maybe?"

"None of your concern, Mr. Starr."

Starr smiled broadly, displaying massive, horse-like teeth. "Call me Gloomy."

A sudden thought struck the Count. "By chance can you fly an airplane?"

"Sure as shootin'. Can ride a horse, too."

"We have—er—a disposal problem. Would you be interested in attending to it for us?"

"How much?"

"Five hundred."

"Dollars?"

"What else?"

"Way you gents talk, I kinda question the currency. No offense."

"None taken, I assure you." The other bowed in courtly fashion. With his cane, he pointed to the brick structure by the water's edge. "The aircraft sits in that hangar. We will wait for you here."

"Glad to oblige," said Gloomy Starr, packing the sheeted form over one shoulder and bearing it into the boathouse.

Minutes passed, then a green-and-white float plane scooted out and took to the skies, engine howling.

They watched the aircraft through field glasses. The pilot showed moderate skill at flying, but that was all that was required for the task at hand.

Before long, a sheeted bundle came tumbling out of the

plane. It made a white splash in the surface of the Sound. Then the plane came about and ran toward them.

"When he lands, we will kill him, of course," said Pippel, who was looking rather greenish after the severe manhandling Monk Mayfair had given him.

The Count frowned. "No. He will be useful."

Pippel's face twisted. "We cannot—"

A gloved hand was raised. "Silence. He sticks out like a sore thumb. He will provide good American company on the voyage south."

Pippel nodded. He was beginning to comprehend the trend of things. His expression told that he did not like it, but he understood his leader.

"Yes, *mein Herr Graf,*" he said crisply, his back stiffening as if in salute.

Chapter XI

CAY BOUND

THE ARISTOCRAT CALLED the Count advanced to meet Gloomy Starr upon his return. The landing was not smooth. Pancaking, the float plane hit hard, all but dipped a wingtip into the choppy waters of Long Island Sound. The hapless pilot, in attempting to taxi toward shore, managed to stub the craft's pontoons against a group of half-submerged rocks.

The final result was that the hulking man was forced to abandon the stricken seaplane and swim back toward land.

The Count asked coolly, "It went well?"

"You saw how well with your own eyes," replied Gloomy laconically. "Sorry about your ship. I was always better at take-offs than landings."

"You mean that your piloting skills did not, in truth, include seaplanes," clucked the Count.

"Now that you mention it, yeah," admitted Gloomy sheepishly.

"No matter, the plane was a rental, and we are done here. I was referring to the disposal operation, by the way."

Gloomy shrugged gigantically. "You saw that, too." From his dull expression, cold-blooded murder was neither a new experience, nor especially nerve-jarring.

The Count smiled unreservedly. "I did, indeed. By the way, my name is Rumpler. Now we must be off."

Turning, he gave orders in a guttural language.

The speed with which the men gathered up their fallen was remarkable. They were carried into the house, which was plainly rented for the purpose of sheltering the group.

Instantly, clothes were packed and suitcases thrown into the trunk of the waiting vehicle. Another car—a sedan—was wheeled out of the attached garage.

"Where to?" asked Gloomy Starr.

"Steamship docks," he was told.

"And after that?"

"You will be told at the appropriate time."

Gloomy Starr went over to the blonde who was very subdued.

"And who might you be?"

"None of your business," snapped the woman.

Gloomy scrutinized her with intensely dark eyes.

"Have we met before?"

"I doubt it," the blonde said frostily.

"I didn't think so," Gloomy muttered.

"I normally keep better company," she added sarcastically.

The Count spoke up. "Miss Hale presents a special problem."

Gloomy pursed thick lips. "She does, does she?"

"We can't kill her, much as we would prefer to."

Gloomy cocked a quizzical eyebrow. "No? Why not?"

"It is a long, tedious story, but your job will be to get her out of the country."

"A kidnap job, eh?"

"If you want to call it that. We wish you to take the young lady to the South Street docks, book passage for the two of you on the packet steamer *Matador*." The Count favored Gloomy with a speculative eye. "Have you got that?"

"*Matador*, right. Bound where?"

"Brazil. That is as far south as the *Matador* travels. That should be good enough."

"And when I get her there?"

"Check into the Alhambra Hotel and wait there until you hear from us."

"Sounds simple enough."

"It *is* simple. And it will pay a cool three grand. Collectable at the Brazilian end."

Gloomy grinned. "I'm game, gents."

"And so there are no untoward complications, we will escort you to the docks and see you off," explained the Count.

"Right kind of you," Gloomy Starr returned.

"Nothing kind about it," returned the Count. "We have no margin for failure."

Glints of interest came into Gloomy Starr's scar-surround-ed eyes.

"And where are you gents gonna be in the meanwhile?" he asked.

"We have a destination of our own in mind."

"Is that right?"

"Yes. One not found on any map."

Curiously, Gloomy Starr looked like he wanted to ask another question. But a problem came up that prevented the asking of it.

"Count," a man said. "Pippel is not feeling right."

"Let me attend to him."

Gloomy followed the noble into another room where the Count went over to a man on a couch. It was that man who wore a rust-colored overcoat, the one called Pippel. He looked ill. His face was pale and his breathing labored. He grimaced with each intake of breath.

"What is wrong, my Ernst?" asked the Count in a solicitous tone.

"I—I think my ribs were stove in by that *verdammt* ape."

"That is too bad. You cannot be moved. And if you cannot be moved, you cannot come with us to the cay."

Gloomy Starr perked up. "Cay?"

He was ignored.

"I would be safe on the cay," grunted Pippel with effort.

"But we will be safer with you out of the picture. I am sorry, Ernst." And with those words still on his tongue, the Count drew his double-barreled derringer from a vest pocket and shot Pippel through the skull. The double report was muffled. The pillow on which the dead man's head had been resting slowly changed color.

Gloomy Starr said angrily, "Was that necessary?"

"Very," said the Count, pocketing the smoking pistol. "You object, Mr. Starr?"

"You're kinda free with your lead slugs and your men's lives," Gloomy pointed out. "Since I'm one of them, that kinda gives me an itch I wanna scratch right now."

The Count smiled bleakly. "Since you will be going to Brazil on our behalf, I think you will be perfectly safe there, Mr. Starr. So long as you do not return before instructed to." The suave man smiled in a friendly manner. "You see?"

Having dismissed the concern, the Count turned to address the others, who had looked on with stiff, unemotional faces. "Now, it is high time that we departed. Yes?"

The men gathered up their things, and one of them took rubbing alcohol and a chamois and began going over the door-knobs, light switches, and other smooth surfaces.

"Clean everything up that could have been touched, rough or smooth," directed the Count. "That iodine-vapor method the American police use will bring out fingerprints on almost everything."

The men fell to work at once. They were very efficient, as if they had covered their tracks in this organized manner many times before.

Watching them, an interested gleam came into the eyes of the pugilist who called himself Gloomy Starr. The pugilist paid special attention to the supervising aristocrat, as if trying to place him in his memory. If he succeeded in this mental inventory, the results were not written upon his horsey features.

Those chores accomplished, the wonderfully efficient men exited, locking all doors. They drove off in the two machines, heading toward Manhattan.

Gloomy Starr was packed into the town car with the blonde. She looked unhappy. Miserable might capture her mood most descriptively.

She was dabbing her red eyes with a handkerchief, obviously fighting back tears.

"She seems kinda upset all of a sudden," commented Gloomy.

The Count replied, "I have just broken to her the regrettable news about poor Pippel."

The blonde woman squeezed her eyes shut. Pain was evident on her pale features. Taking the tear-moistened handkerchief in her trembling hands, she twisted it in her silent agony. In that way, she seemed to get a firm grip on her composure.

Gloomy regarded her with something akin to sympathy. "What got you into this mess, Missy?" he asked.

"I made the mistake of trying to reach Doc Savage," she returned stiffly.

"Doc Savage," said Gloomy Starr, as if tasting the name. "Think I've heard of him."

"Many have," the blonde said vaguely.

"What be your first name?"

"Honoria."

"Nice name," said Gloomy, and left off the conversation. He seemed to drift off into thought as the vehicles made their determined way toward the city.

THE *MATADOR* was scheduled to depart the Manhattan steamship docks at four in the afternoon, stopping at Havana, Curacao, and points south until reaching Sao Paulo, Brazil. It was as popular run and had become even more so since the frantic day two years before when, with the outbreak of war in Europe, passenger liner companies had called back to their home ports all trans-Atlantic vessels. Once the frantic scramble had been completed, the steamship companies had been forced to look south, passenger travel to Europe being out of the question for the foreseeable future.

It was not much of a vessel, but she looked shipshape—if one overlooked the scabs of rust distributed here and there over her dark hull.

Preparations were well under way for departure. There was a lot of scurrying on deck and the gangplank was already unchained and accepting passengers.

The aristocratic Count purchased one ticket from the steamship agent and handed the brown envelope to Gloomy Starr.

"Once you smuggle her on board," he said out of earshot of the girl, "you will hear from a man named Burch. Karl Jon Burch."

"Who is he?" asked Gloomy.

"A contact on the boat. While you will be watching over Miss Hale, he will be watching over you. And we will loiter here to make absolutely certain that you board this rather rusty vessel." Again the Count offered his charming Continental smile that conveyed superficial warmth and nothing of the genuine article.

"I getcha."

The Count grew earnest. "Nothing must prevent Miss Hale from reaching Brazil safely. Is that fully understood?"

"Completely," said Gloomy, collecting Miss Hale, then piloting her to the baggage area, where he intended to acquire a steamer trunk.

Miss Hale seemed to go along willingly, if reluctantly.

After they were gone, the Count left his men on watch and went to a pay telephone. There, he dropped a nickel in the slot. Reaching the operator, he asked briskly, "Yes, I would like to be connected to a long-distance party. Collect. Inform the other party that Count Rumpler is calling him."

After providing the operator with the number, the suave

gentleman waited patiently while the call was put through. He examined his walking stick, noted a nick in the fine wood, and frowned with unconcealed displeasure.

Eventually, the connection was made.

"This is *V-Mann-Fueher* Rumpler," reported the Count, whose name was not really Rumpler. "The immediate problem has been resolved. Regrettably, *Haupt-V-Mann* Pippel had to be liquidated. We are preparing to steam for the staging area."

"Pippel proved to be unreliable," suggested the thickly-accented voice coming over the wire.

"For which he has paid the ultimate penalty," the Count returned coldly. "On a more positive note," he added. "I have just sent the Doc Savage aide named Renny Renwick to Brazil."

"Excellent," returned the other. "Are you certain it is he?"

"Absolutely certain. He is a long-faced hulk of a man with great scarred knuckles. His disguise is good, but not perfect. The truth dawned on me after I had undertaken to hire the brute. A man of *Herr* Renwick's size and countenance should think twice before undertaking to pass himself off as anyone else. I have rather adroitly turned his attempt to infiltrate our little band into a wild goose chase, which we can employ to lure Doc Savage to South America, and so out of our way."

"What about the girl?" the accented voice wanted to know.

"She went along willingly. She does not know the true identity of Gloomy Starr, as he calls himself."

"Wunderbar. Miss Honoria Hale will be taken care of. Arrangements will be made at once."

"Very good," said the Count crisply. "We will see you at the cay in another day, then, *Herr Kapitan.*"

The call was terminated.

The Count looked thoughtful as he returned to his waiting men.

"Matters are coming to a head, my friends," he told the others.

They accepted this information with stony expressions, like

men who have been told they were going to war the next morning. Then they turned their attention to the *Matador,* and watched silently as Gloomy Starr mounted the gangplank and gave the purser his ticket.

"Where is the girl?" wondered one. He had very black eyes in his sunburnt face, and had been the leader of the raid on Doc Savage's warehouse hangar whom his underlings had called Kolb.

"Mr. Renwick has instructions to smuggle her on board, and since it is as important to him to convince us of his *bona fides* as it is that Miss Hale be spirited away to Brazil, I have every expectation that he has complied to the letter."

"What about Doc Savage?"

"Thank you for reminding me, *Herr* Kolb," said the Count, "I must get off a telegram to him at once. Perhaps I will dispatch *der bronzemann* to Buenos Aires."

Kolb frowned. "Won't Renwick wire Savage from the ship to meet him in Brazil?"

The Count shrugged negligently. "Brazil. Argentina. What does it matter?" he scoffed, tossing off a chopping salute in the direction of Gloomy Starr, who returned the farewell gesture with a broad equine smile and a hearty wave of his meaty hand. "Doc Savage will be out of our collective hair for the duration of the operation. After that, it will not matter."

With that, the glum group turned away and sought their automobiles.

Chapter XII

THE SICK WOMAN TRICK

HONORIA HALE WAS being taken care of very thoroughly, just as the mysterious *Herr Kapitan* had boasted.

After making certain arrangements, Gloomy Starr had smuggled her on board in a steamer trunk purchased with her proportions in mind. When the trunk was delivered to the cabin on the B Deck of the *Matador,* Gloomy paid the longshoremen who had set it on the floor and tipped them lavishly.

After they had departed, Gloomy knelt, unlocked the trunk with a brass key and threw the lid open.

Honoria Hale was revealed, trussed, gagged and glaring red-faced fury. She kicked at the trunk's lining with both feet.

When Gloomy Starr lifted her out of the receptacle and dropped her into a chair, showing no more exertion than if he had picked up a sailor's duffle bag, the red-faced woman's features grew fearfully pale.

The gag was removed.

Gloomy grinned. "Since we are going to be cabin mates," he began, "we ought to know more about one another."

Honoria glared at him. Her blue eyes snapped. But a deep fear lay behind her optical sparking.

"Let's start with why those foreign yeggs want you out of the country so bad," invited Gloomy.

"Why don't you ask them?" Honoria Hale said flintily.

"Tried that. No soap. It's your turn."

Honoria Hale—if that was her real name—drew in a long

breath. She seemed to be steeling herself for something.

Gloomy Starr was no fool. He sensed what was coming. Before Honoria could give vent to a cry for help, he clapped his huge hands over her mouth, and kept one paw there while he returned the gag to its original position.

Through the tight cloth, Honoria attempted to give the monstrous pugilist a sharp piece of her mind. Only a muffled honking resulted.

"Now, now," clucked Gloomy. "Be a lady."

Honoria continued her muffled tirade.

"Such language," Gloomy murmured. Apparently, he was a humorist, for the woman's vocal exertions could not be understood in any way.

The *Matador* was by this time leaving port. There was the tooting of foghorns and the usual dockside bustle and uproar. The sounds of gurgling as lines were cast off and the hull shifted away from the busy pier. Soon, the rushing of water came, signifying that the steamer was being guided by tugs out to the Narrows, and thence into the open Atlantic.

Gloomy went to the porthole, peered out. His cartilage-scarred eyes narrowed. He turned to his captive.

"Long voyage ahead of us. Sure you don't want to unlimber with some palaver?"

The look that came into Honoria's frightened eyes tended toward the blank. Her features were by now dull with defeat.

"Talk turkey," Gloomy clarified.

Honoria shook her head vehemently.

"Something was said about Doc Savage. Know him?"

Another head shake came.

"I hear he's bad medicine," Gloomy muttered.

Honoria did not disagree with that opinion.

Gloomy sat down and began making faces that a bulldog might have recognized. He was no beauty. He rubbed his too-perfect nose a few times and pulled on a cauliflower ear.

Abruptly, he stood up.

"I think," he offered, "I will avail myself of a promenade of the deck." Grinning, he added, "You stay put."

As the big man exited the cabin, Honoria stamped a foot in anger.

GLOOMY STARR moved to the nearest companionway and ascended to the main deck. Passengers had gathered at the stern and were waving to well-wishers clustered at the dock. It was the usual *bon voyage* ritual.

Gloomy made a reconnoiter of the deck, his dark eyes searching faces.

After some twenty minutes of this, he failed to recognize any, and returned to the cabin.

"Not much excitement," he muttered upon his return.

Honoria only glowered at him.

Gloomy Starr may have been many things, but a prophet was not one of them. Not long after his casual statement, a sharp knocking came to the door.

Gloomy shot up from his chair and went to the panel.

"Who's there?" he growled.

An unfamiliar voice called, "A friend."

"Name?"

"Blitz."

"Don't know you."

"We have mutual friends."

"Name a few," Gloomy invited.

"Count Rumpler. Pippel. Kolb. Need I go on?"

Gloomy seemed to hesitate, then threw open the door.

A man entered. It could be seen that he was the opposite of the huge hulk calling himself Gloomy Starr. The new arrival had the slim lithe form of a dancer. Such men are sometimes found in the prizefighting ring—in the bantam-weight category.

He sauntered in as if entering his own cabin. Gloomy Starr laid a large, obstructing hand against his chest, arresting the unwanted visitor's attempt to peer about the curtained room.

"You got a longer handle?" asked Gloomy.

The other looked momentarily confused.

"Eh?"

"Full name?" clarified Gloomy.

The bantam-weight smiled a begrudging inch. "Bantam Blitz. Ever heard of me?"

"Fighter?"

"A good guess, my man." He craned his head around the open door and indicated Honoria, whose head had been cocked in their direction since the first knock. "Is that her ladyship?"

"Could be," grunted Gloomy, closing the portal. "What's it to you? She's my headache."

"Did you really think that the Count would entrust you with her care and keeping without someone keeping an eye on you?"

"Makes sense, you put it that way," admitted Gloomy. "But I was told a different name. Burch, it was."

"There is no Burch on the passenger list, which I gave the once-over," advised Bantam Blitz.

Gloomy blinked, as if not sure what to make of that morsel.

Bantam Blitz walked over to the trussed woman in the chair and examined her critically from several angles.

"I rather doubt," he said, "that keeping this dame tied up will be practical all the way to Brazil," he ventured coolly.

"You got a point," grunted Gloomy.

"Suppose that we make other arrangements than these crude ones," suggested the newcomer.

"I'm all ears," said Gloomy.

Bantam Blitz looked over Gloomy Starr with an appraising glance.

"All muscle is more like it."

"It's how I make my living," said Gloomy rather defensively.

"With my muscles."

"I, on the other hand, prefer to rely upon my wits," purred Bantam Blitz.

"Maybe we would make a good team, at that," suggested Gloomy.

"We can discuss this later," said Bantam Blitz thoughtfully. "For now, we must solve the matter at hand."

"Like I said, I'm all—"

"Ears. Yes, yes, I know," Blitz said distractedly. Cupping his chin in one hand, he mused, "I suddenly have what they call a brain storm."

"Yeah?"

Bantam Blitz laughed shortly. "She is desperately ill."

"Eh?" Gloomy appeared puzzled. "How come?"

"Just wait here, friend. I will be back shortly."

Bantam Blitz now left the cabin and was gone some fifteen minutes. He came back smiling widely, carrying a small bottle in one hand.

"Where'd you get that stuff?" Gloomy wanted to know.

"From the medicine chest of the ship's doctor," explained Bantam Blitz. "It is an ordinary opiate."

"Dope, eh?"

"Exactly. We will put her to sleep. A nice, long restful slumber."

Gloomy blinked. "Isn't that dangerous? What if she don't wake up?"

"She will. I am an expert in administering such dosages."

Gloomy looked skeptical. "After we get her ashore, what then?" he growled.

"We put her in one of the Brazilian hospitals."

"Just like that?"

"Once we have this bothersome woman committed to a doctor's care, no one will pay any attention to her ravings," Bantam Blitz said with satisfaction.

During this exchange, the clouded blue eyes of Honoria Hale

jumped from speaker to speaker, her pretty brow growing more worried with each passing moment.

The conversation did not sit well with her, it was clear to see.

Neither Gloomy Starr nor Bantam Blitz gave her much consideration, however. They were arguing over the advisability of such a risky ruse.

"Never work," Gloomy was insisting, shaking his huge head.

"Have you a better solution?" inquired Bantam.

Gloomy sealed his thick lips by way of silently admitting that he had not.

"It's your show," the horsey pugilist said at last.

Grinning, Bantam Blitz produced a hypodermic syringe, removed its protective cork cap, exposing the gleaming needle.

The bottle of opiate was likewise corked, and he jammed the needle into this, slowly extracted the liquid contents until the hypo reservoir was filled.

Setting the bottle aside, Bantam Blitz approached the woman, who began stamping her feet in frustrated fury. She rocked her chair from side to side.

Gloomy moved in, stabilized the chair, preventing an upset.

Seizing one arm, Bantam Blitz prepared to discharge the contents of the syringe.

The woman attempted a final scream of protest. She began chewing on her gag in a frantic effort to remove it.

Something like concern warped the thick features of the towering Gloomy Starr.

"Hold up," he growled, seizing the wrist of the smaller man.

Bantam Blitz glowered. "What now?"

"I'm thinking maybe you aren't any sawbones."

"Guilty. What of it?"

"Suppose that dose you got there is too strong."

The small man shrugged negligently. His smile was cool and unconcerned. "Suppose it is?"

"My orders are to keep her alive," Gloomy pointed out.

"My orders are to keep her from causing trouble," snapped the other, shaking off Gloomy's grip.

"You won't kill anybody!" Gloomy exploded.

"I damn well might!" Bantam snarled.

Gloomy whispered, "Murder ain't nothing to monkey with!"

"Since when did you grow a conscience?" sneered the other. "I understand you already did away with one wren this week."

"That was necessary," returned Gloomy defensively. "There wasn't any other way to get the thing done. I was thinkin' that on a tub like this one, accomplishin' the deed and gettin' away with it is a horse of a different hue."

The crafty eyes of Bantam Blitz narrowed. The hulking pugilist was making sense of a sort.

"Maybe she wants to talk now," Gloomy suggested, dark eyes switching to the fearful girl and back to the fuming Bantam Blitz.

"Maybe she'll spill her guts and fill your ears, too," the smaller man insinuated sharply. "Is that what you're pushing for?"

This time it was Gloomy's turn to shrug massive shoulders. "We'll find that out once we tear off the gag."

The huge specialist in fisticuffs reached out a scarred paw to tug at the well-chewed but intact gag.

Bantam Blitz stepped in, blocking Gloomy.

"In a minute you're going to push me too far, big guy."

"I don't like to be pushed around, Blitz—if that's not a made-up name."

"Do you want trouble?" snarled the small man.

Gloomy drew himself up to full height, which was impressive. "It won't be the first time I've had it."

They glared at each other and there was something in Gloomy's huge size, the fantastic self-assurance with which he conducted himself, that was menacing. Bantam Blitz abruptly shrugged.

"You have brains in that muscle," Blitz said. "Brains are the only commodity in the world that could be worth a million dollars a pound or not a thin dime. Once you learn to take orders, you'll be valuable."

"Then what do you say? Suppose we quit getting into each other's hair."

"Suits me."

But neither of the two strange hard men made a move to shake hands.

HONORIA HALE had been watching this tense exchange with round eyes. Her fear was palpable. Now Gloomy Starr reached out and removed the gag in her mouth. He did so with surprising gentleness.

"Out with it."

Honoria hesitated.

"Snappy," encouraged Gloomy, growing belligerent. His well-scarred face was turning into a storm cloud with dark eyes.

"You want to know what this is all about?" breathed Honoria.

"That measures the matter," grunted Gloomy.

Honoria's eyes went to Bantam Blitz. "But this other man does not wish me to speak, so I daren't."

"Maybe he's curious, too," suggested Gloomy coolly.

"He is with the Count. He will kill me if I talk."

"That so?" demanded Gloomy of Blitz. "You'll croak this frail if she yaps?"

Bantam Blitz seemed to waver.

"Let's hear your song," he said suddenly, addressing Honoria.

The girl maintained a pensive silence.

Gloomy gave her an ungentle shove, saying, "Come on, sister. Spill, spill."

That did the trick. "Perhaps it is time to clear the air, after all," she breathed.

Gloomy grunted, "I was wondering when you would see your way clear."

"I overheard something awful, truly horrifying, while I was with those horrid men," announced Honoria. "I must confess that what they said convinced me something pretty terrible is transpiring."

"What did they say?" prompted Gloomy, horsey face betraying no outward perturbation.

"Words to the effect that the life of no one man, the life of no dozen or score of men, were worthy to stand in the way of their destiny."

Gloomy absorbed this without comment. Bantam Blitz seemed to become acutely interested.

"Did it make sense to you?" demanded the latter.

Honoria shook her head. "No. It did not—by itself. But there was more. Someone had mentioned someone else by name. A very important name. Then there were the whispers about the U-Men—" She hesitated.

"Go on, sister," encouraged Gloomy. "Let's have it all in a nice bundle."

The two men had been so absorbed in Honoria Hale's recital that they failed to pay attention to anything other than the anxious woman. That proved to be their mistake.

For furtive lurkers had begun silently assembling outside the cabin door. They made their move then.

Glass broke. It was the porthole window looking out on the starboard lower deck. The sudden commotion was followed by another shattering sound.

Bantam Blitz swung about, fists coming up defensively.

Gloomy Starr's massive head swiveled, and his dark eyes took in the broken porthole, then dropped to the floor. There, a broken glass bottle was disgorging a quantity of billowing vapor.

"Gas!" Bantam Blitz exclaimed.

Honoria screamed shrilly, *"They're trying to kill me so I don't talk!"*

"We gotta get outta here!" Gloomy barked.

The cabin, quite naturally, offered only one means of egress—the door giving out onto the lower deck. No attempt was being made to batter it down.

"They want to panic us—stampede us into their ambush!" hissed Blitz.

Gloomy Starr nodded wordlessly. His eyes grew crafty.

"You first," he suggested.

Whitish fumes were spreading fast.

From pockets, the two uneasy allies produced what appeared to be bags of cellophane. They drew these over their heads, and the transparent envelopes snapped about their necks with elastic bands sewn into the open ends.

These made serviceable protective gas masks, even if the air supply was necessarily limited with what was enclosed about their heads.

A clasp knife came out, made short work of the ropes tying the girl to her chair. Gloomy wielded the blade.

Picking up Honoria Hale, Gloomy Starr set her atop one beefy shoulder, and clamped her nose and mouth shut to protect her lungs from the fast-flowing fumes.

Plucking an intricate machine pistol from an underarm holster, Bantam Blitz made for the door. Unlocking it, he cracked the panel, and slipped the weapon's muzzle out through the crack.

Depressing the firing lever, he began jerking the weapon this way and that way.

The pistol shuttled, moaned and ejected brass cartridges like a slot machine disgorging pennies. There were a lot of these clattering to the floor.

Outside, men began howling and there came a commotion consistent with a frantic scramble of retreat.

Yanking the door open, Bantam Blitz thrust out his head, craning about. A mistake.

Someone threw a blackjack. It flew true. The weighted portion struck one of Blitz's temples, and he flopped backwards, his unusual pistol falling from nerveless fingers.

Gloomy Starr charged in, pulled the small man back, where bullets could not finish the job of vanquishing him.

A man's voice yelled.

"You in there. Give up the girl!"

"And if I don't?" bellowed back Gloomy.

"We have hand grenades. And the firm intention of using them."

"If I give up the girl, you'll use 'em anyway," the pugilist countered.

"You may take that risk, or you can die with her."

"Who are you, brother?"

"Call me Schmidt—or Burch, if you prefer. Now do your deciding. We have no time to waste on indecision."

Gloomy struggled slightly to keep Honoria Hale perched atop his shoulder. She was wriggling and writhing frantically, feet kicking. The fumes were beginning to get into their eyes. They smarted, as if stung by ammonia.

Gloomy knew that the passing seconds were precious.

"I'm gonna carry the girl out and lay her on deck by the rail," he called out.

"Do it then."

Gloomy eased out, a human monster who cautiously peered both ways before emerging completely.

He set the girl down against the rail, went back to help the insensate Bantam Blitz.

He fully expected a hand grenade to come bouncing down the deck.

He was not disappointed. One did.

The round black object bounced once.

Moving with amazing speed for one so hulking, Gloomy Starr showed how he had earned his reputation in the ring.

Reversing direction, he kicked the grenade. It went flying

between two uprights supporting the rail, and into the water.

The sound of its explosion was not loud. Nor was the spurt of water produced by its detonation remarkable.

But Gloomy had no time to absorb that. For another grenade came sailing his way.

This one he raced to meet, caught it on the fly, pitching it out to sea. It was an amazing catch, worthy of a professional baseball infielder. The pugilist was forced to drop to the deck because this one, set to a shorter timer, detonated before it hit water.

A blast that produced grayish-black smoke mixed with fire made his cauliflower ears hurt.

By this time, the ship was full of commotion. The crew had been roused. A bell rang. Feet pounded up and down companion steps as the ship's complement searched out the source of the battle.

At that moment, another glass bottle like the one that had broken inside the cabin came hurtling Gloomy's way.

He lunged for it, captured it in both hands. But it was a near thing. He had to dive for the clumsy projectile like a football player attempting a flying tackle.

When the second bottle came, it scooted along the deck, not thrown but shoved. It slid along the varnished wood very smartly.

Gloomy's hands were full. Intercepting it was out of the question.

A bullet came along and shattered the glass container before Gloomy Starr could retreat to the relative safety of the cabin.

As it happened—and this was purely by chance—glass fragments raked his cellophane gas mask, rupturing it.

Big hands sought to clutch at the tears, seal them by hand pressure. But there were too many.

The eye-stinging whitish vapor swiftly seeped in.

Nearby, the blonde woman was in the middle of screaming when suddenly the scream turned into a high, howling laughter.

Hearing this wholly unexpected sound, Gloomy Starr wheeled in its direction. Then he began laughing, too.

The pugilist was still emitting sounds of unbridled mirth when he struck the deck, his gas mask coming apart in his clutching hands.

Hard-faced men swept in and seized Honoria, who was no longer laughing. She appeared to have lost consciousness. They bore her away, around a corner to another cabin, whose door snapped shut before the first converging crew members arrived to investigate the raucous sounds of combat.

Chapter XIII

THE CORNER

HONORIA HALE AWOKE in an entirely different passenger cabin.

She was no longer trussed to a chair, but cords were wound around both wrists and ankles, and the tight gag still crowded her mouth. Correction, she realized when she fell to examining her wrists. These were different cords and a fresh gag. It all came rushing back to her. The two men, and attack upon the cabin, her loss of consciousness.

Curiously, the last thing Honoria could recall was screaming wildly, then, paradoxically, bursting into a fit of laughter.

The laughing was strange, bizarre. She did not laugh because she thought her predicament was funny. Quite the contrary, she had been terrified. Yet she had laughed. Then she had evidently blacked out.

Honoria could not explain it. Not even to herself.

By a combination of wriggling and shifting, Honoria managed to maneuver herself so that she was seated on the edge of the bed on which she now lay. This gave her a clear view of her face in a nearby mirror. This showed two things: That her gag was fresh—this one was tan while the other had been white—and there were a few gray hairs in her tousled blonde head.

This latter was probably a figment of her imagination, but that was how Honoria Hale felt about the present situation.

Standing up, she decided, might be achieved. But progressing with her ankles bound together was probably not a smart

110

idea. Nevertheless, she attempted the feat.

Hopping in place proved to be the only sensible method of locomotion, and Honoria managed to jump three times before she lost control of her equilibrium, and fell smack on her face.

Looking about, she came to a startling realization. The cabin was nothing like the one she had previously occupied against her will. This was more modern, the appointments tasteful in the way the other had not been. She began to question if she were not on an entirely different boat than before. The very thought made her wild.

She swore through the gag for more than two minutes. This did nothing to alleviate her predicament, but she felt slightly better.

While she was contemplating her unfortunate situation, a door jumped open. The cabin was a double, with a connecting door.

A man she did not recognize banged in, took one look at her and gave out a holler.

"She is awake!"

This brought another man, also unknown to Honoria.

This second arrival began muttering.

"I understood that the *fraulein* was supposed to be out for a day or more."

"Well, she isn't. Let's get her back on the bed."

The two strangers caught her up, one at the shoulder and the other took her by the feet and actually gave her a couple of hammock-like swings before they let go.

Honoria sailed a few feet and bounced onto the bed, nearly bouncing off it again. The mattress was that new.

Muffled imprecations came from her gagged mouth.

"In case you are wondering," one of the men said, "we are with the Count. I am Mr. Schmidt, and this is Mr. Schwartz. You understand that these are just names for convenience. *Ja?*"

Honoria frowned. One of the men must have been an unconscious mind reader because he seemed to understand the frown.

"Those two who had you before this were fakes," Mr. Schwartz explained.

Honoria's frown deepened.

"The big one who called himself Gloomy was Renny Renwick, a Doc Savage aide," added Mr. Schmidt. "We don't know who the other one was. But we got you loose from them, and now you're going to stay under wraps until the Big Thing is accomplished."

At mention of that, Honoria squeezed her eyes shut.

The two men departed, to return shortly carrying a rather bulky steamer trunk, which had evidently been stored below in the baggage hold. Honoria Hale watched curiously as this trunk was opened.

Inside was much wiring, black insulation panels, knobs, dials, and many batteries taped together in groups. Not until Schmidt donned a telephone headset and seated himself where he could tap a key attached to the apparatus, did the young woman realize the trunk held a portable radio transmitter and receiver.

Schmidt was undoubtedly going to communicate with the other members of his organization. He did not speak but instead began tapping out a message, telegraph-style. Honoria watched him anxiously as he clicked off switches and hung up the radio headset.

"What did you learn?" the other asked anxiously.

The first man was perspiring freely, obviously worried about something.

"Doc Savage has been tricked," he reported. "He was led to believe that Renny Renwick booked passage on a different boat than this one, one whose destination is Buenos Aires in Argentina. This message was sent to his headquarters by telegram. Savage will no doubt hop into one of his big planes and go chasing after that boat to assist his man."

"Which leaves us in the clear?"

"Precisely."

The other looked doubtful. "I'll be damned if I see how Doc Savage can be taken in so readily. That Yankee *supermann* is supposed to be fool proof."

"Savage won't dare risk not following up on the message," the other insisted. "He understands something very large is in the wind. The Count saw to that in his attempt to frustrate Hornetta Hale's foolish efforts to draw him into the matter."

"Brains did the job."

The other nodded. "The Count and his associates are very brainy," he agreed. "It is regrettable that word of Hornetta Hale's escape from that island caused this other one to attempt to reach *der bronzemann*. For Doc Savage has the reputation of a lightning bolt. Sometimes one hears the warning thunder, other times not. Either way, when Doc Savage strikes, he does so with the same irresistible ferocity."

The other man nodded somberly. "Thor the thunderer and his war hammer are no less fearsome, by reputation."

HONORIA HALE took in this byplay with a great deal of interest, first because she was surprised by the terror which mere mention of this man of mystery, Doc Savage, had produced in the unscrupulous pair. Secondly, Honoria was seeing symptoms of a disagreement brewing between her captors, a condition which she hoped might escalate and so draw attention to her own plight.

A hot argument now ensued, Schmidt pointing out jeeringly that Doc Savage was not even upon the trail, and furthermore that the Man of Bronze probably did not even suspect that Honoria Hale had been on her way to enlist his aid.

"How do we know Savage *doesn't* know she was coming to see him?" Schwartz countered.

"We will find out about that, *Herr* Schwartz," Schmidt stated grimly.

The tall, dark man with the guttural voice came over to

Honoria, glared at her, then informed, "If you try to scream, you will promptly receive a knife in your pretty throat, *fraulein.*"

Schmidt produced a pocket knife which had a four-inch blade that *snicked* into view when a button was thumbed. He pressed the cold dull back of the blade to Honoria's throat and made a few other threatening gestures by way of impressing her.

When the gag was removed, the young woman did not cry out; she was convinced these men were thorough villains who would not hesitate to slit her throat to preserve their own skins.

"Were you on your way to enlist the aid of this man, Doc Savage?" Schmidt questioned.

"Yes," Honoria said promptly. She was surprised that she answered at all. It was not her intention to do so. There was not much use denying it and she wanted to worry her captors, anyway. Still, the word "Yes" had jumped off her tongue, unbidden. It was strange.

"What made you think he would believe your story, *fraulein?*" Schmidt persisted.

"I," said the young woman frostily, "have my reasons."

Schmidt scowled. "I will put the question in another way: Have you been in communication with this Doc Savage? Does he know of your existence and your concerns?"

Honoria said grimly, "You will find out the answer to that in the course of time." Which was the truth, if evasive.

"The knife, *fraulein,*" Schmidt warned, holding the blade almost against her rather regally thin nose. "You have not gotten hold of him. You were going to employ a telegram to send a message."

Honoria glared into the gravelly-voiced Schmidt's eyes and requested, "I'll bargain with you."

"How, *fraulein?*" asked Schmidt.

"Tell me what has happened to Hornetta Hale," she requested.

Schmidt spread his hands and murmured, "Most impossible to say, *fraulein.*"

"Then you can go take a flying jump into the Atlantic Ocean," Honoria snapped. "I am not talking any more."

And she did not.

THEY worked along, trying to pump the young woman for the next fifteen minutes, but Honoria displayed an outward courage that Schmidt and Schwartz had obviously not expected; her resistance to their catechizing strengthened proportionately as her belief grew that the sinister duo were not especially anxious to take her life.

"You aren't going to get anything more out of her," Schwartz muttered finally.

"*Ja,*" Schmidt agreed. "She has the nature of a clam."

"This Doc Savage angle isn't something to trifle with," Schwartz warned. "I think we had better put the problem up to *Die Mannner Unter dem Meer.*"

"Yes," Schmidt repeated. "The Men Under the Sea will know what to do."

One of the men went to the steamer trunk and opened it, again disclosing the portable radio transmitter and receiver. He warmed the tubes and snatched up a radio headset.

Honoria did not know the code, hence had no idea of what was being sent and received. She could only watch the expression on Schmidt's rather dark features, a procedure which told her little. Schmidt finally took off the receivers. He was smiling queerly.

"Good!" he chuckled. "Good! The Count will take care of Doc Savage, just in case the young lady did communicate with him. *Herr Kapitan* will himself transmit them."

"But what about the *verdammte* dame herself?" Schwartz growled.

"Our ingenious leader suggested a most effective method of silencing her," Schmidt leered.

Honoria Hale, seized with sudden horror, threw back her head and started a scream of utter fright, a frenzied shriek for aid.

Schmidt, leaping swiftly, managed to smack a hand down over her mouth to cut off the cry.

From a pocket, he produced a glass ampule. He broke the long neck off with a snap of his thumb.

Holding his own breath, he waved the tiny vial under Honoria's quivering nostrils. A tiny thread of whitish vapor licked out. This was disturbed by the woman's escaping air.

When Honoria inhaled, the vaporous tendril was drawn into her open nose. She fought against its unfamiliar smell.

Very quickly, her eyes began to water and her shoulders to shake. Her captor held the distressed woman still for a time, then released her.

When Honoria Hale stood free, the reason for her convulsions became apparent. She had been laughing uproariously. The hilarity which had seized her was an unpleasant, unnerving thing to hear.

She laughed and laughed and then keeled over, as if expiring from uncontrolled laughter.

Holding their breaths, Schmidt and Schwartz rushed in to catch her in the act of falling on her open-mouthed face.

Chapter XIV

RUDE AWAKENING

WHEN GLOOMY STARR returned to consciousness, his dark eyes snapped open and his rather large and shaggy head shifted about.

The pugilist's lips parted and he seemed about to say something, but he caught himself before he could release the utterance, whatever it might have been.

He was in the steamer *Matador's* infirmary. Next to him, sprawled on another hospital bed, lay the man who called himself Bantam Blitz. He was not yet awake.

Rolling out of bed, Gloomy went over to the undersized man and gave him a quick but very professional physical examination for wounds. Finding only a significant bump on one temple, he seemed to relax.

Then the pugilist noticed the ship's wall calendar. It was a day later than he remembered. The sight of the date seemed to hold the man transfixed for quite a long time.

Once more, Gloomy's lips parted, and he caught himself before any sound could emerge. With an effort, the human hulk turned the unspoken thought into music, making a low whistle of astonishment instead of what was about to come out of his rangy mouth.

He went in search of the ship's doctor.

Gloomy did not have to search far. Rounding a corner, he all but bumped into the other. The glum-faced medical man was just returning to the infirmary.

"Good," said the medico. "You are awake. I had begun to question that you would."

"What happened?" demanded the pugilist.

"You missed all the excitement. Or most of it, rather, since I understand that you were in the thick of it when all Hades first broke loose."

"Let's hear it," encouraged Gloomy.

"You, along with your friend, were discovered outside your cabin, dead to the world, but still breathing. There had obviously been a battle—a very serious one. In fact, we are putting into Bermuda to see the authorities there. This is a British ship, as you may know."

Gloomy nodded. "There was a girl named Honoria Hale," he said. "What became of her?"

The doctor blinked. "I have been going over the passenger list with the Captain, with the intention of accounting for the missing. I do not recall that name."

"She was smuggled on board," explained Gloomy.

"This is very serious," clucked the medico. "Especially in wartime. We have missing passengers. During the night, a lifeboat was commandeered and an unknown number of persons went into it. This was discovered only this morning. Most of the missing are from two adjoining cabins. None of the unaccounted-for passengers was a woman, however."

"I think," said Gloomy grimly, "we had better talk with the captain."

THE CAPTAIN of the *Matador* wasn't very happy to speak with the hulking prizefighter. In point of fact, he was downright irate as he demanded answers. Straight ones.

"What the bloody hell went on here yesterday?"

"A group of men attempted to kidnap a woman from my cabin," replied Gloomy.

The Captain placed hard fists on either hip and stuck out his jaw. "You had a woman in your cabin, did you?"

The ship's physician inserted, "The name of Honoria Hale was mentioned by this man."

This brought a dark glower to the skipper's weathered features. "No such passenger on this ship. Can you explain that?"

"She was an unregistered passenger," admitted Gloomy.

The Captain looked the huge tower of a man calling himself Gloomy Starr up and down, canting his head so far to one side he almost lost his captain's cap.

"You appear to have recovered," he appraised. "How do you feel?"

"Fit, but confused," admitted Gloomy. "It appears that I have lost a day of my life."

"You may lose more than a mere day. Since you appear to be in good fettle, I am consigning you to the ship's brig."

"Perhaps it is time to make full explanations," said Gloomy.

"Make them then!" the officer bit back. "But you are going to the brig regardless."

Instead of replying, Gloomy Starr reached up and began peeling away the scar tissue that criss-crossed his rugged features. He removed his cauliflower ears, disclosing outwardly normal aural appendages. Horsey false teeth came out of his mouth.

As pieces of his unlovely countenance came off, more and more the true face of the man who had been calling himself Gloomy Starr came to light. His pasty pale complexion revealed a healthy bronzed hue beneath.

The disguise was excellent. Not until dark glass shells were removed from the eyeballs, revealing irises that glinted with myriad golden flakes, did the truth become evident.

"I recognize you!" chirped the medico. "Doc Savage."

"My word!" exclaimed the ship's captain. "The Man of Bronze in the flesh. So who is the other man we found with you?"

"My aide, Long Tom Roberts, who booked passage on this ship under the pseudonym of Bantam Blitz," imparted Doc.

"Do you care to reveal the details of the matter you are obviously investigating?" asked the befuddled Captain, with more than a trace of respect cutting through his British reserve.

"That matter is confidential," returned Doc, "But I am prepared to reimburse the line for all damages."

"That will be more than appreciated, I am sure. But there is still the awkward matter of answering to British authorities in Bermuda."

"It is vitally important that the lost lifeboat be found," advised Doc Savage.

"Every effort is being made to locate it," the Captain assured him. "As a matter of fact, we have been steaming in circles all morning."

The bronze man asked to use the ship's radio. This permission was promptly granted.

Taking over the radio room, Doc tuned to a frequency used by his men for private communications and began speaking into the microphone. "Doc Savage calling Monk Mayfair. Come in, Monk."

A squeaky voice came back, *"Monk speakin'. Where are you, Doc?"*

"On the steamer *Matador,* heading toward Bermuda."

"We're not far behind you. I got word to hightail it south to Buenos Aires. But no explanation why."

"It was a ruse," explained Doc. "Designed to lure you to Argentina."

"Well, it didn't work. The telegram didn't have our usual code, so we knew it was phony. It was Long Tom who radioed us to head south by boat and wait for word from you."

"Who is with you?" asked Doc.

"Ham and—" Monk hesitated.

"And who?" pressed Doc.

The hairy chemist lowered his childlike voice. *"Pat's with us. And she's madder than the proverbial hornet. Says you took her up in a plane and pretended to drop her into the Long Island Sound."*

"It was to preserve her life."

Ham came on the air, saying, *"You put her under with one of your hypo needles and left her in a plane practically scuttled off Long Island. When she came to, she reclaimed her own bus and came seeking you at headquarters."*

Doc sighed. "This was all explained to Pat before she was rendered unconscious."

"Pat thinks you just wanted her to miss the party," piped up Monk.

"I wish," Doc said fervently, "that my cousin would take up a nice, safe hobby, such as climbing Mount Everest, or diving for sharks."

Pat's angry voice jumped out of the radio receiver.

"No thanks to you, I missed out on whatever I missed out on! What did I miss?" she asked, voice changing from wrathy to intensely curious.

"You missed out on a number of hand grenades blowing up," stated Doc dryly.

"How are your ears?"

"Red," admitted Doc. "My participation in this did not go as planned."

"Try explaining that part."

Doc Savage said, "In my guise as Gloomy Starr, I joined up with the group and took possession of a woman named Honoria Hale. You met her, Pat."

"I'll say that I did!" flared Pat Savage. *"She threw me to the wolves, so to speak. Honoria is not Hornetta, by the way."*

"They appear to resemble one another rather closely," admitted Doc. He continued his recitation of recent events. "Earlier in the week, I had radioed Long Tom to return to the States and remain in hiding in his private experimental laboratory. He did so. Once I had custody of Honoria Hale and had some privacy, I telephoned him with further instructions. In disguise, Long Tom booked passage on the *Matador*. Then he barged in on my cabin, pretending to be one of the gang. We feigned an argument, with me taking Honoria's part. This way we thought she might divulge what she knew of the situation to Gloomy Starr."

"Did she?"

"Very little. But what she did reveal was alarming."

"I'm listening."

"It would be better if you went in search of a lifeboat carrying Honoria Hale and her abductors. They have left this vessel," directed Doc.

"It's a doggone big ocean," muttered Monk.

"The other gang members were supposed to sail south on the liner *Caribbulla*. It's possible the lifeboats are simply waiting in the Atlantic until the ship happens along."

"So you want us to find the Caribbulla?"

"Or the lifeboat," said Doc.

"How is Long Tom?" inserted Ham.

"He has yet to awaken."

"How long were you two asleep?" asked Monk.

"Almost a day," admitted Doc.

"That doesn't sound reasonable."

"It is not reasonable. What is more, before I lost consciousness, I began laughing."

Pat broke in, *"You, laugh? I would expect to see the stone Presidents on Mount Rushmore crack a smile before you burst out in hilarity. Why, the Sphinx would giggle before you would."*

"It is the truth," stated Doc defensively.

Pat's tone grew intrigued. *"What was so funny?"*

"Nothing," said Doc.

"Now, that is funny. You laughing without any reason, I mean," added Pat.

"I do not think so," said Doc Savage frankly.

"One thing is deucedly clear," inserted Ham Brooks. *"This affair is becoming very complicated."*

"Complicated," said Doc, "is a rather mild word for recent developments."

DOC SAVAGE returned to the ship's infirmary and found the *Matador's* doctor examining Long Tom Roberts, the former Bantam Blitz.

"He has not yet awakened," the medical man told Doc.

The bronze man bent over the slender form. He lifted each eyelid in turn, checked Long Tom's pulse at the wrist, and performed other tests.

Indicating the egg-sized lump discoloring Long Tom's left temple, the doctor asked, "There's what put him out."

"A flung blackjack accomplished that," supplied the bronze man. "But after he fell unconscious, Long Tom inhaled a vapor that worsened his condition."

"I take it that you inhaled the same potent brew?"

Doc nodded grimly. "The only reason for my shaking it off so quickly can be attributed to my more robust constitution."

"This man does not appear to have been very healthy from the start. He shows signs of acute anemia and severe malnourishment, if not tuberculosis."

Doc Savage corrected the medico's hasty diagnosis.

"Long Tom has never fallen ill in all the time I have known him."

Doc took a dab of Long Tom's forearm, and gave it a pinch. The slender man did not respond to the pain, if he felt any.

"How do you yourself feel?" asked the ship's physician of Doc.

"Peculiar, although that sensation is fading."

"Peculiar—in what way?"

"Peculiar in that the last thing that transpired before I lost consciousness was that I began laughing without cause."

"How very odd. Did you think that you inhaled a form of laughing gas?"

Doc did not immediately reply, but asked, "Did you administer smelling salts to this man?"

The doctor nodded. "To both of you, but without result, obviously."

From a pocket, the big bronze man took out a tiny vial, broke the stem. He waved the ampule under Long Tom's nose.

This brought immediate results. The other man roused, began shaking his head as if shrugging off a powerful spell.

"What is that?" asked the doctor.

"A concoction of my own devising," returned Doc, without elaborating further.

Long Tom sat up, blinked and peered around. One pale hand went to his stricken temple. He winced.

"How long was I out?" he demanded in a querulous tone of voice.

"Nearly a day."

Long Tom stared.

"I am not joking," stated Doc. "After the blackjack knocked you out, there was a battle, during which another bottle of a mysterious vapor was hurled at us."

Long Tom made a face. "What was so mysterious about it? It smelled of methane."

"Once the fumes entered my nostrils," Doc told him quietly, "I began laughing uncontrollably."

"That's not like you," remarked Long Tom, sliding off his bed.

"Almost a day passed before I woke up here, beside you," elaborated Doc.

Long Tom felt of the throbbing knob discoloring his temple. "I take it they made off with the girl we tried to bamboozle with our play acting?"

"All departed the ship in the night," replied Doc. "Efforts are being undertaken to locate the lifeboat they used to escape in."

"In that case," groaned Long Tom, "our entire charade was a profound bust. We don't know any more about these crazy shenanigans than before."

"On the contrary," corrected Doc. "We know that something

terrible is in progress."

"But what?" snapped Long Tom.

Long Tom Roberts stood not very tall once he was on his feet. He was on the lean side, very slender, and his hair and skin possessed a pallor for which a medical man might prescribe a week in the sun fortified with plenty of orange juice.

But as Doc Savage had revealed, Long Tom had rarely if ever taken ill. In fact, he was a terror in a fight—even if he had been unceremoniously knocked out early during the prior night's battle. His unhealthy looks were the result of long hours spent toiling in a cellar laboratory, where he often conducted experiments.

Long Tom was the electrical engineer of the bronze man's tiny band of experts. He was an electrical wizard of the first order. Those who knew him half-expected the slender experimenter to simply snap his thin fingers and produce sparks. Long Tom had worked with Edison and Steinmetz in his day.

"What's our next move?" he asked Doc.

"This ship is putting into Bermuda, where we are to be questioned by British authorities."

Long Tom squared his jaw. "Can't you pull a little weight on them?"

"Ordinarily, yes. But this is wartime. We will have to submit to British interrogation until they are satisfied. Monk and Ham are following on the *Stormalong*."

"I thought all of our ships and planes were destroyed in the fire at our warehouse hangar."

"Most were. But some proved salvageable. Our boats were held in a water-filled basin that protected them from complete destruction. I had the *Stormalong* rebuilt at great expense."

"What about the other members of the gang—the ones on the steamer behind us?"

"For the moment, we will allow them to think they are not under suspicion by the *Caribbulla's* crew," Doc said. "The liner is no doubt actively searching for that missing lifeboat, as they would be expected to do. The captain had been previously instructed not to hinder the Count and his men, unless their hand was forced."

"You sound very confident of your influence over the other ship's captain," inserted the physician.

"Doc owns the steamer company," supplied Long Tom, applying an icepack to his injured temple. The lump appeared to be going down.

"Oh," said the medico.

NOT an hour later, a radioman knocked on the door of Doc's cabin, which had been repaired during the bronze man's unfortunate convalescence from the mystery vapor.

During that period of time, Doc had removed the last of his Gloomy Starr disguise, and stood revealed in his normal state. The transformation was astounding.

No one could have ever connected the two individuals.

Bits of broken glass had been retrieved for him, and Doc had been studying the remnants of the shattered bottles which had contained the liquid which had vaporized with such volatile and unexpected—not to mention unfortunate—consequences.

Doc was handicapped by a lack of specialized equipment, a regrettable result of inhabiting the personality of Gloomy Starr.

Long Tom asked, "Make anything of it?"

Doc shook his head somberly. He had sniffed the shards, but other than a whiff of something suggesting methane, got nothing out of the procedure.

Long Tom murmured, "Too bad Monk wasn't here. He always lugs that portable chemical laboratory with him everywhere he goes."

"When we rendezvous with Monk and the others, we will subject these specimens to a rigorous analysis," said Doc.

A knocking interrupted.

When Long Tom opened the cabin door for the radioman,

the latter declared, "Mr. Monk Mayfair is on the wireless, and wishes to speak with you, Mr. Savage."

"Thank you," said Doc, following the man to the radio room.

Monk was excited. His boyishly squeaky voice made the radio all but jump.

"We found that lifeboat. Empty."

"No sign of the former passengers?"

"Nothin'. In fact, the thing was overturned. I had to get into the water and flip it over to make sure it was empty."

"Strange."

"Either they had a mishap," Monk ventured, *"or they got picked up and tried to scuttle the boat."*

"Meet us in Bermuda," directed Doc.

The bronze man next radioed the liner *Caribbulla*. The Captain came on and reported, *"All quiet, Mr. Savage. The passengers we were requested to keep an eye on have done nothing out of the ordinary."*

"Continue on your way," said Doc. "When you near Bermuda, put into Hamilton Harbour. Do not announce this change in course until the last possible moment. Make reasonable excuses to allay any suspicion. We will meet you at the shipping pier."

"Yes, sir," said the other captain crisply.

Doc replaced the microphone.

Long Tom tugged at an oversized ear. "The Count and his men are sure going to be surprised to see us."

"Especially since they were led to believe that Renny Renwick was the one who infiltrated their gang."

"Is that why you made yourself up to look like Renny's ugly brother?"

Doc nodded. "In case they penetrated my disguise, having them jump to the wrong conclusion as to my identity allowed for more latitude in proceeding."

"Well, you may not have completely fooled them, but we made a little progress."

"There was another reason," added Doc.

"What's that?"

"It is a virtual certainty that they would have slain Gloomy Starr at their first opportunity, had they known his actual identity. At the worst, they would have held 'Renny Renwick' as hostage against my interfering with their master scheme."

"Whew!" said Long Tom. "The Count sure plays for keeps. But what's his game?"

"We will find out when we all reach Bermuda," said Doc Savage grimly.

Chapter XV

TERROR AT SEA

ONLY ONE SHIP was destined to reach Bermuda, but the bronze man had no inkling of that. Neither did the crew of his own vessel, shadowing the *Caribbulla* as it made its way down the Atlantic Coast.

Ham Brooks was on the bridge of the cabin cruiser, *Storm-along*. He was, predictably, attired for the occasion, wearing an impeccable yachtsman's outfit of tropical worsted with matching ascot tie and white cap.

He had stored his sword cane, since the walking stick was not exactly an ocean-going convenience and Habeas Corpus, no doubt motivated by Monk Mayfair, had twice made off with it—only to be caught by the dapper barrister in the act of trying to drop the cane off the stern and into the drink.

"You might consider," Ham told Monk bitingly, "tying a life preserver to that infernal pest."

"Habeas is too sure-footed to fall overboard by accident," Monk returned blandly.

"What I am considering," snapped Ham, "will not fall under the category of an accident."

Since the ungainly porker was an indifferent swimmer, Monk gave this suggestion some thought. Ham was unusually out of sorts, having had to leave behind his pet ape, Chemistry. The unclassifiable ape had an aversion to boat travel, owing to his distressing tendency toward seasickness. Ham might act out of pure spleen.

Pat Savage came up from below, a vision in white slacks and a cream-colored shirt. She seemed not to mind the relative coolness of the ocean breezes.

"I don't mind taking in the salt air," she remarked, "but I signed aboard for my share of action. Where is it?"

"Once Doc catches up with you, young lady," Ham said reprovingly, "you will have all the action you need."

"Yeah," seconded Monk. "Tryin' to keep Doc from lockin' you in a cellar somewheres. You know he don't like you bargin' into any of our shindigs."

"That glory grabber should learn to share," sniffed Pat, unimpressed by the threats. She had insinuated herself into several of her bronze relative's past adventures, and, despite a hair-raising brush or two with death, never seemed to get enough excitement.

"I wish," she said after a few moments, "I was at the wheel of my three-masted schooner."

"Why?" asked Ham, curious.

"This tub is too slow for my taste. On the *Patricia,* I could catch up with Doc instead of nursemaiding a pokey liner."

Ham made an indignant face.

The *Stormalong,* while technically a yacht, was no pleasure craft. She was an ocean-going cabin cruiser, capable of great range. Sixty feet long, she had plied the South Seas and done exploration work in the mid-Atlantic. Her hull was steel, her bow reinforced so that she could serve as an ice-breaker if need be. She was also equipped with an astounding number of marine gadgets many years in advance of current science.

Nothing like her existed elsewhere, which was why the bronze man had put a crew of shipbuilders to working round the clock until she was restored and made seaworthy after the devastating Hidalgo warehouse fire.

It was late afternoon now, and Pat Savage was taking out her boredom on a swarm of jellyfish.

She had loaded her antique six-shooter with mercy bullets, and was giving the floating organisms a taste of her marksmanship.

Unerringly, she hit every one. The jellyfish immediately went to sleep, although that was a supposition, since they were floaters who drifted with the tides. It was impossible to judge their degree of wakefulness.

"Don't you ever miss?" Monk wondered, eyeing her work with admiration.

"Not in the last three hundred and twenty-seven shots," Pat said confidently.

Monk blinked. "You keep count like that?"

"Missing is something I never forget," the bronze-haired girl said grimly.

"Wonder whatever happened to Hornetta Hale?" the hairy chemist muttered, scratching his nubbin of a head.

"It's not that blonde bearcat that interests me," snapped Pat. "It's Honoria Hale I want a crack at. She helped feed me to the Count and his pack of goons."

Ham Brooks called back from the wheel.

"You say she resembled Hornetta Hale?"

"The two," said Pat, popping a jellyfish dead center, "could be twins."

"Are you sure it wasn't Hornetta Hale in disguise?" asked Monk.

"I know hair, and Honoria's tresses were a darker blonde than the gal I saw in the color newsreels. I run a beauty salon, you will doubtless recall. The face was the same, but the hair was different. And it wasn't colored. It was natural. A gal knows these things."

"If you say so," muttered Monk. "But the idea of there being two Hornetta Hales makes my scalp itch."

"If I ever catch up to either wench," Pat promised vividly, "I won't miss!"

Another jellyfish jumped out of the water and Pat blew a curl of smoke from the muzzle of her sixgun.

A LITTLE before dark, they heard a dull sound.

The noise was coming from the south, in the general direction of the liner they were following at a discreet distance.

"What was that?" growled Monk.

Habeas erected his ridiculously long ears. He sniffed the air with his peculiarly extended snout.

Taking up a pair of binoculars, Ham Brooks conned the sparkling waters before them.

"I did not like the sound of that," he said slowly. "Submarine raiders belonging to one of the warring parties have been known to operate in these waters."

Rushing up to the bridge, the apish chemist snatched the glasses away from the dapper lawyer, saying, "Let me see that, you seagoin' shyster!"

Bringing the eyepieces to his tiny eyes, Monk searched the tossing waves.

Before very long, black smoke began smudging the horizon line.

Everyone saw it. Ham jumped to the controls, threw the throttle to its maximum. The *Stormalong* responded by surging ahead, digging in its stern, and knifing through the waters with her reinforced bow.

The impressive yacht pounded through the whitecaps, as Monk raced for the radio set .

He listened a minute, shouted, "S.O.S. coming through. It's the *Caribbulla!*"

"What happened?" asked Pat anxiously.

"They ain't sayin'! There has been an explosion on board—a big one. The liner is already listin'."

Monk listened further.

"It's bad—plenty bad. They're already orderin' the passengers into lifeboats."

"That *is* bad," mused Ham Brooks. "They appear to have fallen victim to a submarine attack."

Monk was hollering into the microphone, demanding to know what was happening. From the changing expressions on his homely face, he did not appear to be receiving satisfactory answers.

"They're scrambling to get off the boat," he reported hoarsely. "Let's see if we can help out."

Ham wailed, "I have the engines running at their maximum speed."

Monk turned to Pat and said, "Grab a pair of binoculars! Look for a periscope, or wake or anything that tells of a submarine. We could be next."

"Jove!" moaned Ham. The dapper lawyer rushed to the special device called a "listener." This enabled him to hear through headphones the sounds of any underwater activity through hydrophones distributed about the hull, below the waterline. This would include the engines of any submarine.

Clapping the cans over his ears, the elegant lawyer concentrated on the marine noises coming from the activated device.

"I hear nothing that smacks of a submersible," he reported.

Stationed on the flying bridge, Pat was searching the crinkling blue waves. "All clear!" she called out.

"Nothin' here either," reported Monk.

Pat said cautiously, "I don't see *any* sign of trouble."

Grimly, Monk piloted the powerful yacht toward the smudge of smoke that was growing and spreading across the waves. Soon, they could smell it.

Monk sniffed the approaching odors with simian curiosity. "Smells like T.N.T.," he muttered.

"This does not sound like the work of a submarine torpedo," said Ham.

"Remains to be seen," returned Monk.

Pat wore her sixgun on a holster at her hip, Western-style. Lowering her binoculars, she drew the huge weapon.

Monk asked, "What are you aimin' to do?"

"I am aiming to pick off anything that looks suspicious to me," said the bronze-haired girl with steely determination.

"In your excitement," cautioned Monk, "try not to shoot any survivors."

Pat gave the homely chemist a withering look. Then she returned her attention to the smudgy waters.

The black stuff was rolling in like an evil fog bank. The stink of the smoke was climbing into their nostrils, getting into their lungs, clogging their breathing.

Ham began coughing. And complaining.

"Dratted foul stuff!"

The sepia smoke caused Monk to throttle back the engines, while Ham turned on a movable searchlight to pierce the enveloping smudge.

They could see the liner now. It was, in fact, listing to port. Lifeboats were being lowered from davits. There was a mad scramble to get off the ship.

"What are we going to do about this?" asked Pat, features stricken.

Ham said, "Look for injured. The people in the lifeboats should be fine for now. No doubt rescue vessels are responding to the S.O.S. distress call."

They soon came upon the first lifeboat, and called over to those huddled on its bare benches. Passengers were wrapped up in coarse blankets, and shivered visibly.

"What happened?" Ham asked them.

A man cupped his hands around his mouth, megaphone style. "Explosion below decks."

"Any sign of a sub?" yelled Monk.

"No," he was told. "But the explosion was below the water line."

Pat offered, "Sounds like a sub…"

Ham Brooks interjected, "Jumping to conclusions is not becoming of associates of Doc Savage."

"Pardon me," sniffed Pat in a mock-snooty tone of voice.

They moved among the lifeboats, which began pushing away from the stricken vessel. Every shell was full of huddled humanity.

Everywhere, passengers looked frightened, but seemingly were uninjured.

Pat questioned every passing boat.

"Any injured? Did any of you see a submarine in the water?"

The answers to both questions were a resounding No.

Cautiously, moving at a deliberate pace so as not to run down any bobbing lifeboats in the murky pall, Ham Brooks made a circuit of the liner.

In due course, a final lifeboat was lowered, and the black cap of the captain of the ship was visible at the bow. They made for that boat.

Pulling up to that bobbing shell, they accosted the *Caribbulla's* skipper.

"We're Doc Savage's men," identified Ham Brooks. "What happened here?"

"Explosion in the hold, near the hull."

"Torpedo?"

The Captain shook his head. "No. Sabotage."

"Are you sure?" demanded Monk.

"There was no question of it. Someone deliberately blew a hole in the boat from within the cargo hold."

Ham asked, "Where are the passengers you were watching?"

The skipper shrugged helpless shoulders, and admitted, "We have no idea. I personally supervised the loading of every lifeboat. They were not aboard."

"You lost track of them?" complained Ham.

The Captain said defensively, "In the aftermath of the explosion, there was naturally a great deal of confusion. Watching those men was no longer an imperative. Once we saw that the liner was doomed, evacuating the passengers became our chief concern. I assumed that the matter of the missing passengers would sort itself out during the evacuation."

"Was there any missing lifeboat?"

"That, too," admitted the officer, "seemed unimportant at the time. Possibly. I cannot say for certain. But someone on board holed my vessel, and it stands to reason that those persons evacuated at some point, possibly before the explosion."

At that point, the Captain turned and watched his liner list further and further to the point where its smokestacks inexorably sank toward the brine. Silently, tragically, he watched the stacks, still smoking, extinguish themselves amid the waves, like gigantic cigars.

With a surge and a gurgle, the liner *Caribbulla* began slipping beneath the waves. Its bare deck was facing them like a great sinking wall.

It was over in an astonishingly short period of time. Atlantic waves sloshed and crashed around, somewhat obscured by the black smudge. The ship had gone below.

When the Captain was done watching, he turned his emotion-stiffened face back to them. A tear could be seen crawling out of the corner of one eye.

"Mark me," he said hoarse-voiced. "This is sabotage—nothing less."

They believed him.

Cutting in and out among the lifeboats, Monk and the crew searched every face, seeking the aristocratic countenance of the mysterious Count.

No one resembling that worthy—or anyone else who looked suspicious—presented themselves. The survivors appeared shaken and frightened and too preoccupied with their plight to be of much help.

"Good thing there were no casualties," commented Ham Brooks.

"But where did our scalawags run off to?" gritted Pat Savage. "Could they have slipped off the boat before the explosion?"

"That is the only reasonable supposition," returned Ham Brooks. "But where the devil did they slip off to?"

"Probably dropped off in a lifeboat," grunted Monk. "It's gettin' to be a popular stunt around this neck of the Atlantic."

"In broad daylight? They would have been seen."

"We are back to wondering about submarines," complained Pat.

"If a submarine picked them up," said Ham carefully, "why not simply torpedo the ship afterward?"

"Probably didn't want to stir up a war," reminded Monk.

"Well, they sure stirred up something big," predicted Ham Brooks glumly. "Doc Savage will not be happy to hear about this."

Chapter XVI

THE WATER GARGOYLE

DOC SAVAGE WAS most definitely *not* happy to hear about the fate of the passenger liner *Caribbulla*.

His melodious trilling was yanked out of him when the skipper of the *Matador* brought him the news.

"Any loss of life?" asked Doc. It was characteristic of the bronze man that his first thought would have been for the passengers, rather than the loss of a valuable ship of which he was part owner.

"Happily, no," reported the Captain. "All passengers are reported safe and well. We are, of course, changing course to meet the lifeboats and render whatever assistance we may."

"All passengers?"

"Perhaps you had better speak with your man," suggested the *Matador* skipper.

Doc went to the radio room, and Monk Mayfair came on the line.

"This is the scariest thing I've ever heard of!" complained Monk. *"The ship was sabotaged. No question about it. But the guys we were shadowin' got clean away."*

"Clean away in mid-Atlantic?" demanded Doc.

"They ain't among the lifeboat passengers. We checked all the way around, and the crew agrees with us. They got away scot free. Probably before they blew up the tub."

Doc Savage said grimly, "If the passengers are safe, see if you can hunt up any sign of the dory on which our quarry evacuated."

"Gotcha, Doc. Monk signing off."

Doc Savage turned to the Captain of the *Matador*. "How long until we reach the lifeboats?"

"No sooner than midnight."

The bronze man seemed dissatisfied. "It is urgent that we locate those missing men."

"I will request that a British naval cutter look into it."

"Thank you," Doc Savage said sincerely.

THE PACKET STEAMER *MATADOR* reached the zone of thinning smoke where the *Caribbulla* had gone down long after darkness had descended upon the Atlantic. By this time, a few of the women passengers had grown hysterical. But the men were holding up. In fact, except for an individual here and there, most were holding up remarkably well. Nerves were understandably frayed and on edge. They all knew that they were sitting ducks in the event of a submarine attack—which was not entirely unlikely given how a certain enemy nation of the British had been harassing and sinking shipping for some months now.

The securing and raising of the lifeboats onto the deck of the *Matador* was executed with admirable British efficiency. It took less than two hours; soon the extra lifeboats were littering the afterdeck of the steamer.

There was some discussion of what to do with these latter shells, the *Matador* not being designed to carry twice its customary complement of lifeboats.

It was soon realized that in the event of further trouble they would need all those boats to handle an evacuation of the *Matador,* so they were organized where they would be as much out-of-the-way as humanly possible.

With the Captain's permission, Doc Savage and Long Tom went among the grateful passengers, who were being given strong coffee or tea, as well as sandwiches, as they became accustomed to their new vessel.

After a thorough search, Long Tom came up to Doc Savage and said, "Nobody out of the ordinary that I can make out."

"The Count and his men either went down with the ship, or got off before the explosion. If the latter, then that implicates them in the sinking."

Long Tom fingered his jaw forcefully. "Sounds like they are guilty, all right. Do you suppose they smuggled that T.N.T. on board just to scuttle the ship?"

"It is difficult to say," admitted Doc Savage. "The entire affair is difficult to comprehend. The objectives of this group remain murky, to say the least."

Doc Savage went to confer with the *Matador's* skipper. They did so in the captain's quarters, talking at great length.

In the end, the Captain said heavily, "It is clear that something is transpiring which requires deep investigation. I think that, given present circumstances, and in light of the acute assistance you and your men have rendered to the Crown, your presence in Hamilton may be put off until later."

"Thank you," said Doc Savage. "We will escort you to port. However, we may join you in Hamilton, once we have concluded our search."

"That would be much appreciated," said the skipper. "In the meantime, you and your man may board your own vessel at your convenience. With our best wishes."

DOC SAVAGE found Long Tom Roberts in the radio room, exchanging reports with Monk on the *Stormalong*.

Doc Savage told the slender electrical engineer, "We will put off in one of the surplus lifeboats."

This was thought to be the most prudent way to go about it, for bringing the steamer about to rendezvous with the *Stormalong* would be to invite attack—if there were in fact any hostile raiders lurking in the vicinity.

Doc and Long Tom lowered the lifeboat by themselves in order to accomplish the task without calling attention to their departure. Once in the water, they pushed off, and watched the *Matador* steam onward.

The *Stormalong* was informed by radio of the position of the tiny lifeboat. Having discovered nothing of interest, it cut through the waters at its best speed, and before long it had located Doc's lifeboat, navigating in the darkness with ease.

Ham Brooks hailed them from the cabin cruiser's bridge saying, "No luck. No luck at all."

The two vessels maneuvered until they were floating side by side. Long Tom came up the pilot's ladder, followed by the bronze man.

Doc looked around the open cockpit aft. "Where is Pat?"

"Hiding below," Ham said dryly. "We put the fear of your wrath into her headstrong noggin."

"That was unnecessary," replied Doc.

Monk offered, "Considerin' that she was after *your* scalp in the first place, it seemed to be a smart thing to do."

"Yes," added Ham. "Pat has been blaming you for what Gloomy Starr did to her."

"Even though you saved her life," added Monk.

Upon consideration, Doc decided not to go below.

Taking the wheel of the *Stormalong,* he thrust the throttles ahead, executing a smart maneuver that cut a deep wake across the wrinkled face of the Atlantic, taking the yacht away from the drifting lifeboat.

"No sign of anything unusual?" he prompted.

"None," said Ham. "However, if the rascals got away, they did so very thoroughly and completely."

The *Stormalong* was running along a brilliant track of moonlight. There was a fair breeze, and it wasn't too cold, despite the lateness of the season.

They followed along in the wake of the steamer. Doc Savage was intent, concentrating on the headset earphones of the listener device, whose receiver was installed in the bridge for convenience.

Positioned along opposite rails, Monk and Ham had their binoculars clapped to their eyes, scouring the dark horizon in all directions, seeking any hint of a periscope, or other sign of a lurking vessel.

"Except for the steamer," Monk remarked at one point, "there ain't nobody around."

"If there is," Ham said tightly, "we are sitting ducks."

"Ducks," Monk growled, brandishing his superfirer, "don't shoot back."

At that point, Pat Savage decided to poke her bronze-haired head out of the lower deck.

"Did someone say something about shooting?" she inquired brightly.

"Figure of speech," grunted Monk.

Pat pretended to notice Doc Savage for the first time, and said cautiously, "Oh, hello, cousin. How goes it?"

Headset clamped tightly to his ears, the big bronze man did not respond. It may have been the intensity of his concentration, or it may simply be that he did not wish to respond. Pat Savage had many times disobeyed him. Her antics had been growing tiresome of late.

Pat shrugged and said casually, "Anything for me to do? I'd like to be useful."

Ham suggested, "Find a flashlight and scour some light around. Periscopes are hard to see at night."

Pat frowned. "Do you think there is a sub lurking nearby?"

"We cannot be sure. But we need to protect the steamer."

"In that case," Pat said, "I'll go below and point it out the portholes there so I can get a better look."

Pat returned below, and after that, light blazed from various portals in the lower hull and to port as she moved about the cabin below, searching with her powerful flash ray for any sign of activity on the ocean surface.

Pat was very diligent about this. The flashlight moved about constantly.

"Speaking of sitting ducks," Monk said to Ham, "she's makin' us into a pretty fair target."

Hearing this, Doc Savage commented, "It is better this way. We will attract any first torpedo launched, which will warn the *Matador* crew."

The bronze giant sounded very matter-of-fact about it, but there was an undertone in his voice, a kind of steely edge, that made them all feel chilled up and down their spines.

Ham inquired, "Doc, if there was a sub, that device will detect the sound of its engines. Correct?"

"Only at a reasonable distance. Do not forget, some modern submersibles are rigged to run silently via electric motors."

That made Monk and Ham redouble their efforts with their binoculars.

It was getting to be a long night, when from below Pat Savage let out something that sounded like a yelp. It had a choked off quality, but when she got her vocal cords back in working order, she let out a piercing scream.

Monk lunged for the below deck, howling, "What is it?"

Pat came charging up, face twisted in a kind a horror. She said, "I saw a head in the water!"

"A head?" gulped Monk.

"Yes! It was hideous!"

Pat went to the starboard rail and pointed in the direction she had seen the head. Her flashlight was gripped in one hand and she sprayed illumination about liberally.

Doc Savage turned the boat in that direction, asking, "What did the head look like, Pat?"

"Inhuman." Pat shuddered the length of her bare arms.

"Was it a severed head?" demanded Ham Brooks, training his binoculars on the patch of illumination that was now in their direct path.

Pat seemed to struggle to put her words together. "It—it was shaped like a human head, but the details were anything but.

The eyes looked like silver dollars with bullet holes in the center. It was more like the face of a frog or a fish or—I don't know what it was!" she said at last, plainly rattled.

Stationing themselves on either side of the boat, Monk and Ham used their own flashlights. They had their supermachine pistols out, stood ready to bring them to bear.

They saw nothing unusual. Just moonglade on the heaving Atlantic. The cool night air plucked at them, brought out goose bumps along the arms—although the skin prickling hadn't been there a few minutes before. Perhaps it was the vivid description Pat had gasped out that brought about the alteration in their exposed flesh.

After a few minutes, there came a splash. All heads turned, flashlights darting this way and that.

Then they saw it.

Something like a fishy tail flashed into the water, shaking itself.

"What was that?" Pat demanded.

"Fish," Monk said nonchalantly.

"Are you sure?"

"I know a fish tail when I see it," Monk retorted. "That was a fish I saw. A big one, but a fish's tail for sure. Might be a swordfish."

Doc Savage caused them all to freeze in their tracks at his next words.

"That was no ordinary fish."

They waited for him to elaborate.

"What was it then?" Ham asked when the bronze man offered no more.

"That," said Doc, "remains to be seen. The tail was very large, but it did not resemble anything known to live in these waters."

"What do you suppose it was?" Ham asked tensely.

The bronze man declined to reply. It was a habit he had, when he did not wish to answer a question—or had no answer to give. Doc maintained his grim silence as he piloted the big oceangoing cruiser around in careful circles.

Finding nothing untoward, Doc Savage placed the sleek *Stormalong* on a heading that took it back into the wake of the steamer *Matador*.

"Guess it's gone," Monk said, "whatever the heck it was."

"Any guesses?" Ham asked no one in particular.

Monk muttered, "First Pat spies a floatin' head, then we spot a fishtail that doesn't belong in these waters." He scratched his rusty head in puzzlement. "Say, Pat, that head you saw. Did it look like a girl's head?"

Pat shook her head firmly. "It was so ugly I couldn't tell what it was. Instead of hair, it looked like it had kelp or seaweed growing out of its scalp. Why do you ask?"

"Maybe it was a mermaid," Monk said thoughtfully.

"No such creature exists!" Ham retorted unkindly. "The very idea is a pure fantasy."

"I dunno," Monk muttered. "Sailors the world over have been reportin' silkies and nixies and the like for centuries. Maybe there's somethin' to it."

Long Tom, who had been a silent participant up to this point, said, "Didn't that stubborn blonde, Honoria Hale, say something about the U-Men while we were giving her the third degree?"

"She did," said Doc Savage. "However, it is unclear what the remark meant, for she had no time to complete it before we were besieged in our cabin. But she seemed troubled about these individuals, whoever they were."

"Doggone it!" squeaked Monk. "Do you suppose she was tryin' to warn about mermen livin' underwater?"

"Nonsense!" snapped Ham. "Utter rot!"

A little more time passed. They were making fair progress. Doc had no trouble pacing behind the steamer. In fact, Doc had to keep the *Stormalong* throttled back so she didn't overhaul the vessel. The cruiser was very fleet and nimble. It had been designed by Doc Savage himself, and was undoubtedly a decade ahead of its time.

It was rather deep into the night when Doc Savage again placed the locator headset over his ears, seemed to become interested in sounds the hydrophones were picking up.

"What's up, Doc?" Long Tom asked.

Doc Savage waved an admonishing hand, requesting silence.

Suddenly, something shot out of the water just ahead.

Not everyone saw it clearly, but Doc Savage had the best view.

The thing looked to be over seven feet in length, an iridescent green, and nearly human.

The head was a mass of seaweed. Long scale-covered arms projected forward like someone diving into the sea, except this fantastic form had jumped *out* of the sea.

Wriggling in its wake was a great silvery-red tail, like that of a deep-sea swordfish, but also remindful of the fluked tail of a mermaid under the circumstances.

The creature—if that was what it was—described a high wave-clearing arc long enough to be seen, then it dropped back into the water, making a very respectable splash.

In that fleeting moment, they thought they spied a great reddish dorsal fin running along its curving back. The resemblance to a shark fin was marked.

After the tail disappeared, the swells returned to their normal heaving rhythm. Despite their alert watchfulness and the penetrating glare of their searchlights and flashlights, the fin-backed thing did not show itself again.

Long Tom broke the silence that held them all spellbound.

"I don't believe in mermaids," he said peevishly.

Pat Savage retorted archly, "I got a good look at that thing. That was no mermaid. That was a mer*man*."

Chapter XVII

THE MEN UNDER THE SEA

THE BRITISH STEAMSHIP *MATADOR* reached the port city of Hamilton in Bermuda without further complications.

The *Matador* pulled in around daybreak, with the cruiser *Stormalong*, piloted by Doc Savage, trailing not far behind her.

A delegation of customs officials and other high dignitaries were there to meet the two vessels.

Doc Savage was commended for his efforts, but was told that he would be required to submit to a formal interrogation. Evidently, the British authorities had changed their minds about giving the bronze man his liberty until the sinking of the *Caribbulla* was solved.

The bronze man consented to this without outward objection.

Doc's three men and Pat Savage went along. Official cars conveyed them to a government building situated amid the white roofs of downtown Hamilton. The streets were quiet, the hour being early.

There, Doc Savage met privately with several high British officials.

Sympathy was expressed for the loss of the liner *Caribbulla*, and the bronze man was questioned closely about all that he had witnessed on the high seas.

Doc Savage freely admitted to having seen no signs of any submarine activity.

"It is my conclusion," he stated, "that certain persons of

foreign extraction who had booked passage on the *Caribbulla* had come to suspect that they were being watched, and took matters into their own hands."

"By blowing up the entire boat?" one official blurted out, aghast.

"So it would appear," Doc replied calmly.

"Rather extreme, would you not say?"

"I would," admitted Doc.

"What do you think these rotters were about, that in order to escape they would sink a passenger ship and manage to vanish in mid-ocean?"

"A reasonable person," returned Doc thoughtfully, "would assume they had a boat or a submarine, which they radioed, and managed to make rendezvous with."

"But you say there were no signs of a submersible?"

"My vessel is equipped with sensitive listening devices, and I detected no sound consistent with Diesel or electric engines belonging to an underwater vessel."

"Do you have any inkling of their scheme?"

"Only that it is of the highest importance to them and that they will stop at nothing to bring it to fruition—or to eliminate anyone in their path," advised Doc.

"But you do not know the particulars?" pressed one official.

"No."

Another asked, "Have you any reason to suspect that these people are working against British interests?"

"I have no data one way or the other. But they were headed south—how far south is open to speculation."

They conferred until noon with the bronze man patiently fielding question after question, seeming to talk freely, but in fact volunteering no usable information beyond the gravity of the situation as it had already developed.

Doc Savage thought it prudent not to mention the sighting of the merman—or whatever the oceanic gargoyle was.

At length, the official stood up and said, "Thank you for your cooperation in this unpleasant matter. You are free to depart Hamilton at any time."

Doc Savage stood up and thanked everyone, saying, "Since we do not have a definite destination in mind, we may stay in port some while before we depart."

"Be careful to apprise us of any developments which may affect British interests," reminded the chief official. He was very grave in his tone.

"Yes," added another. "Concealing information of vital interest to the Crown during wartime would be very inadvisable. Very."

With that not-so-veiled threat hanging in the air, the bronze man left the building.

DOC SAVAGE collected his men in the waiting area, and said, "Let us repair to our boat."

Puzzled, Ham asked, "We are not being detained?"

"Our services are very much appreciated, so we have been let go with a warning."

"They have some nerve warning us," grumbled Long Tom.

"Nonetheless," said of the bronze man quietly, "it would be best if we took possession of the *Stormalong* immediately."

The official car was waiting to take them where they wished to go. They rode in silence back to the waterfront. By this time, news of Doc Savage's arrival in Bermuda had reached the fourth estate. There was a crowd of reporters ready and eager to interview the notoriously publicity-averse bronze man.

"All of you go ahead," Doc said quietly, after instructing the driver to drop him off some distance from where the *Stormalong* lay anchored. "I will join you directly."

The car door opened and closed so quietly that it was several seconds before Pat Savage gasped, "He vanished!"

"That's Doc Savage for you," grinned Monk.

Upon arriving, they quitted the car, thanked the driver, and made their way to the *Stormalong*.

The local press had been keeping their eyes peeled for a Herculean bronze man with golden eyes, so they were not immediately recognized.

By the time the party got to the pier, they rushed on board, and repaired to the lower deck where they held a conference. They were astonished to find Doc Savage waiting for them there, his hair only slightly wet from his swim. For the big bronze man had obviously gone into the water, swam some distance, and climbed aboard the yacht unseen. His close-lying bronze hair possessed the peculiar quality of shrugging off moisture as if it were greased.

Doc had already changed into fresh clothes. The wet ones were sitting on a bench, neatly folded.

"You move mighty fast for someone so tall," Pat said admiringly.

Doc addressed his cousin. "It is time to assemble what little we know about the situation. Starting with you, Pat."

Pat shrugged. "All I have are some scraps and rags."

"They may be important," invited the bronze man. "Proceed."

Pat sat down, and began, "While I was eavesdropping on the Count and his men, they said something about a lagoon."

"Did this lagoon have a name?" queried Doc.

"If it does," returned Pat dryly, "it was never mentioned in my presence. But they were talking about going to the lagoon. Or so they claimed."

Doc said, "The Count also let slip something about a cay. Cays are a Caribbean term."

"Are lagoons found in the Caribbean?" wondered Pat. "I seem to connect them with South Seas atolls in my mind."

"Coves are more common," admitted Doc. "But lagoons are not unheard of."

Monk offered, "Sounds like he's headed for a cay that has a lagoon in it. Does that sound about right?"

Doc Savage reminded, "Hornetta Hale was picked up on a tiny cay in the Caribbean. She is the trigger for all of these unsettling events."

"Did that isle have a lagoon?" asked Pat. "Perhaps we should start there."

"It would make perfect sense to do so," allowed Doc Savage. "But from the descriptions in the newspapers, that particular cay was so tiny a lagoon would be not a natural feature for it."

Pat Savage eyed her bronze cousin skeptically, asked, "Have you a better lead?"

"I have not," admitted Doc. "Prepare to cast off. We will take the *Stormalong* south, and see what we can discover."

Long Tom grumbled, "Sounds like the beginning of a wild goose chase, if you ask me."

"Yeah?" challenged Monk. "Got a better idea?"

"Yes," said Long Tom. "I'm going to dig up some ice for this knob growing out of the side of my head."

Monk quipped, "From the size of it, I'd hunt up an iceberg."

"Keep your opinions to yourself," snapped Long Tom. "Unless you'd like a shiner to match my bruise."

The hairy chemist subsided. Long Tom was in a foul mood, and when he was thus agitated, one risked his wrath at their own peril.

They cast off, pushed their way out of Hamilton Harbour, and plotted a course south to the Bahamas, which was the closest island group.

Once out in open water, Ham Brooks was complaining, "Cays stretch from the Bahama Bank all the way south to the tip of Florida and around into the Gulf Coast. The Bahamas group alone comprises hundreds of islands. Without a name for this cay, or any inkling about this lagoon, we could be months plying these waters."

"Not to mention the fact that everything we overheard might've been designed to deceive us," reminded Pat.

Doc Savage said, "It is conceivable that what the Count told Gloomy Starr was designed to confuse and confound him. But the fragment you overheard about a lagoon, Pat, was spoken in an unguarded moment. Therefore, we are looking for a lagoon. Unavoidably, this points to an island or cay or some similar spot."

"Doc makes sense," Ham allowed. "Let us head south and see what luck we have."

What luck they had, as it turned out, proved to be very mixed fortune indeed.

THE HOUR was late, and the *Stormalong* was skirting the maze of small islands of the Bahama Bank as the sun began to set like a slow comet.

Monk had been testing the shard of the glass bottle that had released some potent vapor that produced first, high hilarity, followed by unnervingly deep unconsciousness. The apish chemist availed himself of his wonderfully versatile portable chemical laboratory. Long hours he toiled, but the only result was to deepen the furrows in his minuscule forehead.

Doc Savage looked in at one point. "Any progress, Monk?"

"These traces don't give me much to work from, but I think it's a gas that has been concentrated under pressure to make a liquid. Break the bottle, and it turns back into a gas again."

"Natural? Not man-made?"

"That's my guess. Pretty volatile stuff, too. There's traces of carbon dioxide, hydrogen sulfide, methane, and a bunch of other things. It's a real witch's brew."

Doc Savage's trilling piped up briefly, but the bronze man declined to offer any hint as to his conclusions, if he had any. He might only have been surprised by Monk's findings.

Not much else transpired until a strikingly colored seaplane flew overhead.

Pat Savage was the first to notice it, Doc having gone below for reasons of his own.

The bronze-haired girl lifted a pair of binoculars that she had hung around her neck. She trained the powerful lenses on the overflying craft. It was a small sport job, equipped with floats. Its colors were a distinctive canary yellow—cowl ring, tail and other elements trimmed with black.

"If I didn't know any better," Pat told the others, after she called their attention to the highflying plane, "I would swear that yellowjacket crate belonged to no less than Hornetta Hale herself."

Ham lifted his own field glasses. "I spy the name *Hornet*." He frowned. "Whatever would she be doing way out here?"

As if in answer to that interrogative, the bumblebee-like ship performed an expert maneuver and came flying back toward them.

It buzzed the cruiser at a low altitude, then took to the skies, waggling its wings.

On the second pass, the trim aircraft tilted so they could see the blonde tresses of Hornetta Hale hunkered at the controls.

She tossed out a bottle as she zipped by, motor snarling. The snappy aviatrix was attempting to land the bottle on the deck. But she missed.

The bottle made a splash off to port. Momentarily slipping beneath the waves, the object bobbed back to the surface. Ham and Monk trained their binoculars on it, saw that it was a common quart milk bottle, sealed with candle wax.

By this time, Doc Savage has come up on deck. He needed no binoculars to see that the bottle appeared to contain a message.

Stripping off shirt and shoes, the bronze man plunged into the ocean, struck out for the container, seized it in one mighty fist, and brought it back to the *Stormalong*.

Once on deck, Doc uncorked the bottle, brought forth a curled note. One word was marked in pencil:

TRUCE?

Peering at the note, Pat Savage sniffed disdainfully, "Give me the word, Doc, and I'll clip her sassy wings for you."

Pat brandished her antique six-shooter.

Doc shook his head, found a flare gun, and shot a greenish rocket into the sky.

Pat asked Doc, "Is that a yes or a no to the note?"

The yellowjacket ship was an amphibian, and capable of landing on water. Doc throttled the *Stormalong* back until it was wallowing in the swells.

Hornetta dropped her ship to the lightly-rolling waves, spanked down hard, and coasted in their direction.

Once the prop stopped spinning, Hornetta stuck a blonde head out and asked jauntily, "Permission to come aboard?"

"Permission granted," Doc called over.

"No horseplay," admonished Hornetta.

Ham called out, "We could ask the same of you."

The blonde grinned. "Deal."

Hornetta swam over to the *Stormalong* and climbed aboard, acting as if it were nothing at all. Her attire was very abbreviated—shorts and a halter top.

Doc Savage wordlessly offered her a towel with which to dry herself off. Hornetta applied it to her face and hair, as strings of water dripped off her clothing. She was dressed for warm weather. Apparently, she was some sort of optimist.

"It is high time," Hornetta announced, "that we trade information."

"You first," Pat said tartly.

"Who are you?" Hornetta demanded, giving the bronze-haired girl the once-over.

"Pat Savage."

"Never heard of you," said Hornetta thinly. She turned her attention to Doc Savage. "I lost the trail, so I need to take it up with you."

"Trail to what?" questioned Doc.

"Her name is Honoria Hale."

"We have met her," admitted Doc. "What is she to you?"

Hornetta seemed reluctant to divest herself of any facts. Heaving a reluctant sigh, she said, "My big sister, if you must know."

Doc said, "She could be your twin."

Hornetta appeared to be struggling with her tongue. Another sigh came. She spoke.

"She *is* my twin. Honoria's three minutes older than me."

Doc Savage said, "The last we saw her, Honoria Hale had been abducted by men in the pay of an individual who was calling himself Count Rumpler."

"Never heard of him," snapped Hornetta. "Hear anything of the gent named Lancelot Lacy?"

"No," said Doc Savage. "Who is he?"

"The biggest phony-baloney you ever could meet," snorted Hornetta.

"Perhaps you need to start at the beginning," suggested Doc.

"First things first. What happened to my twin sister?"

"She was abducted aboard the steamer *Matador,* but was spirited away last night. Her abductors took her off in a lifeboat. The boat was found overturned, floating in the Atlantic, with no sign of anyone who had formerly been on board."

"The Men Under the Sea got her!" snapped Hornetta.

"Who exactly are the Men Under the Sea?"

Hornetta made a stubborn jaw. "If I told you," she returned, "you would not believe me."

"Her abductors appear to be very dangerous men, intent upon a very alarming mission," Doc pointed out.

"Don't I know it?" gritted Hornetta. "How Honoria got mixed up in all this, is all the fault of that rascal, Lancelot Lacy."

"We are going around in circles," Doc pointed out. "What is behind all of this?"

Again Hornetta made a stubborn square of her jaw. She was thinking.

"My bossy big sister fell for this Lancelot Lacy—which I don't even think is his actual name. They are up to skulduggery. Serious skulduggery."

Pat interjected tartly, "If you don't shake loose with some details, I might come over there and box your ears proper."

Hornetta Hale took that as a challenge. Instead of shrinking, she marched over to Pat Savage and attempted to flatten her nose.

Pat hauled off and connected with the point of Hornetta's sharp chin.

The sassy blonde went flying backwards, and pitched over the rail.

Doc Savage rushed to the rail, looked down.

There was no sign of the woman. Only disturbed blue water.

Doc leapt in, fearing Hornetta had been knocked unconscious and was at risk of drowning.

Once underwater, the bronze giant rushed about, looking for any sign of the woman. To his amazement, he saw none.

Working his way around to the bow of the boat, Doc broke the surface.

Hornetta was on the other side of the boat, swimming toward her rolling amphibian.

Doc struck out in her direction, swimming madly.

Hornetta had only a fair head start, and Doc soon overhauled her, grasping her by one forearm, arresting her in the water.

"We had a truce," admonished Doc. "You promised to share information."

"That was before your brassy girlfriend socked me," spat Hornetta.

"You were attempting to throw the first punch," Doc pointed out.

"Either way, the truce went overboard when I did. Now let me go!"

Instead of replying, Doc Savage began swimming back to

the *Stormalong*, towing the girl by one arm.

Hornetta had no appetite for returning to the vessel. She began kicking and clawing, spitting and screaming in the manner of an enraged wildcat. Doc Savage had been in many battles in the past. But this was something new.

Hornetta Hale was, as Pat Savage once remarked, a genuine bearcat. It was as if the bronze man got hold of a hurricane in female form. The feisty blonde tried to stick her thumbs in his eyes, poke fingers in his ears, pulled at his hair, twisted his nose and generally made a miserable nuisance of herself.

Doc let go, dived underwater, came up on the girl's blind side and attempted to get hold of her neck.

Alerted by the rush of water, Hornetta turned around and attempted to bite the bronze man's fingers. She had very strong teeth. They snapped like castanets.

Brandishing her frontier peacemaker, Pat Savage called over, "Say the word, Doc, and I'll pot her with my trusty hogleg. You know I never miss."

"Never mind," Doc called back.

Reluctantly, Doc Savage allowed the girl to return to her amphibian. Slamming the door shut, Hornetta kicked the engines to life, producing a great deal of exhaust smoke and engine noise. The engine was sorely in need of an overhaul.

As the bronze man watched, various parts of his anatomy smarting, Hornetta Hale sent the amphibian scooting across the water, then droning into the air. She pointed the screaming prop south and settled in for a flight to an unknown destination.

Doc Savage's men were waiting for him when the bronze man returned to the deck of the *Stormalong*.

Pat Savage said triumphantly, "Now we know who wears the pants in the Savage family. You let that brazen hussy slap you silly. *I* put her over the rail with one clean sock!"

Doc Savage had nothing to say to that. He looked thoroughly disgusted, and more than a trace embarrassed. The bronze man had been trained by a seemingly endless cavalcade of scientists and other singular experts from the point in life where he had just begun to walk. No expense had been spared, nor any necessary skill deemed suitable for his life plan of roaming the globe, rendering humanitarian service to those in need, and dealing out uncompromising justice where lawful authorities could not reach, was unlearned.

This extensive training had continued relentlessly until adulthood. It was an audacious and demonstrably risky endeavor. That it had been wonderfully successful was proven by the type of man Clark Savage, Jr., had become, and the great works that had attached themselves to his legend.

There had been only one glaring flaw in the undertaking.

No scientist, nor other learned expert, had ever satisfactorily explained the female of the species to Doc Savage. Having been handed off from one tutor to the other, with frequent moves from country to country, learning chemistry, botany and other specialized disciplines, Doc's social life naturally suffered, and no one had thought to correct this oversight when it came to the opposite sex.

Thus it was that, in adulthood, Doc Savage could design a modern aircraft and perform delicate brain surgery, but women in general baffled him. It was as close to an Achilles' heel as the big bronze fellow possessed. It explained his perpetual difficulties with his untamable cousin, Pat—as well as giving insight as to how Hornetta Hale had heretofore managed to run rings around him.

Grimly, Doc took the controls and drove the *Stormalong* deeper into the southern reaches of the Caribbean Sea.

Chapter XVIII

HORROR IN THE HOLD

THE HOUR WAS now very late, and a brittle half moon rode high in the night sky. A chill laced the ocean breezes as the *Stormalong* beat further southward.

Doc Savage stood at the controls, the listener device headphones clapped to his ears. From time to time, a light rain speckled the roof of the bridge, but it didn't amount to very much. The skies remained as clear as a black velvet curtain dusted with diamonds.

From time to time, the bronze man steered the boat off course as if probing for underwater noises.

His silence, as well as the fact that he kept returning to course, indicated that he detected nothing of the sort.

Sidling up to him, Ham Brooks said quietly, "You are worried about submarines, aren't you?"

Doc replied, "For the last year or so, there have been unconfirmed reports of foreign submarine activity in the Caribbean. Rumors of refueling bases and resupply depots. None of these have ever been confirmed, however."

"I have read the same reports," said Ham. "They appeared in reliable periodicals."

"Reliable magazines have proven to be in error in the past."

Below, Long Tom and Pat were taking turns shining torches down an ingenious window that was built into the bottom of the *Stormalong's* keel.

This portal of glasslike composition material was big enough to offer an excellent view of the waters beneath the cruising yacht. It had many useful applications. Not the least of which was that it afforded the ability to examine the ocean floor in the type of shallow depths toward which they were headed.

Another value was the ability to make out various underwater life-forms, and of course any submarine that might have been passing beneath them. Despite the narrowness of the window, the portal, combined with the moving lights, showed any disturbances such as would be made by the wake of any silently cruising submersible.

After several hours of observation, Pat Savage remarked, "I don't see anything—not fish nor fowl."

Long Tom blinked. "Fowl? Underwater?"

Pat winkled her entrancingly pert nose. "Something sure smells foul when we all see a merman cavorting in the pale moonlight."

Long Tom had no reply to that. He was still examining the mental image of the catapulting creature that had shot out of the water and dived back in.

"What happens if we *do* spy such a creature?" Pat asked. "What do we do about it?"

"Bait our hooks?" Long Tom grumbled.

Pat regarded the puny electrical wizard dubiously, "With what, pray tell?"

"If I know Doc Savage," Long Tom said carefully, "he will go after it with his bare hands." He pointed back in the direction of a projecting pipe—a tall round tube of a hatch which had been dogged shut.

Pat had noticed it before, but had not investigated. Now she wondered, "What is that?"

"Diving well. You open it up so you can enter the water quietly and unseen."

Curious, Pat moved over to investigate. It looked like an ordinary hatch that might have been found on a submarine or similar vessel. It was rather small. It would allow only one person at a time to enter or leave via this route.

Compelled by her feminine curiosity, Pat undogged the hatch and threw it back, using both strong hands owing to its heaviness.

Staring down the pipe, she heard rushing water and after her eyes adjusted to the darkness, she was able to discern the sea swirling past. It was unusually tranquil.

"Very clever," she remarked. "This well is so tall the water can't get up and spill over."

"It's similar to the escape tubes found in most modern submarines," advised Long Tom.

Pat shut the hatch, gave the wheel a careless spin, and got back to her feet.

Eyeing the bulkhead overhead, she observed, "I don't like this one bit. Doc is too quiet."

Long Tom frowned. "Doc is always quiet."

"True," Pat admitted. "But he hasn't blistered my hide yet, or confined me to my quarters for barging into this screwy mess."

Long Tom was concentrating on the glass porthole underneath him. He had taken to squatting on the port itself, and moving his flashlight all around.

"This is as dangerous a mission as I can remember," Long Tom said grimly. "You can tell by looking at him that the big fellow is very preoccupied with getting to the bottom of things."

"Still," grimaced Pat, "I can feel my spanking coming."

"You might want to sit down then," suggested Long Tom. "And stay that way."

Pat made a face composed of thoughtful lines. "Maybe I should turn in for the night."

"Good idea," said Long Tom. "We're going to have to take turns on watch. Maybe you should grab your forty winks so you can take the morning watch."

The *Stormalong* was spacious enough below decks to boast

private staterooms. These were very small, barely more than a bunk and a few other items. Pat selected one, and closed the door. She did not bother to lock it. In the event of an emergency, she would need to get out in a hurry.

Long Tom went back to his underwater scrutiny.

After a while, Monk Mayfair came down, toting Habeas Corpus by one oversized ear. He yawned like a steam shovel getting ready to grab a large boulder.

"Where's Pat?" he asked Long Tom sleepily.

"Turned in for the night," said the slender electrical expert.

"That's what I come down for. Doc said to get some shuteye. He and Ham will keep an eye on things."

Long Tom doused his flashlight, and stood up.

"I have the same idea," he said. "There's nothing down there except fish. And not many of those."

Monk peered down into the blue depths. "See anythin' interestin'?"

Long Tom shook his pale head. "Sand shark or two. The usual."

Monk grunted, encouraged Habeas Corpus into one of the staterooms. "Sure it wasn't a mermaid?"

Long Tom favored the apish chemist with a sour glance. "You know there isn't any such animal!"

"I knew that yesterday," commented Monk. "But today, I ain't so sure...."

With that, the hairy chemist closed his door quietly and before long the sounds of his snoring could be heard.

Long Tom stuffed some cotton into his ears so that he could get some needed sleep. Before long he, too, was gone from the world of wakefulness.

HOURS passed. Dawn was far off. The passage of the *Stormalong* down the Atlantic Coast wended through the multitudinous islands of the Bahamas, with its lonesome coral atolls and strange sandy cays, proved to be entirely uneventful.

At the controls, Doc Savage stood like a statue cast of metal, listening intently to the underwater listener. He turned to Ham Brooks and suggested, "Why don't you wake up Monk, and get some sleep yourself."

"Righto," the dapper lawyer said. He did not look so much like a lawyer now in his nautical outfit and, despite the situation, seemed to be enjoying the voyage. It was suspected that Ham— had he his druthers—would have spent more time at sea had not the pressing work of his demanding legal practice and his association with Doc Savage kept him on dry land.

Ham plucked his sword cane from its place of concealment, where Habeas Corpus could not capture it, and went down the hatch into the lower hold.

He was not down there very long. There came a kind of a screech. Ham came rushing up, waving his stick excitedly.

"Doc!" he howled.

The bronze man turned. "What is it?"

"Pat! She's *missing!*"

Doc Savage plunged for the hatch, banged down the companionway so fast he nearly bowled the dapper lawyer over. Ham followed him down.

The other cabins disgorged their occupants—Monk and Long Tom, looking sleepy and annoyed at the same time.

"What the heck is going on?" demanded Monk.

The answer was not long in coming.

The floor was wet, and there were tracks.

These tracks were not human. They were splayed, larger than a human foot, and had some of the qualities of a duck. Or perhaps a goose. No duck or goose or similar waterfowl possessed such monstrous appendages, however.

The tracks came from the escape well and went directly to Pat Savage's stateroom, whose door lay open.

Doc entered the cubicle, found rumpled sheets, but no one was lying in the bunk. He touched the mattress. Still warm.

Tracks led back to the escape well, which had been left open by whatever had stolen aboard the yacht and carried away Pat Savage. Doc Savage read that story in a glance from the myriad weird tracks, and by Pat Savage's distressing absence.

While the truth of the matter was sinking in, the bronze man's trilling began to issue from his parted lips.

It had a strained, almost agonized tone. It was nothing like his men had ever heard wrenched out of him. They detected myriad emotions threaded through it as the sound circulated about the narrow confines. Shock, anger, confusion, and something that they took to be a weird species of grief.

Without hesitation, Doc stepped out of his shoes and went down the well.

Monk plunged for the companionway, went up to the rail, and also dived into the water.

Neither man said a word. Concern for the missing Pat Savage impelled their frantic behavior.

Doc and Monk swam about as the *Stormalong,* robot helmsman engaged, beat on into the night. Doc had set the automatic controls before abandoning his post.

Realizing what was transpiring, Long Tom raced for the controls, and threw the boat back in the direction that Doc and Monk were treading water.

While Long Tom raced about, making wild circles on the face of the Caribbean, Ham Brooks, after dogging the hatch, was liberally shining his flashlight through the hull-bottom portal.

Doc Savage, he saw, was floating by the stern landing stage. He called for a diving outfit.

Ham Brooks, hearing this shout, got one out of the locker, and brought it to the rail. He handed it down to the waiting bronze man.

This consisted of a mouthpiece and spring nose clip, to which was attached a breath purifier pack. There was nothing more to it than that. But the contrivance allowed Doc Savage to stay submerged longer than his usual extended period of time, the bronze man having a remarkable lung capacity, the result of a childhood spent among the pearl divers of the South Seas.

Another outfit was handed over to Monk Mayfair, who began diving, submerging and resurfacing time and again.

Over an hour passed before silently and reluctantly, Doc Savage and Monk returned to the *Stormalong*. They all went below.

Removing his breathing apparatus, Doc Savage looked like a stricken man.

The flake-gold of his eyes seemed to have become unnaturally still, as if the suspension medium in which the flakes normally whirled—or gave that appearance at any rate—had congealed.

Monk exploded, "What the heck could've happened to Pat? Where could she have gone?"

Ham Brooks said thickly, "Those tracks were not the tracks of anything human. Nor were they made by swim fins. See those points? I will wager those are claw marks."

Everyone bent down to see the tracks more clearly. At points at the edges of the racks, there appeared to be the unmistakable moist indentations of very large claws.

Long Tom Roberts tugged at an oversized ear, and murmured, "I still don't believe in mermaids, but—"

"Do not be ridiculous!" snapped Ham. "That merman creature we saw possessed a fishy tail. The kidnapper had feet that were like those of wild geese."

Monk muttered, "That don't make any more sense than a fishtailed merman."

Everyone looked to Doc Savage for answers. The bronze man's face was something frozen in metal. He seemed at a loss for words. Finally, he regarded them with a voice like chilled steel and intoned, "We will find Pat Savage whatever it takes, wherever it takes us."

It was not an answer to the conundrum, but it gave them a

rising confidence in the face of the baffling unknown thing that had transpired.

Wordlessly, Doc Savage regained the controls, pointed the *Stormalong* south, and pushed the throttle as far forward as the mechanism permitted.

The powerful cruiser surged ahead, just as dawn began breaking.

Chapter XIX

THE CROSS THAT
WAS CROOKED

THEY REACHED THE sandy speck of a cay in the Caribbean just before noon that day.

The tiny isle proved to be on no marine chart—not even the authoritative *West Indies Pilot* listed it. Thus it had no name, and no history they could ascribe to it.

Doc Savage located the cay by radioing the liner captain who at first stumbled upon it during the rescue of Hornetta Hale. From this individual, he obtained its exact longitude and latitude. It was nowhere near the spot where the blonde firecracker's seaplane had been discovered, floating abandoned—a suspicious circumstance in itself.

There was no question but this was the correct island, for it matched the description given in the newspapers—a pitiful little hump of sand surmounted by a couple of forlorn palm trees. Not much else. Not even a sand lizard.

They circled the tiny spot, but that was just a precaution. It was so small they needn't have reconnoitered it to determine a fact that was obvious to all.

Ham spoke up after a while. "No lagoon. Not even a tiny cove." He sounded disappointed.

"Heck," snorted Monk, "it ain't but a sand spit, if that."

Nevertheless, Doc Savage brought the *Stormalong* to a suitable spot for anchorage, halted the engines, and lowered the stainless steel anchor by a mechanical windlass.

They were east of the tip of Florida. Somewhere northwest

of Cuba, many nautical miles south by west of Great Abaco Island in the Bahama island group.

While the others remained behind to guard the cruiser, Doc Savage and Monk Mayfair got into the water, waded for shore and investigated the little dab of an island.

There were, of course, signs of recent habitation. A few cracked coconut shells. Some remnants of the shell of a crab. Most of the rest were broken shards of pink shell and dark husk proving that Hornetta Hale had subsisted largely upon conch meat and coconut milk during her enforced exile.

Peering about, homely Monk scratched his rusty head, and made a perplexed face.

"Well, love a duck. That blonde fire eater must be one tough babe in order to survive on this sandpile the way she done."

Doc Savage nodded. "She has quite a reputation."

Doc searched about for any signs of why the blonde-haired adventuress had been marooned on this tiny cay. Of course, there was nothing. Whatever had compelled unknown persons—probably the Count and his crowd—to strand Hornetta Hale in a remote corner of the Caribbean in this manner, and not kill her, those answers would be found elsewhere.

This did not stop Monk Mayfair from trying to puzzle it all out.

"Who ever done this, they didn't want to kill her, but maybe they didn't care whether she lived or died," he ventured.

"A reasonable conjecture," admitted Doc Savage. The bronze man was scratching about in the sand with the toe of one shoe, looking for any evidence, sign of writing, or even a distress marker.

He found a few sun-bleached stones carefully arranged in the shape of an S.O.S., but they were too few to properly spell out the letters. It was only by chance that the liner *Amberjack* had wandered close enough to spy Hornetta's flag of rags.

The flag was still there, consisting of a piece of driftwood stuck in the sand. The pennant was what was left of a summer skirt.

Doc Savage examined this. There were no pockets, no writing. Nothing in the way of a message.

Examining the boles of the two palms, the bronze man looked for signs of writing. It would be possible to scratch out something with one of the pink conch shell shards, if one put their mind to it.

Indeed, the bronze man found a number of broken shards at the base of one tree, evidence that this was attempted.

The smooth, silvery bark of the palm proved to be too tough for anything in the way of a message.

Glancing over the attempt, Monk grumbled, "Looks like she gave up on it."

Going to the next palm, they found more evidence of an attempt at writing. This palm was younger, somewhat stunted, and therefore softer of bark.

Five words Hornetta had managed to scratch out. They read:

BEWARE!
MEN UNDER THE SEA

That was all.

"For the love of mud!" exploded Monk. "She could be talking about the fish-man we spotted!"

Doc Savage offered nothing. He was examining another mark below the letters. It was not a letter, but a symbol.

Crude, of unequal lines, it might have been simply a hash mark, or a first attempt to test the bark before carving the other message.

Monk wrinkled his simian face in perplexity, tilting his rusty head this way and that, until it hit him.

"I know what that jigger is supposed to be," he gulped.

It was a cross. Its arms were bent a clockwise manner. A crooked cross, a twisted thing of harsh right angles.

"This hooks up with the Count and his boys, all right," Monk stated grimly. "But what does all this have to do with men livin' under the sea?"

"That remains to be seen," said Doc. "My hunch is that Hornetta Hale left these marks as a warning to others in the event she perished here. No doubt whatever she can tell us will have an important bearing on the mystery behind all this—the motive, the reason for what is happening in the Caribbean." Doc Savage was silent for a time. He was studying the strange twisted cross.

"Let us return to the boat," he said abruptly.

They made their way back to the *Stormalong*, and shared this latest information.

Dark eyes glowing, Ham Brooks said, "Everything we have encountered or witnessed so far appears to tie together. Yet it makes absolutely no sense."

"No apparent sense," corrected Doc Savage. "This does not mean that there is no sense to be found at the bottom of the matter."

"If so," Ham said, twisting his polished sword cane in his hands, "we're going to have to dig very deep to find it."

Long Tom spoke up. "This is a dead end for sure. Where do we go from here?"

Doc Savage said, "We have three clues. There is a cay with the lagoon, and the Count and his cohorts appear to have a hideout or a base there. It is imperative that we find this unknown cay."

"What about Pat?" asked Monk, voice stricken.

"The fact that these men were too squeamish to do away with Hornetta Hale could imply that they will hesitate to bring harm to Pat. If they wanted her dead, there would be no necessity of abducting her. It is a slim hope. But it is all that we have."

"Do we know that the Count and the mermen are connected?" wondered Ham.

"We do not," Doc said flatly. "But we can hope that one trail converges with the other. The fact that Honoria Hale and her captors disappeared from a lifeboat mid-Atlantic, in a manner similar to Pat's vanishing, suggests a tie-up."

"But not much of one," muttered Monk. "This sure is a screwy fish stew."

Going to the controls, Doc Savage raised the anchor, reversed the engines, and piloted the powerful cruiser away from the nameless island.

Ham got out all the marine charts, and was poring over them. They had been doing this previously, in the hope of locating a cay possessing a noticeable lagoon. But now they became very intent upon the task.

"Deuced needle in a haystack," he muttered.

"What is?" asked Long Tom.

"Finding the correct cay with the accompanying lagoon."

Doc Savage surprised them by announcing, "The cay we are seeking is volcanic."

How the bronze man had arrived at this conclusion was a mystery, but no one questioned it. Doc often came to correct conclusions through what appeared to be magic, but was in reality sound deductive thinking.

Suddenly, Monk snapped his blunt fingers, saying, "Those vapor traces that I analyzed. All of that stuff are products of volcanic action! I shoulda realized that myself."

"Some lagoons are created by water eroding the extinct cone of an underwater volcano," mused Ham. "Are there any extinct volcanic cones in this immediate vicinity?"

"None," asserted Doc. "But it is possible that an ancient volcano, overgrown by tropical greenery, and worn down by perpetual action of the tides, could exist in this region, undiscovered. You will both recall our troubles on such an island two years back, when we fought a battle on a volcanic spot such as we now seek." *

"That don't help us now," snapped Monk. "What difference does it make what kind of isle it is? We're lookin' for a lagoon, ain't we? Then let's get to it. Pat needs rescuin'!"

---

* Poison Island.

The *Stormalong* worked its way amid scattered islands. Shoal cays and coral atolls were plentiful. Many were simply forlorn mangrove swamps, overgrown with the tough water-seeking roots, home to lizards and tropical birds. They were clearly uninhabited, if not uninhabitable, by humans.

They discovered nothing of interest along the way.

It was a little bit further along in the afternoon when they came upon the yellow-and-black amphibian plane roosting upon the waves. It looked like a tired duck resting after a long flight.

Monk trained his binoculars on it, and squawled, "Hey! That's Hornetta's bus!"

DOC SAVAGE sent the *Stormalong* hammering in the direction of the amphibian. He cut in the silencing mechanism for the motors, but it was of limited value. The powerful Diesels, even throttled down, made considerable noise despite the ingenious baffles.

As they drew near, Doc throttled back the engines to reduce the noise, hoping not to give away their approach.

The sleek cruiser slipped up on the amphibian from its tail section, where visibility was nonexistent from the point-of-view of the cockpit.

Still, something alerted the pilot, for suddenly the exhaust stack spat sparks and began belching grayish-black fumes. The seaplane began shuddering and moving forward.

Advancing the throttles, Doc raced to get in ahead of the craft.

The famous *Hornet* had been a champion in her days, and had come in second in two consecutive Schneider Cup races. But that was years ago. She was showing her age.

Prow throwing up spume and spray, the *Stormalong* soon overhauled the thundering amphibian. Doc, perhaps desperate for a lead, lunged toward the port wing of the amphibian as she tried to climb up on step.

The pilot—they could see clearly that it was Hornetta Hale—flung the amphibian to starboard. In this way, she avoided a collision, but lost headway.

Doc veered the *Stormalong* in a great sweeping circle, attempting to get in front of the plane's buzzing nose.

Each time Hornetta attempted to bring her ship around and resume taxiing, the *Stormalong* intercepted it.

Finally, Hornetta realized the futility of escape. She shut down the engine. The spinning prop froze, and she slid open a window.

"You win!" she called out.

Doc Savage called over in a voice that carried with amazing clarity, "It is time to parley."

"I don't seem to have much choice in the matter. You stiffs are in my way."

Reluctantly, Hornetta stepped out of the cockpit and onto a pontoon. Without hesitation, she threw herself into the water and swam with the agility and speed of an Olympic diver for the waiting yacht.

Monk and Ham raced one another to be the first one to help her on board. Hitherto they had considered the blonde adventuress to be the female equivalent of the devil, complete with horns, spiked tail, with a tongue like a pitchfork. But now their initial impression subsided, the blonde girl's evident charms providing the motivation.

To Ham's slack-jawed surprise, Hornetta spurned his offered hand and accepted Monk's assistance onto the heaving deck of the *Stormalong*.

Monk beamed. Ham frowned.

"We meet again," Hornetta said boldly.

Long Tom warned her, "Watch your step around me, unless you want to be knocked into the drink for all the trouble you bring."

"Pick on someone your own size, you shrimp," sneered Hornetta. "I only fight them that's in my weight class." Looking around the deck, she snapped, "Where's that gal that socked me? I want a rematch right here and now."

Doc said somberly, "My cousin Pat was abducted in the middle of the night."

Hornetta hesitated before replying. She seemed at war with herself.

"By the Men Under the Sea, apparently," prompted Doc.

Hornetta's snapping blue eyes popped in surprise. She bit her tongue.

Doc said, "Given the uncanny manner in which Honoria Hale vanished in mid-ocean, we might conjecture that both women are being held by the same persons, possibly in the identical location."

"Where is she?" Hornetta yelped. "You tell me this instant, you copper-faced wooden Indian!"

Doc ignored the insult. "At last report, Honoria Hale was a prisoner of a man calling himself Count Rumpler. What can you tell us about these Men Under the Sea?"

"They are not what they seem to be," Hornetta supplied sullenly.

"If you are speaking of the same type of creature we encountered," Doc Savage returned simply, "one of which we saw under moonlit conditions suggested a merman. But last night an aquatic marauder stole aboard this vessel, leaving behind footprints like those of oversize geese."

"The Men Under the Sea," said Hornetta slowly, "come in two varieties. The web-footed ones, and the fishtailed ones. They're pretty ugly customers, as I'm sure you realize by now."

"Where do they dwell?" pressed Doc.

"That's what I'm down here trying to find out!" snapped Hornetta. "But you clowns keep cramping my style. I need to be free to act! My sister's life is at stake!"

Doc Savage said calmly, "We appear to have a common cause."

Hornetta subsided. Her facial contortions showed that she was doing considerable thinking. She gave her bedraggled blonde locks an annoyed fluffing.

"It all goes back to the time Honoria took up with that phony-baloney Lancelot Lacy character," she began.

"Tell us about Lacy," Doc requested.

"Lancelot Lacy," exclaimed Hornetta Hale, "is as vain as all the peacocks in Siam. He struts about like some kind of upper-crust swell, when in fact he's a dirty low-down dog. My opinion."

"Was Lacy the one who stranded you?" asked Ham.

"No other. He wanted me out of the way because I knew too much. But he refused to knock me off."

"Why not?" inquired Doc.

"Because of my stuck-up sister, Honoria," snapped Hornetta. "She's sweet on the rat."

"You had better begin at the beginning," suggested Doc. "We would like to hear a full account of your recent activities."

Hornetta looked as if she had swallowed poison. She began spitting out words.

"My sister and I are twins. But we didn't like being twins. What's more, we are as different as a pineapple and a peach. I like the limelight, adventure, seeing my name in headlines. Honoria, who was nicknamed 'Honeybee,' was the exact opposite. She likes the nightlife, gay parties, socializing. She had an affinity for European royalty. She took up with a number of them, during the period she lived in Europe. Then came the war, and she had to return to America. You probably remember that fuss the week the war broke out."

Doc nodded. "All nations recalled their vessels back to their home ports. There was a scramble to evacuate Europe by tourists visiting the continent. For a few days, the Atlantic was choked with passenger liners and refugees fleeing the outbreak of war."

"Honoria returned to the U.S. on one of those panicked

liners," supplied Hornetta. "With her came that no-good Lancelot Lacy. He promptly joined one of those Bunds you read about, where they grow identical trick mustaches, go off to weekend camps and dress up like pretend soldiers."

Doc Savage said, "I have looked into your background. I find no written record of your having a twin sister."

"That's because Honoria and I could barely stand one another. Sure, we're sisters. But we are exact opposites. Our parents died, and we were separated. Honoria was raised down in Virginia, where she took on the buttery manners of a Southern Belle. I landed in Jersey. Because Honoria was three minutes older, she thought she was better than me. She tried to pretend that I didn't exist, so I returned the favor. It's as simple as that. This goes back to when we were young. Get me?"

"I get you," returned Doc. "Please continue."

Hornetta was looking at her nails, plainly still upset over her predicament. "Lancelot Lacy is the rottenest of bad apples. Strictly Fifth Column material, if you take my meaning."

Then her crystal blue eyes shifted up over their heads.

Doc was the first to notice this. He turned his head.

The bronze man's vision was sharper than it seemed possible for human optics to be, the result of a lifetime of intensive training for all of his senses.

"What is it?" asked Long Tom, peering in the same direction.

"Passing mail plane," explained Hornetta. "Probably nothing."

Still, the blonde adventuress did not take her eyes off the approaching aircraft.

Suddenly, Doc Savage rapped out crashing orders. "Everyone go below! Take cover!"

Doc plunged for the controls, got the engines going, and began driving the *Stormalong* in a zigzag line, changing direction frequently as if attempting to slice up the Caribbean seas into sections.

Sunburned arms flailing, Hornetta Hale tumbled off the stern—whether by accident or design was never known. Once in the water, she struck out for her own amphibian, the *Hornet*.

Maneuvering wildly, sweeping in half circles alternating with sudden shifts in course, Doc Savage spotted the approaching plane. It was a very modern craft, whose wings were bent in a fashion that had become feared all over Europe. It was now flying very high, climbing hard. Then, suddenly, it rolled its canted wings, dived straight down.

There came an unearthly screaming.

"Dive bomber!" moaned Long Tom, recognizing the sound.

The bronze man had already determined that from the canted configuration of the warplane's wings.

Hurtling down out of the clear sky, the alarming howl grew nearer. Doc steered to port, then starboard, desperate to avoid what was coming next.

The dive bomber, fortunately, carried only one bomb slung to its undercarriage. There was no telling when it would release, or where it might land.

Finally, this let go.

Their first certain knowledge that they were under attack came when a great upheaval disturbed the coral-hued Caribbean waters off to starboard. A gush, followed by a fountain of water came—so close that chilly spray spattered their faces.

Monk and the others had by this time unlimbered their superfirers. The tiny weapons made thunder on the open water, but it was all show. The ingenious pistols did not have the range needed to pepper their attacker.

Doc Savage had rushed below, and came up with a .220 rifle, which the *Stormalong* carried for potting sharks.

Bringing this to his shoulder, the bronze giant fired two shots, clipping one wing fuel tank, then the other. It was amazing shooting, and it had a marked effect upon the pilot, who might have been about to trip his machine guns.

The screaming warplane leveled out, and headed south. It carried only one bomb. And that had missed. With precious fuel stringing behind, it had no more business to conduct.

They all saw that it was painted a flat battleship gray and bore no markings whatsoever.

"Where the heck did *he* come from?" bellowed Monk, emerging from below. "This ain't Europe!"

Doc Savage, pushing the *Stormalong* hard, attempted to come around in an effort to head off Hornetta Hale, who had already climbed back into the cockpit of her yellow-and-black amphibian.

The engine was still warm, so Hornetta got the propeller spinning smartly. It sounded like a buzzsaw getting ready to rip through timber. She propelled the trim ship across the face of the Caribbean, got smartly on step, and went howling up into the sky.

The headstrong she-hornet pointed her amphibian in the direction of the retreating warplane.

"Brave," muttered Monk.

"Foolish," retorted Long Tom, who was no admirer of the distaff sex.

Grimly, Doc sent the *Stormalong* charging after the fleeing planes.

"At least," said Monk with undisguised relish, "we got us a trail to follow at last."

Chapter XX

DEAD END

AS A RACE, it was not much.

Despite being armored and no longer encumbered by its undercarriage bomb, the foreign warplane pulled away from the speedy *Hornet,* which was hampered by the fact that the latter ship hauled two plump Edo pontoons on its underside.

The warplane was soon lost from sight.

Taking up the rear, the yacht *Stormalong* was no match for either aircraft, given the fact that it was thundering over placid waves. Friction drag of the sea ensured that its streamlined hull was no substitute for wings slicing freely through the air.

Still, Doc Savage refused to give up. He kept the yellow-jacket amphibian in sight at all times, as steely fingers like a bronze vise held the yacht wheel locked in a dead-reckoning position.

Before long, the bronze man's eyes began shifting to the turquoise waters. A flicker of a concern touched his metallic features.

Ham scrambled to pore through the charts. He sensed what was coming.

"We are approaching the region where the waters are extremely shallow—dangerously shallow," warned the dapper lawyer. "There are blackheads, coral reefs. If we're not careful, we could tear the bottom out of our keel."

Hearing that, Monk Mayfair rushed below and manned the hull-bottom porthole which looked down into the amazingly clear waters.

There was a speaking tube down there. He used it.

Monk's voice bellowed upward, "I can see the bottom plain as day. Blackheads everywhere you look. This is gettin' dangerous."

Doc Savage called into the speaking tube, "Guide me best you can."

Monk worked his way around so that he could shine a light ahead of the boat at an angle. It was not much warning, but it was something. He yelled into the tube, "Hard to starboard!"

Doc Savage flung the wheel, carving a new course. Then Monk called up, "Now sheer off to port!"

Doc rocked the wheel in response. The yacht again changed course.

They got about five nautical miles in twisting fashion, losing headway, as the yellowjacket amphibian dwindled to a black dot in the azure sky.

Finally, Monk called up, his voice twisting, "Back off! Back off! Blackheads everywhere you look!"

Doc Savage reversed the engines. The ship shuddered. He sheared off, and probably by scant inches, avoided scraping bottom by the barest of margins.

Monk came climbing out of the lower deck to join the others watching the yellow amphibian vanish into blue nothingness. The high drone of its engine had already ceased to echo over the waves.

Long Tom stared after the departing aircraft.

"Mark my words. She's gone for good this time. If we catch up to that high-flying hussy, I'm going to turn her bag of tricks inside out for good."

Monk turned to Ham and said, "My money's on Long Tom. He don't like women much and this one's gotten his goat for sure."

To which the dapper lawyer responded, "Twenty dollars says that Hornetta Hale will pick Long Tom's pockets without him suspecting it."

They shook hands on it, each man convinced he would get the better of the other.

A profound gloom descended upon deck. Doc Savage brought the *Stormalong* to a dead stop.

They looked at one another. Monk and Ham exchanged sharp glances, as if on the verge of a new quarrel. However, their spirits were by now very low indeed. No argument commenced.

Ham Brooks examined his sword cane thoughtfully and asked a supercilious question. "What do you suppose Hornetta Hale is going to do if she manages to overhaul that warplane? It could shoot her down on a whim."

Doc Savage replied, "No doubt but she is attempting to locate the warplane's landing strip. Evidently, that base may be the key to this entire mystery."

"What buffalos me," Monk muttered, "is why that warbird just didn't turn around and blast her out of the sky on general principles."

"It is something to ponder," returned the bronze man thoughtfully.

Ham Brooks said, "The Count and his crowd have stopped at nothing, not even wholesale murder and destruction, yet they won't lay a hand on either of these Hale women."

"Nor, it is to be hoped," said Doc, "Pat Savage."

They were going over marine charts, trying to come up with a solution to their vexing problem of having no clear destination, and no way to get to that destination if it lay in unusually shallow waters, when a sputtering came to their years.

"Someone's returnin'," warned Monk.

Ham and Long Tom grabbed binoculars, and began scanning the seemingly endless horizon.

Long Tom was the first to spot it. "Hornetta's crate! Must be she ran out of gas."

Minutes later, the yellow-and-black amphibian came scooting over the waves, struggling to stay aloft. One wing dipped alarmingly, then righted. The other started to sag. It was, to all appearances, low on fuel.

Then the engine gave the final pop, and the propeller jerked to a halt. Now it was gliding.

By expert manipulation of the controls, Hornetta Hale managed to pancake the bumblebee amphibian onto the surface of the Caribbean Sea. It was a good job. It helped that the water was smooth. Of course, the Caribbean Sea is almost always smooth, other than during hurricanes.

They watched as the tiny *Hornet* bounced along a bit and began wallowing. Then the hatch popped open.

Out came a stick decorated with a white rag.

Long Tom grinned widely. "She's surrendering!"

Doc urged the *Stormalong* over to the helpless amphibian, and eased up alongside, reversing the throttle, and bringing the heeling cruiser to a slow, sliding halt.

The vessel bumped the pontoon, and Monk reached out to take hold of a wing strut, arresting the *Stormalong's* tendency to drift.

"I guess I can't shake you, so I might as well join you," Hornetta said disconsolately. "That bum got away from me."

This time no one offered her assistance to board the yacht. Hornetta jumped up from the pontoon, and managed to do it with an agility that didn't come from playing tennis on the courtyards of the wealthy. She bounded over the rail nimbly, showing her fiercely sunburned legs.

"I'll bet you want me to start at the beginning," said Hornetta in a forlorn tone. Her shoulders were sagging. She wore an air of utter defeat.

Doc Savage said, "We already heard the beginning, take us to the present. There is no time to lose, unless I am very much mistaken."

"You? Mistaken?" scoffed Hornetta, a little of the former fire returning to her voice. "The Man of Bronze is hardly ever mistaken, from what I hear."

"Enough of your tart tongue," snapped Ham. "This is a very serious matter."

"Yeah," seconded Long Tom. "Bottle that sass and give out with some dope."

HORNETTA HALE'S crystal blue eyes sharpened cunningly, and it could be seen that she was thinking hard.

"Tell you what," she said slowly. "I'll make you a deal."

Ham sniffed, "She sounds like Pat."

"You stay out of this, you overdressed dude!" Hornetta snapped back.

Ham clenched his cane angrily while Monk Mayfair grinned at the cutting jibe.

Curling her lip in Monk's direction, Hornetta added, "What are you dreaming of—banana and coconut soup?"

Monk glowered while Ham brightened.

Doc Savage interjected cautiously, "What deal do you propose?"

"You tell me how you got out of my van, and I'll get around to spilling the beans."

Doc Savage said, "If I am not mistaken, this was explained to you."

"All that you coughed up was that you had that particular trick pulled on you before. Which explains exactly nothing."

Hornetta folded her arms defiantly.

Ham Brooks quipped, "You should know that a magician never reveals his tricks."

To which Monk Mayfair added, "Yeah, that's right. Not only that, but Doc's secrets keep him alive."

Hornetta Hale flounced around, presenting her attractive back to them all. She looked over one raised, sun-blistered shoulder.

"You know my terms. They stand just the way I do. If you want me to turn around, start yakking."

Doc Savage heaved a tiny sigh—which was a mountain of emotion where the bronze man was concerned.

"Getting out of the sedan was no effort whatsoever," he began.

Hornetta whirled. "That van was sealed so tight you couldn't open the car doors a crack once you were trapped in the back. So don't hand me that hooey!"

Doc Savage continued patiently, "As you know, we have fallen for that trick in the past. So my new automobile was designed with that future eventuality in mind."

Hornetta eyed the bronze man skeptically. "In other words, it was built so you could get out if it ever happened again?"

"Precisely," remarked Ham Brooks.

Doc Savage looked at Hornetta Hale in the hope that she was satisfied by that explanation.

But the blonde spitfire was not. She wiggled her fingers at the bronze man, saying, "Give."

Doc Savage gave what was for him a rather long speech.

"The interior of the sedan was rigged so that the driver, by pushing back on his seat, could crawl into the rear seat, and by removing the seat cushions, thereby wriggle into the trunk."

Hornetta looked very interested.

"Once in the trunk, it was a simple matter to actuate a catch, which caused the trunk to spring open."

"I get it now," Hornetta crowed. "But that does not explain how you got out of the van interior. It was locked tight."

"By standing on the sedan's hood, it was possible to apply acid with a special tool on the underside of the van's roof."

Hornetta cocked a dubious eyebrow. "Acid?"

"By painting a nearly complete circle in the roof," continued Doc, "a large hole was created. It was then possible to push up the top of the roof in the same way that the lid of a soup can might be opened after the application of a can opener."

"Clever," said Hornetta. "But how did you get the vehicle out of the van?"

"By crawling to the back end, hanging upside in front of the door, anchored by a small grappling hook and line I always carry, and picking the padlock. Once the doors opened, it was possible to swing into the van interior."

Hornetta made nearly comical faces as she processed the mental pictures created by Doc's succinct account.

"I drove along the whole time, and I didn't hear anything. Spill."

Doc Savage said, with more patience than he possessed at the moment, "I climbed back into the car, engaged the motor and released the brake when you were on an uphill grade, and the sedan rolled out the back."

"I would've heard that!" Hornetta snapped. "I'd have seen you out my rearview mirror."

Doc Savage related, "You may recall that Monk's pet pig was putting up quite a fuss at the time. This covered any noise we made. Furthermore, the sedan was equipped with aviation-style shock absorbers. This allowed it to land safely without a ramp. With the engine running, the sedan shot ahead rather briskly. After following the van closely for a time, we waited for you to go around a tree-shaded bend in the road. At which juncture, we pulled over to the side of the road, and parked. Possibly you noticed the vehicle then, but failed to realize it was the one that had been inside your truck."

"Impossible!" raged Hornetta.

Monk Mayfair inserted, "Like it or not, that's how it happened."

Fuming, Hornetta fretted for almost a minute as if searching for a retort. It was clear that the salty female was smarting from having been outwitted in such a spectacular fashion.

"One second, buster! Who closed the doors to the van?"

Doc Savage hesitated.

"Out with it!"

"It was necessary to fool you into thinking that nothing untoward happened."

"Watch what you call me. I do not like that word, fool."

"Just a manner of speaking," the bronze man reassured her. "My associate, Monk here, climbed out onto the sedan's hood and reclosed the doors, replacing the padlock, which I had previously pocketed."

"You never suspected a thing," chuckled Monk.

Hornetta Hale was struck, for once, utterly speechless. Her brow began to furrow, and she appeared to be searching her memory.

"That tangled-up yarn you just spun," she said archly, "does not make a whole sweater."

Doc asked, "In what way?"

"When I flung open the doors, I didn't notice any hole in my roof."

Doc Savage admitted, "I neglected to mention that I left my coat over the roof in order to mask the outlines of the lid, which I forced back down into place."

By this time, Hornetta Hale was almost lobster-red with indignation.

"No sale!" she snapped at last. "I don't buy any of that hogwash you just slopped over me."

With that, she placed two fingers against one corner of her mouth and made a sideways zipping motion, leaving her lips completely sealed.

"Double-crosser!" raged Monk Mayfair.

Long Tom spoke up. "Let me shake some truth out of her, Doc."

Doc Savage regarded the woman with the sealed lips as if facing one of the most intractable problems he had ever encountered outside of a scientific laboratory.

"We are going to be stuck with one another until the end of this affair," he said with just a trace of steel edging his voice. "Cooperation will be essential."

Hornetta Hale said acidly, "Go climb up your right leg and

slide down your left. Don't forget to tighten your shoelaces while you're about it."

With that, she once more presented them with her defiant but very sunburned back.

"That," fumed Ham Brooks, "seems to be the end of that."

Chapter XXI

HORNETTA STINGS AGAIN

HAD HIS COUSIN, Patricia Savage, not gone missing under such mysterious circumstances, it is unlikely that Doc Savage would have behaved as he did now.

The bronze man strode up to Hornetta Hale, seized her fiery red shoulders, and spun her around until the startled blonde was facing him.

The strength of the Herculean bronze man was undeniable. Hornetta Hale momentarily lost her facial composure. She looked on the verge of being afraid of the towering metallic Samson who stood over her.

"My cousin is missing," Doc Savage said harshly. "It is imperative that we locate her without delay."

"I don't know where she is!" Hornetta retorted hotly, her naturally feisty female personality reasserting itself.

"You know a great many answers to our questions."

"What if I do?" she sneered.

"Has this anything to do with your having antagonized a certain foreign dictator years ago, when you flew rings around his nation's passenger dirigible?" queried Doc.

"No comment," snapped Hornetta.

Doc Savage's ever-active flake-gold eyes were boring into Hornetta's strikingly blue ones. The bronze man modulated his vibrant voice until it became quiet but compelling.

"You will explain why you were so anxious to obtain a submersible."

"What are you doing!" Hornetta demanded, trying to look away.

The bronze giant would have none of it. He forced her to meet his penetrating gaze, then demanded, "Why were you marooned on that island in the first place?"

"That's my business! I tried to hire you, but you wouldn't make a deal."

"Who are the Men Under the Sea?" Doc questioned. "And what have they to do with the sign of the twisted cross?"

"How do you know about that?" Hornetta flung back.

"Do you not remember the message you carved into the palm tree on that Caribbean cay?"

"Oh. So you checked the island out, did you?"

Not taking his whirling eyes off the blonde girl, Doc Savage nodded firmly. "Tell me about the ones who live under the sea," he directed.

Hornetta Hale found herself unable to tear her eyes away from the bronze man's compelling orbs. They fascinated. They seemed alive in a very strange way, as if their animated depths were full of radiant lights like aureate stars. There might have been a galaxy of golden sparks in either eye.

The more Hornetta peered into them, the more they seemed to expand, enlarge, and all but swallow her.

"They—they are hideous," Hornetta blurted out. "Monsters. Spawn of a terrible civilization. They aim to take over the world."

"Why did you carve that symbol?" pressed Doc.

Hornetta seemed on the verge of divulging a modicum of truth, but abruptly she shook her head and snapped her eyes shut.

"Stop trying to hypnotize me!" she spat.

Doc released her abruptly, his features dark with suppressed emotion.

Monk Mayfair interjected, "Do we have any truth serum on board?"

Doc Savage told Monk, "Go look."

The apish chemist went below, rummaged around for a time, and came back holding a hypodermic needle that had been fully charged with a rather murky-looking chemical.

Monk asked seriously, "Should I just jab her with this?"

Doc Savage nodded. "I will hold her for you."

Hornetta Hale began flailing frantically, attempting to wrest out of the bronze man's metallic fingers, but it was no good. The grip was unbreakable.

Monk ambled over, and seized Hornetta's right arm at the elbow. Her arms were bare, so there was no necessity of lifting sleeves.

"No! Stop! Wait!" Hornetta snapped. "I'll talk. Just put that needle away."

In the act of introducing the truth serum, Monk looked to Doc.

Doc Savage told Hornetta, "Last chance, young lady!"

"That symbol I carved. You recognized it? You know what it means?"

Doc Savage nodded. "It is the political sign emblazoned on the flag of one of the warring European nations."

"It's more than that," Hornetta returned. "That mark is as old as civilization. I found it on Hopi pottery and Navajo blankets. In temples on the Indian subcontinent, and elsewhere."

Doc Savage nodded. "It is an ancient symbol, having many meanings. The significance of the symbol varies from nation to nation, depending upon the era."

Now that things were taking a conversational turn, Hornetta began subsiding.

"There is an island in the Caribbean, and on that island is an ancient ruin," she informed them. "That mark can be found on that island."

"What is the significance of this island?" asked Doc.

"It is the isle where the Men Under the Sea dwell," replied

Hornetta matter-of-factly.

Ham Brooks was listening very closely, and said, "This is not the first wild tale she has attempted to tell us." Suspicion threaded his well-bred tones.

"This time I'm leveling with you," insisted Hornetta. "Find that island, and you'll find your cousin. That's my guess. If the mermen took her, that's where they would hold her."

DOC SAVAGE searched Hornetta Hale's fiery face, as if searching for signs of truthfulness. He did not speak, but the bronze man would have been the first to admit—assuming he was willing to be so uncharacteristically forthcoming—that he was an utter failure at reading the female face.

"Can you lead us to this island?" he asked finally.

"Turn me loose, and I will. It's a promise."

Ham Brooks objected vociferously. "Doc! You can't possibly trust this woman after all she has said and done!"

Monk Mayfair added, "She's poison. She's shown that a bunch of times. Don't listen to her. She'll just fly away on us."

Although normally impassive of countenance, Doc Savage's expression twisted slightly at the corners of his mouth and around the eyes. His normal emotional reserve was cracking. He was genuinely torn.

At last he said, "Time is of the essence."

"No fooling," murmured Hornetta. "Do you let me go, or do you jab me with that thing, and lose some of the who-knows-how-many-hours of search time?"

With evident reluctance, Doc Savage released Hornetta Hale and said, "Take us to the island of the Men Under the Sea."

Monk and Ham began objecting in raw voices, talking over one another to such a vociferous degree that their precise words blended and mixed in a verbal confusion.

It was Long Tom Roberts who became the voice of reason.

"Doc's right," he said. "If we're ever to find Pat, it's now or maybe never. And that never probably means forever."

That silenced everyone. Hornetta Hale backed away from them all, turned to the rail, and made a great splashing dive into the Caribbean Sea.

She wasted no time in backstroking to her waiting plane. Climbing aboard, the prickly blonde started up her overpowered engine, and was soon running the plane into the soft Caribbean headwind.

Doc Savage lunged for the controls, began jazzing the big Diesel engines.

As they watched, Hornetta's yellow-and-black ship with its Wasp radial engine went banging along the water's surface. It jumped into the air, started spiraling upward, evidently to give them time to orient the *Stormalong* in the proper direction.

Hornetta flew south, staying low, only one thousand feet high. Doc Savage sent the *Stormalong* surging after her.

Long Tom muttered, "We're taking a long chance, but it's the only chance that makes sense."

"I still don't trust that glory hound," Monk growled.

"My sentiments exactly," added Ham Brooks.

It was rare that the two friendly foes ever agreed upon anything, even rarer where they did not fall over themselves putting halos on himself and adorning his romantic rival with horns and a spiked tail in an effort to impress a beautiful woman.

That Hornetta Hale was a delectable morsel no red-blooded man could deny. But her fierce personality, her stubborn contrariness, and other quirks of her free-spiritedness, had cooled any fires of desire Monk and Ham might otherwise be harboring.

"Count me in as part of your chorus," Long Tom echoed. He snapped his fingers suddenly. "Say, didn't that dame say she was out of gas?"

Doc Savage pointed out. "Hornetta said no such thing. However, she put on such an acrobatic aerial act as to lead us to that conclusion."

Long Tom said philosophically, "So much for that."

Monk turned to the puny electrical wizard and demanded, "What was all that tall talk about whippin' Hornetta the next time you saw her? You didn't lay a dang glove on her."

"Aw, you're just sore because you lost another fool bet with Ham."

Ham frowned darkly. "Without doubt," he fumed, "Hornetta Hale is the most infuriating female I have ever encountered in my life."

"The word infuriating," barked Long Tom, "is too good for that wily wasp."

Doc Savage drove the thundering cruiser southward, rarely taking his golden eyes off the little hornet-hued plane which now seemed to be the only hope of recovering Pat Savage from her strange and bizarre captors. Whoever or whatever they might be.

Chapter XXII

DOUBLE SNARE

FOR NEARLY TWO hours, they followed the yellow-jacket seaplane piloted by Hornetta Hale.

Hornetta maintained a reasonable airspeed, and flew low enough to be visible and within sight at all times.

This prompted Monk and Ham to reevaluate their opinions of the slippery amazon.

Ham offered cautiously, "Hornetta appears to be adhering to her part of the bargain."

Monk grunted, "Much as I hate to admit it, the shyster may be right. That screwy dame ain't tried to shake us yet. And she's had plenty of chances."

To which Long Tom contrarily suggested, "Unless that firecracker female is leading us into a trap."

Doc Savage contributed nothing to this discussion. He was becoming visibly tenser as each nautical mile reeled behind them.

It was a warmish afternoon, and this part of the Caribbean appeared to be both vast and deserted. They saw no passing ships, and of course no airplanes, these remote reaches not being on any airline route.

Ham Brooks, noticing Doc's concerned expression, put forth the question. "Hornetta is leading us somewhere. Do you think it is a trap?"

Doc Savage shook his head. "That is not my chief concern," he said.

"Then what is?" wondered the dapper attorney.

Before Doc could answer, a thin muttering carried over the waves toward their ears. At first, only Doc Savage appeared to notice it, because he waved a metallic hand for Ham to be quiet.

Ham looked up, empty hands clenching. His sword cane was stored away for comfort and safety.

Abruptly, Doc Savage killed the Diesel engines.

The speedy cruiser continued knifing forward, momentum carrying it along.

Quiet followed. Before long, the sighing of the Caribbean winds became mixed in with that sultry song, and resolved into a growing sputtering.

Flying low, Hornetta Hale's trim little amphibian plane bumbled into sight.

Monk exploded, "She's running out of fuel for sure!"

At the radio, Doc attempted to raise the *Hornet*. He found the correct wavelength swiftly enough.

Out of the speaker came Hornetta's succinct ripping complaint.

"I really ran out of gas this time."

"Attempt to land near our boat," Doc advised her.

No reply came. No doubt the acerbic aviatrix was too busy managing her stricken steed. The colorful craft began to wobble its wings, and lost additional altitude.

Banking, the *Hornet* swooped back around in their direction. They could see that its propeller blades were clearly defined, no longer spinning.

Hornetta glided along the surface of the Caribbean, smacking the ship down on its fat pontoons, executing a respectable but bumpy landing that made the yellow wings dance.

The ship soon wallowed, its wingtips rocking with the undulating waves.

Restarting the engines, Doc Savage sent the *Stormalong* in the crippled craft's direction.

By the time they reached the plane, Hornetta had clambered down onto one pontoon and jumped into the water.

She began swimming in their direction, obviously there being no other recourse left to her.

As she swam, Hornetta wore an expression of extreme agitation. She was not the most pleasant person they had encountered in their years of adventuring, and they were used to her rather unfeminine facial expressions. But now she looked truly upset.

Doc Savage throttled down the cruiser and veered in the trouble-prone blonde's direction in order to pick her up.

It was while the bronze man was executing this maneuver that a very strange thing happened.

Hornetta was swimming furiously, doing a dog-paddle, her blonde hair sometimes being the only thing visible between her flashing forearms.

Abruptly, she disappeared from sight.

Ham Brooks reached for a pair of field glasses. He clapped them to his eyes.

Something thin was cutting through the blue water like a blade. It resembled the fin of a shark, but sharks the world over are uniformly dull colors such a gray or brown.

This fin was a gangrenous reddish-green!

Then Hornetta's head resurfaced, but she was screaming. *"It's got me!"*

"Who?" howled Ham.

Doc Savage advanced the throttle to its maximum. The engines roared, throwing up a violent wake, sending the cruiser lunging in her direction.

"Monk!" Doc rapped out. "Take the controls."

The hairy chemist dived for the wheel, yelling, "What got her—a shark?"

Doc Savage did not reply. Kicking off his deck shoes, he flung to the rail. It was evident that the bronze man was going to jump into the water as soon as the cruiser reached the spot where Hornetta was flailing and thrashing in the waves

Before the prow knifed into position, Hornetta disappeared again. This time she did not resurface.

The liver-colored fin had also vanished beneath the sea.

MONK MAYFAIR killed the engines, gliding the last stretch of water to the spot where Hornetta had vanished, while Doc Savage pitched himself over the rail and knifed into the cool coral waters.

Immediately after, a startling apparition came up from below decks, throwing open the deck hatch. The figure made enough noise to be heard, so all heads turned at once.

Long Tom stood at the stern, so he was the first to yell out an identification.

"It's that Count!" he howled.

It was indeed. The immaculate figure of Count Rumpler—as he styled himself—now stepped up from below, as if he had just come topside after an afternoon nap.

He wore his usual elegant ensemble, and a neat Tyrolean hat was perched jauntily on his head. He also sported a fresh cane. This one was cut from wood so that a spiral groove ran down its length.

The Count pointed his knurled stick held in one gloved hand at Long Tom Roberts and did something which caused a spurt of pale vapor to strike the slender electrical expert in the face.

Taken by surprise, Long Tom took a step backward and then began laughing uproariously. Tears welled up from his eyes. Overcome by this fit of laughter, he pitched forward.

DOC SAVAGE had meanwhile gone under the waves in search of Hornetta Hale.

He saw nothing at first. No shark. No blood. No sign of the troublesome blonde.

Then, fifty yards off, something could be discerned to the south.

It was a great bluish shadow, as large as a small whale. The bronze man knew that blackfish—otherwise known as killer whales—could be found swimming in these waters. Blackfish were, quite naturally, ebony of hide with ivory markings.

This thing was an aquamarine hue—so closely blended with the coral color of the Caribbean Sea that its outlines were indistinct. It possessed a dorsal fin, not unlike that of a shark, but this fin was bluish-gray, not red.

What became of Hornetta Hale and the red-finned thing that had apparently snatched her was utterly baffling. But the blue creature gliding away was the only trail Doc Savage had, so he began swimming after it.

A strange thing happened as soon as the bronze giant arrowed toward its blur of a tail.

A jet of water, so powerful that it knocked Doc backward dozens of yards, struck him full in the chest with irresistible force, driving the air from his mighty lungs.

Air bubbles boiled from his mouth. A tightness clamped about his muscular chest.

Recovering his underwater orientation, Doc fixed his gaze on the uncanny thing.

It was even more indistinct now. Catching up to it would be impossible.

Reluctantly, Doc resurfaced for air.

The sounds of combat emanating from the becalmed *Stormalong* caused his metallic head to turn. Seeing the commotion on deck, the bronze man rushed toward the diving stage at the *Stormalong's* stern, and grasped it with both hands, preparatory to climbing aboard.

To his utter astonishment—for the bronze man had been entirely unaware of the situation on the *Stormalong*—the clever Count swung in his direction.

Doc Savage had the presence of mind to hold his breath, thus when the jet of gas came his way, he was initially unaffected.

Seeing this, the Count drew a lean-barreled foreign automatic from his coat and pointed it at Doc Savage's face.

The bronze man abruptly veered to the left, avoiding the spiteful snap of the weapon and its vicious bullet. His reflexes made his body a bronze blur. He vanished beneath the waves.

Meanwhile, Ham Brooks had not been idle. He swept up his sword cane, exposed the glittering blade, and came charging at the dashing gallant.

There followed a very strange duel as Ham's blade collided and clashed with the Count's sturdy cane barrel.

The Count was not a bad fencer. He might have won some awards in the past, but he distinctly belonged to the saber school of the art. He parried Ham's first lunge expertly, and performed a riposte that sent the dapper lawyer gingerly dancing back and henceforth exercising greater caution.

Blade and barrel banged and clashed, while Ham Brooks fought to press the advantage against the hacking attack.

The problem turned out to be that the blade was not as sturdy as the barrel. And each time Ham struck, he found its edge slithering against the barrel, becoming caught on one of its spiral grooves.

Redoubling his effort, Ham lunged and lunged again, features working.

But nothing the determined lawyer could do appeared to defeat the debonair Count's strong defense.

Stepping back a moment, Ham paused, seeking an opening.

It was at that point the resourceful Count pressed a stud on his cane and out from the far end jutted a tiny steel needle.

With a casual sweep of his hand, the Count brought the sharp tip slicing along the back of Ham's outstretched fist.

The swipe drew blood, and Ham let out a yelp of pain. In that startled moment a spurt of white gas took him full in the face.

The expression on Ham's face changed immediately from twisted anger to high hilarity. His laughter was on the high-pitched side, and rolled out in peals and peals and peals as if he were steadily losing his mind.

Then the dapper lawyer collapsed, joining Long Tom sleeping on the deck.

Monk now came on roaring, his upraised fist ready to pound his adversary to the deck floor.

Casually, the Count holstered his automatic, and this time brought forth a small glass jar filled with liquid from a pocket.

He drew back to throw it, and the jar smashed ahead of Monk's pounding feet. The contents immediately vaporized, producing a spreading white cloud. The Count backed down below deck, locking the hatch behind him.

Monk began laughing almost at once. It was a great bellowing laugh. It shook his barrel chest and made him convulse and double over as if he could not contain his belly-quivering mirth.

Doc Savage got back aboard, reached into a pocket, and extracted a portable gas mask, which he drew over his head. It was another one of his pliable transparent cellophane hoods which sealed about his neck with an elastic.

Thus it was that when the vapor filled the cockpit of the cruiser, he was entirely unaffected.

Lunging for the hatch, the bronze man tried it, discovered that it was locked. He began using his bronze fists on the wood.

Metallic knuckles reduced the hatch to a broken shambles. Doc plunged downward.

Below deck, he was not greatly surprised to see the hatch of the diving well flung open.

Around the device, seawater stood about in fresh puddles. There was no question that the Count had entered the *Stormalong* by this means.

What appeared to be utterly baffling was how the debonair antagonist had done so and how he had managed to show up on deck, as dry and immaculate as if he had strolled off a seaside dock.

Doc Savage bent to one knee at the well, and peered downward.

There was little enough light, owing to the well's high sides, so it might be excusable that Doc did not notice until it was too late the needle-tipped cane jutting up and swiping at his eyes, a strike which ruptured his cellophane protective mask.

The jet of vapor that followed quickly insinuated itself into the pliable shield, and reached the bronze man's nose and mouth.

Caught off guard, Doc quickly suppressed his breath. He could hold it for a very long time.

But apparently sufficient quantity of the vapor crept into his nostrils so that, despite his iron will and absolute determination not to inhale, the bronze giant's mouth fell open and he began laughing in a strange and uncontrolled manner....

It was a distinctly hideous sound.

Chapter XXIII

HADES CAY

MONK MAYFAIR SNAPPED awake with a start. The simian chemist had been dozing, making the most amazing sounds as he snored. It was as if a flock of geese had formed an orchestra.

Now those sounds turned into a snuffle, followed by a succession of snorts, as Monk became aware of a scratchy sensation in his mouth and nose.

He sat up, and peered about. His tiny eyes narrowed suspiciously.

"Where the heck am I?" he muttered to himself.

Sitting up, the hairy chemist saw that he lay in darkness. He looked to the left.

There Ham Brooks lay sprawled, apparently slumbering. For the sound of his regular breathing was audible.

Over to the right, Long Tom Roberts was likewise asleep.

Since the undersized electrical expert was closest to hand, Monk reached out with one of his overlong arms and gave him a hearty tap.

Long Tom was no heavy sleeper. The slap jarred him awake, and he jumped to his feet, wielding the first thing he could get his hands on, which proved to be a thorny stick of some sort.

Long Tom almost brained Monk Mayfair before the hairy chemist sprang to his own feet, waving his arms, saying, "Whoa! It's me—Monk."

It was dark, and there was a moon. The moonlight probably

saved Monk Mayfair from one of the most serious beatings of his entire life. For Long Tom Roberts, while he could be classified as a bantamweight, was known to take on four or five grown men at a time and beat them within an inch of their lives. He had quite the temper.

"Where are we?" Long Tom demanded when he got control of himself.

"Beats me," admitted Monk.

Long Tom noticed that his nose and throat felt scratchy. He gave the air an experimental sniff.

"Smells like we landed in Hades," Long Tom ventured uneasily.

Monk said, "I smell fire all right, but not the brimstone part."

They searched their clothing and discovered they had no weapons. Long Tom produced one of the tiny flashlights that Doc Savage and his men always carried. These were operated by a spring-generator that required only a brisk winding to produce strong illumination.

After digging it out of his sock, where it had been secreted, Long Tom speared illumination all about.

At first, it looked as if they had landed in some kind of charcoal pit. The ground was charred and blackened by fire. The fire was recent, for the stink of burning wood hung heavily in the warm night air.

Investigating, Long Tom discovered what he initially mistook for a great horny tentacle, that ran for some length around and along the ground. It, too, was black and charred. Casting about, he discerned more of them, traveling in all directions. It was as if great beanstalks had caught fire and fallen in tentacular profusion. The sprawling protrusions had an otherworldly look to them.

Monk walked up to the ugly thing, and rubbed it with his hairy paws.

Burnt charcoal resulted, smearing the palms of his hands. Monk sniffed them.

"Smells like creosote, or something like that," Monk said.

They woke up Ham Brooks, who started awake with wide eyes, the expression on his handsome face suggesting he had been having nightmares.

Looking about, the dapper lawyer saw and smelled that they were no longer aboard the *Stormalong*.

"Where are we?" he began thickly.

"Your guess is as good as ours," Long Tom informed him.

Ham got up, found no trace of his sword cane or any weapon on his person and began flapping his hands, which he did whenever agitated or feeling helpless. The lack of a sword cane always made Ham feel helpless. The others suspected that he slept with the thing under his pillow.

They began exploring, guided only by the penetrating ray of Long Tom's flashlight. He had to stop and wind it periodically, but unlike a battery-powered torch, the device would never fail to produce illumination.

As they walked along, they began coughing and hacking, the result of continuing to inhale the low-lying haze that had been produced by what had apparently been a very recent fire.

"What the heck happened here?" Monk wanted to know.

Long Tom said, "I think I see water ahead."

They followed him, craning their heads this way and that, unsure what to expect.

Every man remembered the seemingly miraculous appearance of the Count who had sauntered up from the hold of the *Stormalong*, as dry as a flag, and overcame them all with his trick cane.

Now they were here—wherever "here" was. They had no idea. Nor did they know how many hours had passed since they had fallen into laughing fits, followed by a black unconsciousness.

At last they came to shore, and their feet crunched on the immaculately white sand that suggested crushed sea shells.

They followed the pearly beach for a bit, and soon the moonlight showed them the *Stormalong*, which was lying at anchor, as calm as can be.

"Our cruiser!" Ham bleated. "What the devil is it doing here?"

Long Tom said sourly, "The better question is—what are *we* doing here?"

Since no one had an answer for that, they decided to investigate the cruiser.

They had to roll up their pants legs and wade out to the vessel. The water was very cold, but tolerable.

MONK arrived first, and boarded by the simple expedient of climbing the anchor chain. He reached the foredeck in jig time, clambering into the bridge.

Long Tom followed, and Ham came last, apparently reluctant to commit himself to the indignity of climbing the cumbersome links. He worked around and used the pilot's ladder.

Once on deck, they initiated a thorough search.

The boat appeared for the most part to be intact, but Long Tom started swearing when he discovered that the radio tubes had been smashed.

Many things were missing—weapons and other equipment that would prove useful. Miraculously—at least according to Ham's lights—he discovered his sword cane. It was lying in two sections, blade and barrel.

Picking them up, the dapper lawyer made the stick whole. His handsome features grew very pleased.

Monk commented, "A lot of good that done you against that Count's trick walkin' stick."

"I will know what to do next time," Ham said stiffly.

Going below, they discovered Doc Savage, lying on the floor near the diving well. The bronze giant appeared to be asleep.

Monk attempted to rouse him, but Doc slumbered on.

He placed one hand over the bronze man's chest, and felt a very strong, steady heartbeat. He appeared very relieved.

Monk offered, "Doc musta gotten a bigger dose than the rest of us. Normally, he's the first one to come out of anything."

The hairy chemist fidgeted uneasily, and looked around some more.

Detecting scratching sounds from the lazaret door, the simian chemist threw it open. Out popped Habeas Corpus, the pig. The homely shoat had taken to sleeping in the space, and no doubt had passed the last few hours therein.

"Hog," said Monk proudly, "leave it to you to stay out of trouble!"

The pig jumped into Monk's waiting arms and cast a beady glare in Ham's direction. This made Monk suddenly suspicious.

"Shyster, did you lock him in there?" he demanded of Ham.

"Nonsense," denied the elegant attorney. "That misbegotten insect is smart enough to hide from trouble on his own account."

This unexpected compliment made Monk's tiny eyes narrow and his suspicions grow.

"It appears as if the vessel has been stripped of anything in the nature of weapons," Ham observed, veering away from the subject of Habeas.

"Yeah," allowed Monk. "But how did it get here? How did *we* get here?"

Again, there were no answers.

Monk sat down and waited for Doc Savage to come back to life. Ham and Long Tom went topside to continue their investigation.

After a while, they discovered the Diesel fuel tanks had been drained.

"Bone dry," reported Long Tom in a dispirited voice.

"That means we're stranded," said Ham grimly.

"Marooned is the technical term," Long Tom corrected sourly.

Ham stood watch while Long Tom went back below and waited for Doc Savage to return to consciousness.

Impatiently, Long Tom asked Monk, "Isn't there some

stimulant you can give him?"

Monk shook his bullet head. "No. We ain't got any idea what Doc was dosed with. No tellin' what reaction he might have if we try. Better to let him wake up on his own account."

ANOTHER hour passed before the bronze man showed signs of activity. He began to stir. His eyes snapped open, came into clear focus.

Without a word, Doc stood up, looked around, but said nothing. Not even his customary trilling issued forth.

"We're stuck on some Hellforsaken island somewhere," Monk informed him.

Doc Savage seemed not to hear. Despite the clearness of his eyes, he seemed a little out of sorts, as if still half-asleep.

"You O.K.?" Long Tom asked him.

Finally, Doc Savage spoke.

"Precautions are not always sufficient," he said simply. There was a trace of disappointment in his metallic tones.

Monk said, "It got us all. The heck of it is, we don't know how we landed here, how our boat got here, but they took away anything we could fight with, and drained the fuel tanks to boot."

Doc Savage seemed to want to unburden himself of something. The bronze man addressed no one in particular. He simply began speaking.

"I took the precaution of swallowing an oxygen tablet before donning my gas mask. I assumed that would protect me from the laughing vapor, in the event the mask was breached, or the period of exposure went on too long. I was in error."

"What happened?" Monk asked him.

"I followed the Count down below, but apparently he escaped through the diving well. When I looked down, his sword stick licked up and ripped my mask. Then came the jet of vapor which produces uncontrollable laughing, followed by unconsciousness."

"Yeah?"

"The oxygen tablet allowed me to continue breathing without having to respire normally."

Monk grinned. "Yeah, they are handy little gadgets at that."

"Unfortunately," added Doc Savage, "they are only good for twenty to thirty minutes. I feigned unconsciousness, awaiting another move by our enemies."

Long Tom looked interested. "What happened?"

"As I lay there, playing possum," reported Doc, "the sounds of strange flopping feet on deck came. I could hear things moving about. But I saw nothing, of course."

Doc seemed to be searching his memory.

"I waited for a chance to make a move. I feared doing so prematurely, lest any of you be harmed in your helpless condition."

"So what happened?" pressed Monk.

"Our adversaries are as clever and determined as before," Doc said with a trace of ill-concealed disgust. "While there was scurrying about above deck, someone tossed a jar of the vapor down the hatch, introducing a great quantity of the stuff below decks. I decided it was necessary to enter the water, but before I could do so, I was overcome by laughing. I had only pretended to laugh loudly the first time I was gassed, but the second time I was not in control of myself, so consciousness was lost, with the end result that I accomplished exactly nothing."

Monk clucked, "Well, you gave it the old college try."

Doc Savage seemed not mollified by the homely chemist's pronouncement. Moving suddenly, he went topside, and made a thorough investigation, verifying the fact that the tanks were empty and the vessel stranded. He looked about him in the night and saw the dark shape of a mangrove-covered island.

Doc took to the rail, went into the water, and waited until the others followed him, Monk carrying Habeas the pig above his blunt head triumphantly.

They reached the beach of pearly white sands without incident.

Doc Savage had borrowed Long Tom's generator flashlight and was using it to pick his way around the island.

Monk offered, "This hickey on the Caribbean looks like a stray patch of Hades."

Doc Savage said nothing, merely worked his way around, examining the burnt terrain, the great charred profusion that resembled horny, groping elephant trunks reaching everywhere.

Then the bonze man looked up and began studying the waning moon and stars.

After a while he ventured, "A day has passed. It seems that we are still in the Caribbean."

"What part, though?" wondered Long Tom. "That takes in a lot of territory."

Doc Savage did not answer directly. Rather, he said, "This island appears to have been fire-blackened and scorched by a recent lightning strike. The blaze has burned itself out, but the air remains heavy with the resulting smoke."

That explanation relieved their minds no end, since their initial impression suggested that they had been deposited into some kind of Purgatory.

They were on the flat side of the island, which sloped upward to a kind of broad hump covered in unchecked green growth. Doc Savage ignored the rise, and simply walked around the beach, which soon became obstructed by tangles of thorny brush, some scattered cactus, and woody mangrove roots. One end of the isle was choked with red mangrove swamp, whose tough, twisting roots dipped into water's edge as if attempting to escape the awful place by walking into the sea.

There was absolutely no life. No birds. No insects. No tropical lizards of any kind.

It was a little uncanny.

Reversing course, the bronze man followed the beach around in the other direction, only to discover another tangle of mangroves.

There was no point in attempting to negotiate the tough root system, so Doc began mounting the high summit of the island.

Glancing about, Ham Brooks ventured, "There doesn't seem to be any kind of lagoon here."

"Why does that matter?" asked Long Tom peevishly.

"With all the talk of lagoons," Ham explained, "this might be the place to find one. But there's nothing of the sort along the shore."

Doc Savage led them up the rise, which was thick with grass, and when he got to the top, his eerie trilling began to filter through the night air. It wafted briefly, trailed off in an intrigued, curious sound.

When the others joined Doc, they discovered the reason for this expression of surprise.

What they took to be a hill was in fact a great hollow crater, at the bottom of which lay a pool of placid water, dark and unmoving in the moonlight.

"Blue hole," said Doc Savage.

"What?" asked Ham.

"A natural formation in this part of the world, as well as in others," Doc Savage explained. "We are looking at a body of water which no doubt leads to one or more underwater caves. Sometimes there are networks of tunnels feeding seawater into these so-called blue holes."

Monk peered downward and remarked, "Looks greenish to me."

Indeed, as they watched, luminous patches of faint green showed here and there, deep in the depths of the dark pool, as if creatures were stirring the waters.

"Sea fire," ventured Ham. And to prove his point, the dapper lawyer kicked a loose stone over the edge.

Where the stone made a splash, a zone of disturbed water sprang into vivid luminescence, which turned a spectral green before dying into darkness again. It appeared almost alive, which in a way, it was.

Doc nodded. "The pool is undoubtedly brimming with minute marine organisms which, when agitated, produce temporary phosphorescence. They are already subsiding."

Doc began to walk along the lip of the depression, and his flashlight showed that the soil was black and rocky, some of it very shiny ebony glass.

Monk reached down, then picked up a chunk of this. He looked at it closely.

"Obsidian! This isn't any valley. This is the cone of an extinct volcano!"

Long Tom excavated some growth with the toe of one shoe, revealing igneous rock.

They looked at the formation with new eyes. Apparently, a volcano had existed on this spot, but had gone extinct possibly thousands of years ago. It had filled with rainwater, if not seawater, which infiltrated through lava tunnels.

Doc Savage said, "The Lesser Antilles is predominately comprised of volcanic isles such as this. That could place us in the West Indies, in the westernmost portion of the Caribbean Sea."

Doc shone the intense pencil beam of his flashlight down into the water. He did this for quite some time.

"What are you looking for?" wondered Ham Brooks.

Doc Savage did not reply. It was characteristic of Doc not to respond when he preferred to keep information to himself.

He said only, "This blue hole bears investigating."

ABRUPTLY, the bronze giant retreated down to the shore, and made his way back to the anchored cruiser.

Rummaging through broken equipment cases, he unearthed a diving helmet that was remarkable in the extreme.

It was no clumsy affair of stainless steel and glass ports. Instead, it resembled one of those tall crystal glass covers that are placed over old-fashioned desktop clocks to protect the intricate gearworks from dust and dirt. Except for a shoulder plate of formed aluminum, as well as leather straps to go under the armpits to secure the thing, the diving helmet was entirely transparent. It was not glass, but of a clear composition stronger than steel produced in Doc's fabulous laboratory at the North Pole.

From a drawer he took a handful of white pills that resembled ordinary aspirin. These, however, were more of the oxygen tablets Doc had devised many years ago.

Cradling the helmet under one arm, Doc returned to the water and waded back onshore.

He joined his men and they took up a position under a palm tree that was black with soot but otherwise unscorched.

"What I have in mind is best accomplished after sunrise."

"So we wait?" questioned Long Tom.

Doc nodded.

Ham had a sudden thought. "It has just dawned on me that the Count and these web-footed creatures must be in league with one another."

"They are," said Doc. "Furthermore, I recognized the Count. His name is not Rumpler. Rather, he is Count Runo von Elmz, a Prussian aristocrat of some renown. I have never met him, but in pictures I have studied, he was always bearded. With his face shorn, it took a second encounter until I was able to place his identity."

"Spy?" asked Ham.

"Without question," said Doc.

Long Tom grumbled, "None of this adds up to much."

Monk looked about him, and then up into the crown of the palm tree which was rustling in the soft breeze. He muttered, "I wonder if there's anything to eat around here?"

Ham sniffed, "You *would* think of your stomach at a time like this!"

Monk snapped back, "If we're stuck here any length of time, we're all going to be dreamin' of grub."

That sobering thought made Ham grow silent.

Long Tom looked out across the water at their anchored cruiser and rubbed his jaw in perplexity.

"I still can't figure how we got here, boat and all. We didn't pilot it in our sleep, that's for sure."

No one seized the conversational hook dangling in the darkness until Monk Mayfair suddenly asked, "What do you suppose happened to that waspy Hornetta Hale?"

"Shark most likely got her," Long Tom said without sympathy.

The thought of the feisty blonde having been devoured by a shark did not bring any cheer to their collective mood. Doc's men again lapsed into silence.

While they waited for the sun to rise, Monk Mayfair grew restless and stood up.

"I need to stretch my legs," he remarked to no one in particular.

Doc Savage cautioned, "Do not go very far. Stay in sight."

Monk shrugged resignedly and said, "This whole dang island ain't much more than a half mile in any direction."

The gorilla-like chemist ambled off.

Hardly five minutes passed before Monk came charging back, waving his long, furry arms and saying, *"Ye-e-ow!"*

Doc rushed up to meet him, demanded, "What is it?"

Monk did not immediately reply. He was too agitated. He made noises that the bronze man recognized as inarticulate panic.

When the hairy chemist got himself under control, he asked Doc Savage a simple question.

"Are you sure this place was scorched by lightning?"

"Absolutely. Why do you ask?"

"Because I just saw the Devil."

"The Devil?" Doc Savage prompted.

A weird horror was in the homely chemist's tiny eyes. His

hairy forearms actually trembled.

"This devil didn't look like the Devil you see in picture books. He was worse."

"Describe this devil," Doc Savage instructed.

Monk made wild gestures of description. "He stood nearly eight feet tall. Had a row of horns all around the top of his head, not just two in the front like you would expect a decent devil to have."

"Jove!" Ham breathed. "Monk has lost his mind."

Doc Savage gestured for silence. "Continue, Monk," he invited.

"Like I said, eight feet tall and he was green as a grasshopper, not red. I think he had a tail, but he was starin' directly at me, so I didn't see that part for sure. Yellow eyes. They were not a good yellow. A witch's black cat might own such eyes."

"Did he have a pitchfork?" demanded Long Tom, apparently in all seriousness.

Monk had to think about that. "No, it was more like a trident. Like King Neptune would carry."

Ham Brooks, ever eager to pick apart a story, said, "You are describing an underwater Satan."

Monk had to think about that for a moment. He admitted, "I am at that, aren't I?"

Doc Savage said, "Take us to this devil."

Monk Mayfair hesitated. His hairy arms still trembled. "I don't think I ought to," he said vaguely.

Doc Savage gave Monk a strong shove, by way of propelling him on his way.

Reluctantly, Monk got going, and they followed him.

When they got to the palm tree where Monk had encountered the green devil, there was no sign of any such creature.

Doc Savage speared his flash beam about, looking for signs of tracks. He discovered none. But in moving around some more, he found something that brought Ham to a dead halt.

"Look," he said to the others.

The bright ray disclosed a sandy area where the ground went down to the beach. There were messy-looking tracks that were certainly not human feet or cloven hooves. They were wet.

Ham remarked, "Looks like geese have been walking around here."

"Mighty big geese," muttered Monk.

Doc Savage said, "These tracks bring to mind the ones we discovered in our hold after Pat vanished."

"They do, at that," said Long Tom. Turning to Monk, he asked, "Did the thing you saw remind you of that merman we saw?"

Monk shook his head in a violent negative. "No, not unless it was the king of them."

Doc Savage poked around, looking for more tracks or signs of anything stalking about. He found nothing. Returning to the grotesque webbed footprints, he seemed to be committing their weird watery contours to memory.

Ham Brooks was down on one knee, examining a splayed print and said to no one, "These were not made by diving fins. But I cannot tell if these tracks are coming out of the water, or going back into it."

Monk grunted, "My vote is for goin' back into it. I never want to see that emerald Satan again. It was taller than Doc."

Ham Brooks pressed him. "The creature you saw, did it have skin, or scales?"

"What's the difference?" snapped Monk. "It was awful-looking."

"The difference," Ham returned, "is that scales would make it a relative of the merman."

"Nothing like that hob-seagoblin should have any relatives," Monk said with a trace of trembling fear in his voice.

Long Tom turned to Doc Savage and asked in an undertone, "What do you make of Monk's story? He's always been on the superstitious side. Think he's embellishing what he saw?"

"It is difficult to say for certain," Doc Savage admitted. "But Monk is convinced that he encountered such a monster."

They went back to the doubtful shelter of the palm tree and returned to awaiting the dawn.

It was a difficult wait, for the haze of smoke rasped at their throats and made them scratchy. Their nostrils felt as if they were clogged with sand. From time to time, the air seemed to carry unusual odors reminiscent of sulfur, or brimstone. Given their Hellish surroundings, it was not a cheering thing to breathe into the lungs.

Long Tom happened to be looking toward the surf when he thought he saw something moving in the water. It was still dark, so he could not be certain. Moonglade on the waves, stared at long enough, can produce confusing optical effects.

The puny electrical expert stared carefully at the spot that seem to be disturbed.

There was phosphorescence in the water, and it produced a weird greenish effect as if underwater fireflies were dancing in the shallows.

Long Tom nudged Ham Brooks. In a low voice, he whispered, "Look out where I'm pointing. What do you see?"

Ham peered through the darkness, hissed, "I see something moving, but I'm not sure what it is."

"Looks like a mermaid to me," Long Tom breathed.

Doc Savage caught this exchange, and turned his attention in the direction of Long Tom's pointing finger.

"Something out there all right," he said. Then the bronze giant was up on his feet, and moving toward the water.

The others were not far behind him.

Running alongside, Long Tom made a strangled sound and blurted, "Is that real?"

Ham cried out, "I can't see it clearly! What is it?"

Long Tom's voice lifted wildly. "Don't laugh at me, but it

looks like a mermaid. An honest-to-goodness mermaid. She's wearing seashells and her hair is as green as kelp."

Ham squinted hard, murmured, "I can barely make anything out, except some *thing* is floating in the water!"

"Are you sure it's a mermaid?" Monk demanded.

Long Tom barked back, "I'm not sure of anything! But unless I'm dreaming—*the mermaid looks just like Hornetta Hale!*"

Chapter XXIV

CONFOUNDMENT

DOC SAVAGE REACHED the surf ahead of the others, and plunged in.

He waded out, legs churning, until the water was deep enough to swim in, and then he threw himself upon the dark rollers charged with wavering sea fire.

It was clear to the others that the bronze man had spotted something in the water as well. For he arrowed out into the deep, then disappeared beneath the waves for a time.

There followed a splashing and thrashing and crashing of violently disturbed water. Doc Savage surfaced, clutching something that squealed and flailed and fought him madly.

Monk and the others charged out to give assistance to the bronze man.

But when they reached him, the battle was already over.

Doc Savage was treading water, and the thing that he had captured was floating placidly beside him, its distressed squealing having subsided.

Even in the moonlight, it was difficult to discern clearly. It was almost as long as an average man, but beyond that all resemblances to anything human ceased.

Monk Mayfair, swimming with the brine up to his barrel chest, stopped propelling himself forward and suddenly began to jerk backwards, momentarily taken aback by the ugly creature floating there.

It was long and fat and grayish-brown, with a blunt snout,

all of it covered with thick, leathery skin like a walrus. But it was no walrus. For one thing, there were no tusks.

"What the heck is that thing?" the hairy chemist sputtered.

"Manatee," Doc Savage said calmly.

Long Tom pushed his way forward, and glared at the beast.

"That," he insisted, "was *not* what I saw. It was a mermaid. It looked like Hornetta Hale. And that's final."

Doc Savage said simply, "Manatees, or sea cows as they are also known, are sometimes mistaken for mermaids by superstitious sailors."

"I am not superstitious," blazed Long Tom. "Keep looking! That mermaid is around here somewhere."

Doc Savage shook his head. "There is no mermaid. There is only this solitary manatee."

As they trod water, the manatee got its strength back and began paddling away. It was very placid-looking animal, and now that they could see it more clearly, its resemblance to a human being was at best general.

Doc Savage struck out for shore. The others followed.

Long Tom was not finished defending himself. "She had green hair, like seaweed. She wore seashells to protect her modesty. And her face was just like Hornetta Hale's thin-nosed puss."

"Did she have scales or skin?" asked Ham sharply.

"What difference does it make?" returned Long Tom hotly. "I saw what I saw."

"You saw a manatee," corrected Doc Savage without a trace of reproval. "At a distance, and under present conditions, it was an understandable mistake to make."

"Either that," inserted Ham, "or you dozed off and had a nightmare."

"If that was a nightmare," defended Long Tom, "it was very vivid."

"My devil was pretty vivid, too," added Monk Mayfair sheepishly. "Maybe Long Tom saw what he saw."

They all turned to look at the simian chemist. Monk Mayfair was among the bravest men they had ever known, but his encounter with the Satanic version of Father Neptune had reduced him to a quivering wreck.

"I think you were both imagining things," Ham insisted.

An argument broke out between the three of them as they beached themselves and started wringing seawater out of their clothes.

Doc Savage left them for a time, and resumed his reconnoiter of the island. The first peep of dawn light was breaking across the water and now that he could see more clearly, the bronze giant wanted to investigate the terrain more closely.

Doc first looked over the spidery sprawl of horny fire-blackened tentacles.

Along their charcoal surfaces were sharp protrusions, rather resembling the tough surface of a pineapple, but of immense size. The light was bright enough to show details clearly, The extensions—for that is what they were—lead back to a central stalk, also barbed and blackened.

Long Tom had drifted up by this time, drawn by the spectacular sight.

"Looks like a petrified giant tarantula, or something worse," he hazarded.

Doc Savage shook his head. "The ground-traveling roots of a species of Philodendron bush, which had been blasted and burned by lightning strikes. You can plainly see the charred leaves lying about, after having been burnt off."

The puny electrical expert looked down. The ground was covered in great leaves resembling blackened elephant ears, he now realized.

"That's a relief," he exclaimed. "Monk thinks we landed on an outer isle of Hades."

"This species is native to the Lesser Antilles," Doc pointed out. "This erases all doubt as to our approximate location."

"I'll go tell the others," offered Long Tom. "It will take a load off their minds."

As Long Tom turned back, Doc Savage pressed on with his tour of the queer cay.

He was soon lost from view.

MONK AND HAM'S argument had pretty much ended when Doc Savage's trilling suddenly sounded, carrying to their ears through the tropical night. At first, the others thought it was the song of a tropical bird, but after a few bars, they knew differently. The eerie sound drew them inland.

They found Doc Savage among the mangroves where the going was difficult, to say the least about it.

The bronze man had used his hands with their remarkable tendon strength to excavate something that was overgrown.

It was a stone temple, very ancient. Constructed along the lines they all recognized, but were also very unusual. Great basalt blocks comprised the structure, over which something like stucco had been applied. The stucco surface had largely fallen away over time, exposing the foundational blocks.

This temple had been all but reclaimed by the growth of many generations, if not centuries. Sinuous creepers had entwined it in a verdant web. In the back, a runt palm was growing out of the riven rock at a drunken angle. The thing was an utter ruin.

Monk offered, "Must be the ruin that doggone she-hornet told us about."

"You should talk—about pests, that is," jibed Ham.

Long Tom remarked, "Looks kind of Egyptian."

Monk contradicted him, saying, "Reminds me of the temples down in the Valley of the Vanished, where the Mayans who supply us with our gold dwell." *

---

* *Early in Doc Savage's career, the bronze man came into contact with a fabulous civilization hidden deep in the mountain fastness of the nation of Hidalgo. There, he encountered remnants of the ancient Mayan people, still living as they did thousands of years ago, en-*

To which Ham Brooks inserted, "The architecture is a peculiar blend of both."

But that was not what drew their attention as Doc Savage worked.

For over the entrance were cut a series of symbols—four of them in a row. They were the same symbols that Hornetta Hale had carved into a royal palm trunk back on the sandy island on which she had been marooned.

Ham Brooks said darkly, "I don't like the looks of that mark."

"You mean that *swastika*," corrected Long Tom.

"Whatever it is," Ham sniffed, "I don't like it."

Doc Savage reminded them, "This symbol may not be what it appears to modern eyes. Remember that it was carved long ago."

"What would it mean in this part of the world?" wondered Ham.

Doc Savage was thoughtful. "In the far east, the swastika is considered to be an auspicious sign, rather like a good luck charm. South of here, the Cuna people of Panama and Columbia use it to represent the octopus deity whom they believe created the world."

"Did they build temples such as this one?" asked Ham.

"They did not," said the bronze man, returning to his investigation of the weird ruin.

Doc got to the point where he could access what appeared to be an entrance. He brought out his flashlight and directed the light around.

To his disappointment, the light disclosed only a choke of jungle growth and old vegetable debris. The interior of the temple was largely awash with water and mangrove roots. Small

tirely isolated from modern civilization. In gratitude for a past service rendered, and in honor of Doc's father, who had originally discovered this hermit enclave, the good Mayans agreed to give Doc Savage the benefit of their enormous reserves of gold. Periodically, burro trains of the precious metal are sent to the outer world, to be deposited in a bank account owned by Doc Savage. This seemingly endless supply of wealth is what funds Doc Savage's worldwide operations.

fish darted between the roots—gray angelfish and blue tangs predominantly.

The bronze man found a stick, and attempted to stir the tangle, with the only result being that it became clear to him that whatever lay within the temple, it would be impossible to get at it without the proper tools. Mangrove roots were tough stuff, and brute strength alone would not dislodge them.

THEY stood back, marveling at the ruin. It appeared to be ancient.

Ham Brooks asked, "What do you make of it, Doc?"

"You will remember several years ago when we discovered a vault at the bottom of the Atlantic, not far from Nassau in the Bahamas."

Ham nodded. "We always wondered if it wasn't some remnant of something akin to Atlantis, the continent reputed to have sunk beneath the waves centuries ago in a terrific cataclysm."*

Monk scratched his furry head and said, "It wasn't long after that that we discovered that dome under the water where people who descended from those original builders still lived."**

Long Tom asked Doc Savage, "Do you suppose that these mermen or whatever they are, are kin to that race of people?"

"It is too soon to tell," admitted Doc Savage. "But it is very worthwhile exploring."

Ham considered this and said, "It may well be that the Count and his men are on the trail of some treasure or scientific knowledge to be found in these ruins, or similar ruins nearby."

Long Tom added, "It would explain a lot, wouldn't it?"

"Yeah," Monk said slowly. "That big vault we discovered was filled with scientific knowledge that we weren't able to get out of there before the roof fell in."

"Those ruins are very far from here," reminded Doc.

But to every one of Doc's men, the pieces began to come

---

* Mystery Under the Sea.
** The Red Terrors.

together in a way that made a certain sense. Doc Savage's remarkable oxygen pills had been developed as a direct result of his discoveries in that underwater realm that had once stood on dry land and harbored a great scientifically advanced civilization in a long-ago era before recorded history.

Those thoughts in mind, they returned to the more habitable part of the island, which under the rising sun took on a very weird aspect. The tropical light, very gory, looked like it was setting the charcoal ground back alight.

The air seemed more breathable than before, which did not make it very palatable. It stank of smoke.

Doc Savage retrieved the transparent helmet and its harness, and began mounting the overgrown slope of the dormant volcanic cone. The others followed not far behind.

Reaching the summit, Doc swallowed three oxygen tablets, which he washed down with the milk of a coconut he had found.

The manner in which he cracked the coconut would have astonished a circus strong man. Doc merely balanced the coconut husk atop one metallic palm, and brought the edge of his other hand down sharply.

The coconut split with an audible *crack!* Swiftly, Doc took it up, and drank milky fluid from the breach.

That accomplished, the bronze man set the heavy helmet over his head, and connected the straps under each shoulder. This created a very tight seal. No air could get out, but inasmuch as his system was charged by the oxygen-generating chemical pills, he would not have to breathe for over an hour.

On one wrist he wore an ingenious leather strap on which were several instruments, including a dial watch, a compass and a depth gauge. These would come in handy if Doc discovered any underwater tunnels. All three instruments were painted with radium so they could be read under unfavorable conditions.

Doc removed his shoes, and placed his flashlight in one pocket. Without another word or gesture, he turned and prepared to plunge in.

Before he could do so, the bronze man was stopped by a remarkable sight.

There was a bubbling kind of disturbance in the water below. The surface had been very placid up to this point, but now it roiled.

Something bobbed up from below.

Doc pointed, but said nothing. No sound could escape his sealed helmet anyway.

Up from the deep came a green-haired head. They all saw it.

The owner of the head flung her hair back, snapping long green tresses that shook off seawater the way a dog sheds rain from its coat.

A face looked up. It was a face they all recognized.

Monk bellowed, *"Hornetta Hale!"*

"And pipe this!" exploded Long Tom. "She's got the mermaid hair I told you about!"

Chapter XXV

SNAGS

THERE WAS LITTLE question that it was Hornetta Hale emerging from the depths of the algae-green blue hole.

Neither was there any doubt that her hair was as green as seaweed, exactly as Long Tom had described hours before.

While Doc Savage and his men were taking in the strange sight, the strange vision began stroking toward the side of the extinct cone.

She reached what looked like a wall of cooled lava and remarkable scrambling up, but the same agility that had allowed her to climb coconut trees and survive on a remote tropic isle for several weeks failed her now.

Monk lowered a hairy arm to assist the green-haired girl up to the rocky rim of the cone. The blonde hesitated at first, seemed to shrink from the sight of the gorilla-like chemist, but finally accepted the offered paw.

Setting the thin-nosed woman on her feet, Monk demanded hoarsely, "Where did you come from?"

They all saw that she had two perfectly formed legs with matching feet, and not the long fishy tale of a mermaid. Nor did she wear sea shells.

Her hair, however, was an unearthly green.

Doc Savage removed his diving helmet and asked, "Explanations would be appreciated, Miss Hale."

The green-haired blonde looked as put out as a spinster in a rowdy saloon.

"Whatever you do," she said fiercely, "do not go down there."

"Why do you say that?" asked Doc.

"Because *they* are down there," she said thinly.

"Who are they?"

"Do I have to spell it out for you? The U-Men—devils who dwell under the sea."

Ham Brooks said curtly, "Stop giving us the runaround. What happened to your hair?"

The green-haired girl made a distasteful face. "Don't ask me to explain that now."

Doc Savage added, "We discovered the old ruin with the strange symbols carved into it."

Hornetta said, "That was only a clue as to the location of this place. Those ruins are just the tip of the most terrible iceberg you could ever imagine."

Her voice tone caused Doc to remark, "You have been issuing such dire warnings since we first encountered you. Is it not high time to reveal the facts behind your threats?"

"I… can't," she said with a struggle.

"Here we go again," said Long Tom sourly.

"Do you recall how you got here?" demanded Doc.

"Recall it? I'll probably never forget it! I was swimming for your boat when I could feel slimy hands grab my ankles and pull me down."

"I take it these were the so-called Men Under the Sea?" Ham prodded.

"In all their fishy glory," she shot back. "You have no idea what it's like to be manhandled by those…things."

"Where did they take you?" asked Doc. "And while you are answering, how did you get to this island?"

The former blonde spitfire sat down as if tired. "I don't even know where to begin."

Ham sniffed, "The runaround again."

She sighed very deeply and said, "I'm done."

Doc regarded her steadily. "Done?"

"As in beaten. Defeated. Shanghaied. And marooned. Once more."

"Say again?" asked Ham.

"This time I want to talk. I want to talk so badly my teeth hurt. But if I do, Honoria will suffer. Your cousin, too."

"Where is Pat?" Doc asked sharply.

"Alive. That is all I can say."

"Safe?" demanded Doc.

The girl shrugged sun-reddened shoulders. "Only as long as the Men Under the Sea keep her that way."

They seemed at an impasse. Then the trouble-prone girl looked up with imploring blue eyes. These were very different orbs from those which had previously shot sparks every time they lanced in their direction.

"I suppose you figured out a lot of this already?" she murmured.

Doc advised the woman, "It suggests all this fuss is over a great treasure, yet to be unearthed."

"You are not far from correct. About the treasure, I mean."

"It is a wonder that we were not murdered when we were helpless," Doc stated simply.

"You and me both, big boy."

"In New York, every effort was made to slay us," continued Doc. "But in this instance, we were transported to this island alive. It is very puzzling. Why were we spared?"

The green-haired girl began wringing out her seaweed-hued tresses. "I am sure that I do not know. I'm stuck in the same boat as you shipwrecked stiffs."

It was not a satisfactory response, and the expression on the bronze man's face mirrored that judgment.

Reaching down, Doc Savage lifted the woman to her feet. They were bare. Fresh cuts laced them, obviously from climbing the sharp obsidian walls.

Doc Savage scrutinized her formerly blonde hair, saw that

the green hue was running, turning her face and neck into a splotchy chlorophyll wash.

"Dye," he concluded.

"I trust so," quipped Hornetta. "I would hate to think I was stuck with green hair the rest of my days—however long or short that may be."

Doc demanded, "Who did that to you—and why?"

"What makes you think I didn't do it to myself?" she countered.

"We seem to be at an impasse," said Doc Savage.

"How so?" retorted the other.

"You cannot speak freely for fear of your sister's life. We are inhibited from taking overt action, lest we risk my cousin's safety."

The erstwhile adventuress said flatly, "That's about the size of it. And it's a pretty miserable package."

Everyone stood around in silence, lost in their individual thoughts.

DOC SAVAGE showed no further inclination to dive into the blue hole, which promised to contain many of the answers to the mysteries which had engulfed them so thoroughly.

After a bit, their captive wondered, "Anything to eat around here? I'm famished."

"Coconuts," advised Doc.

Hornetta sighed. "As long as it isn't conch. Take me to these monkey fruits."

They walked down the slope to where a few scattered coconut palms waved in the breeze. Morning was full on, and the air seemed fresher. Lingering smoke haze still nipped at their nostrils.

Picking her way along the charred and blackened ground, skirting the fire-ravaged Philodendron roots, she asked a natural question.

"Did your campfire get out of hand?"

Monk mumbled, "We woke up in this charcoal pit. Doc says lightning started a blaze."

"I don't know any different, so don't look at me," returned Hornetta.

When it came to gathering coconuts, all eyes turned to Monk Mayfair. He had the general physique for it. So the simian chemist began going up one coconut palm after another, uprooting the dark shells and dropping them to earth.

Doc repeated his amazing stunt of cracking them open with the sharp edge of his hands.

Hornetta's eyes went wide in spite of herself. "You must really be made out of metal," she said wonderingly. Her fire seemed to have gone out.

Firm-lipped, Doc offered her the dribbling coconut shell.

Hornetta drank it greedily, tossed the husk aside, and wiped her mouth clean.

"Got another?"

Doc Savage repeated the procedure. The woman drank her fill.

When she was done, she looked at them all with a mixture of concern and confusion.

"What do we do now?"

No one offered any idea. So Hornetta asked, "I don't suppose any of you have a deck of cards in your pockets? I'm a shark at poker."

Their stony expressions wiped the patently fake grin off her face.

"In that case, I'm going for a walk," she told them flatly.

If she expected anyone to stop her, Hornetta Hale was vastly disappointed. She walked down to the beach and pretended to be looking for seashells.

They were not plentiful, as she discovered during her perambulations. So when the green-haired girl exhausted all opportunities offered by the white pearly sand, she drifted inland.

Doc Savage directed, "Monk, keep an eye on her."

"Gotcha, Doc." Monk ambled off.

Before the hairy chemist could get more than a few yards, a strange sound rippled out in the morning air.

It was preceded by a clatter that made them think that Hornetta Hale had tripped over one of the charred pieces of wood that lay strewn about as if Hell itself had exploded. This was followed by the convincing thud of a body tumbling to earth.

Then came an uproarious peal of laughter. Very feminine laughter—even if it had a bit of a hard edge to it.

There was no doubt but who was emitting the maniacal mirth.

Doc Savage's voice crashed out, "Monk, do not approach her."

"You don't have to tell me twice!" the homely chemist returned. He came charging back, his healthy respect for the laughing phenomenon uppermost in his mind.

Doc Savage put on his transparent helmet, buckled it tight, and went in search of Hornetta Hale.

He found her sprawled atop a strange earth formation, entirely unconscious.

It appeared to be a shattered dome about the size of a human hand. Doc Savage recognized it as an old lava bubble. Hornetta had evidently struck it with her foot, shattering it.

Doc picked up the green-haired woman, and bore her back to the shore. There, he laid her carefully on the white sand.

The others drew near.

"What happened?" asked Ham Brooks.

"Miss Hale discovered one of the sources of the laughing fits," explained Doc.

They looked at him in perplexity.

Doc Savage elaborated, "There are pockets of volcanic gas

fumes trapped here and there in cavities in the caldera. Places where bubbling lava cooled long ago, forming thin domes that are easily broken. Some of those bubbles contain pockets of gas. Miss Hale evidently encountered one, and in breaking it, released a small quantity of the gas that causes uncontrolled laughing fits, followed by swift unconsciousness."

Long Tom murmured, rubbing his jaw, "So now we know where the Count found his concoctions."

"Yeah," added Monk. "I'll bet there's a lot of other valuable stuff to be found on this dang island."

Recognizing that the woman would be unconscious for some hours, Doc Savage said, "She cannot interfere with anything we do."

Ham asked, "What makes you think she would be of such a mind?"

"She believes she is protecting her sister with her silence."

"Is she?"

"That," said Doc Savage, his golden eyes flashing to the moonlit rim of the nearby volcanic cone, "remains to be discovered."

They all understood what the bronze man meant by that statement. He was going to dare the volcanic pool, regardless of the risk.

Chapter XXVI

GREEN HOLE

DOC SAVAGE DID not ordinarily deceive his men. Nor was it his nature not to reveal his plans when it was essential for them to know his intentions.

As the inflamed sun climbed higher into the sky, hurling a chaotic array of splendor over the heavens and across the sea, the bronze giant picked up his diving helmet and told them a half-truth.

"Guard the girl while I return to the cruiser to look into its seaworthiness."

Monk said, "Sure, Doc. How long do you think you're going to be?"

"Difficult to say," said Doc, tucking his helmet under his muscular arm. He cleared his throat rather noisily, doing so twice, as if in anticipation of going for a dive.

Monk and the others swapped strange looks, but said nothing.

Without any further comment, the bronze man went down to the water and waded out toward his waiting ship. He set the helmet on the stern landing stage, and clambered aboard.

Carrying the transparent thing into the cockpit, he seem to be looking around it for something in particular.

Apparently not finding what he searched for, the bronze man disappeared below.

He took the fantastic-looking helmet with him.

Anyone watching from the shore would assume that Doc Savage had become preoccupied with the condition of the *Stormalong.*

From time to time, Monk and the others glanced in the direction of the stationary vessel.

Ham remarked, "I wonder what Doc is doing down there?"

Monk shrugged, saying, "Beats me."

To which Long Tom added, "One thing's for sure, he's not taking a nap. We've all had so much sleep we won't need any shuteye for a week."

They spoke rather loudly, the way men do when they find themselves in uncomfortable circumstances and feel the strong need to keep up their courage.

Had Doc Savage's men possessed eyes with the penetrating properties of an X-ray machine, they would have been slack-jawed in amazement.

For the bronze man was no longer aboard the *Stormalong*. He had donned his transparent helmet and gone down the diving well.

With his lungs charged with chemical oxygen, Doc Savage swam slowly underwater, circumnavigating the weird volcanic cay. He kept himself close to the sandy ocean bottom, the weight of the helmet and its harness rig assisting him in that operation.

Swimming in toward shore, Doc investigated the mangrove tangle that dipped its weird woody roots into the water to feed off the ocean currents in the fashion of such swamps.

It took some time, but the bronze giant found a spot where reef coral formed a very large maw. This proved to be an underwater cave, apparently entirely natural. Long ago molten lava had streamed out into the sea and deposited itself on the ocean floor, forming a strange cooled surface. It was this solid magma which gave the bronze man his first clue.

Doc eeled into the tunnel, using his flashlight sparingly.

There were tropical fish darting around in the underwater passage, but not many of them. Their colors were a riot of neon.

Doc Savage swam with powerful strokes and, while the helmet was cumbersome, it had the advantage of not releasing air bubbles which might give away his approach, should he slip and exhale unnecessarily. It had been specially constructed for use with the chemical oxygen pills.

The tunnel did not run in a direct line, but twisted at one point, devolving into a fork in the passage. Doc kicked backward, arresting his progress, and showed every indication that he was uncertain which way to go.

The bronze man checked the illuminated dial of his wrist compass, and this helped his decision-making. Doc swam to the left.

From time to time, Doc grasped the sides of the tunnel, and pulled himself along on the theory that this produced less noise and turbulence than swimming and kicking with hands and feet. Sound carried far underwater, and the bronze giant was cognizant of the fact that he was swimming into the unknown.

This way, he approached the crater-bound body of the so-called blue hole, which was almost entirely landlocked, other than this reservoir tunnel.

Doc pulled himself out of the passage and found himself suspended in a great emerald pool. The waters were not as clear as he would have liked. There were a lot of algae and seaweed strands—enough to discolor the water in the direction of green-ishness. No doubt erosion created by rainwater and storms washing silt and debris down the inner walls of the cone had also polluted the naturally pure body. Caribbean waters have a reputation for crystalline beauty. Not so here.

Doc swam about, no longer needing the flashlight. Brilliant sunlight charged the water with a measure of jade-green clarity.

Below, he spied something moving with a sinuous, serpentine fashion. A deeper green than the surrounding waters, it all but blended with the murky bottom of the crater.

It was a moray eel, about four feet long, opening and closing its mouth lazily so that its rows of vicious needle teeth could be counted. It moved away, like an undulating green ribbon waving in an underwater current.

Here and there, Doc Savage saw what appeared to be other

passages or possibly underwater caves on the inner side of the caldera.

He swam toward one of those, taking care not to inhale or exhale at any time.

The oxygen tablets were a wonderful aid to underwater exploration. They freed a diver from such encumbrances as an oxygen hose or other artificial breathing apparatus. But the lifelong habit of respiration is not one easily suppressed. The instinct to draw life-giving air into the lungs runs very deep. Over time, minute quantities of carbon dioxide gas tended to seep from the mouth and nose, filling the diving helmet. To inhale too much of this, Doc discovered through experimentation, interfered with the action of the oxygen tablets.

So Doc had to focus on the unnatural discipline of holding his breath, lest he draw into his lungs pure carbon dioxide.

As he approached, the bronze man restricted his movements to the minimum swimming effort necessary to propel him along. Barracuda dwelt in underwater dens such as these and, if disturbed, could inflict a nasty bite.

Instead, out of one cave came a great turquoise-and-tan thing like a disembodied bladder, but possessing many whipping arms. A tropical octopus. Many roamed among the coral reefs.

Doc recognized the species as not dangerous, although its many-suckered arms could create complications if they wrapped themselves around him.

On the boat, Doc had donned a belt of many pockets which he had unearthed from a concealed compartment known only to him, which had escaped the raiding party. This was the equipment kit he wore whenever his gadget vest was impractical. He reached into one pocket now.

From it came a tiny device with attached nozzle. Doc pointed the nozzle in the direction of the approaching octopus, whose hooded eyes appeared inhumanly curious.

Octopi are infamous for squirting clouds of sepia ink into the faces of any potential predator that approaches them. Perhaps this was on the mind of the aquatic creature.

If so, this particular octopus must have been startled—for it was Doc Savage who squirted a cloud of sepia potion in its direction!

The billowing black pall struck it full in the face. The octopus suddenly convulsed, propelling itself back into its warren via a jet of violently expelled water.

This told Doc that this particular cave was probably otherwise untenanted.

The bronze man moved onto another cave, which was much larger, and consequently more interesting to him.

DOC SAVAGE had been accused in the past of possessing clairvoyant abilities. Nothing could be farther from the truth. But he did have a strong sense of caution, and the wariness that came from walking danger trails all over the world.

Approaching the large cave mouth, Doc slowed, kicked backwards, and moved about, scrutinizing the cavern from different angles preparatory to entering.

This was purely precaution on his part.

What happened next proved that sensible precautions could be prescient.

For out of the cave projected a pair of blood-red feelers. They resembled those of the Caribbean crawfish, a lobster-like sea creature considered a delicacy throughout the many islands.

But these waving stalks were of immense size!

Doc approached with care, calculating the probable size of the crawfish to which those monstrous feelers belonged. It verged on the impossible.

In a swirl of air bubbles, out shot three swimming figures, great muscular arms edged with long spiny fins and capped by claw-tipped talons reaching out and scooping water as they advanced.

Reddish-green, covered in scaly, crablike plates, they were substantially greater than the size of grown men. Two possessed webbed feet and the third boasted a heavily-muscled torso that tapered down to a lean, sleek fishtail. All of these appendages jerked spasmodically. Each of the trio sported blood-red dorsal fins running along their backs. Above jutting lower jaws filled with pointed teeth, their flat, fishy eyes glinted with the queer brilliance of freshly-minted quarters.

Their inhuman gaze was fixed on the bronze man. Suddenly, the approaching forms began convulsing in the violence of their swimming.

The strange creatures were not retreating, rather they were arrowing in Doc Savage's direction.

Doc had been floating in place, kicking his feet, treading water and using his hands to keep his balance. His weird trilling began to fill the confines of his transparent diving helmet. He stifled it.

Gathering his great muscular body, Doc turned into a human torpedo and swam hard in the direction of the trio, whose faces were hideous with waving fins and gleaming teeth.

This bold action took the approaching creatures by surprise. They broke in three directions. Doc knifed after the one closest to hand.

Legs scissoring, he lunged for the kicking claws that were so much like the feet of wild geese, except for their reddish-green color.

Doc was a powerful swimmer, even if he lacked fins and webbed appendages. He soon overhauled his target. Metallic hands swept out, and grasped an ankle that was slick and metallic to the touch the way fish skin is.

The creature doubled up, thrashed, and from somewhere on its person pulled out a crude dagger that appeared to be made out of obsidian lashed to a spiral seashell handle.

The glassy black blade prove to be viciously sharp. It sliced out, scraping across Doc's transparent helmet with a thin shriek that pierced his eardrums.

Doc swept out of hand, found the wrist back of the knife, and gave a violent twist.

Fishy fingers released the shell handle, and the blade went sinking out of sight.

Doc next reached out for the creature's neck, clamped over what felt like thick gill slits. The skin there felt very slick, and the bronze man struggled to locate the nerve centers that, in a human being, could produce unconsciousness when pressed a certain way.

That he failed to find those nerve centers did not entirely surprise him. The anatomy of the grotesque thing diverged from the human in striking ways.

Doc switched tactics. He pressed metallic palms against the merman's gills, sealing then shut.

Expelling bubbles from its fishy mouth, the creature struggled, but could not shake Doc's powerful grasp. It reached up with its webbed hands and attempted to rake the bronze man's face, but to no avail. The thing began a frantic flailing. Its massive claw-tipped hands strove to find skin, scored metallic forearms with the needle-like weapons. Crimson began to billow in long, thready clouds.

As the creature fought to break Doc's iron grasp, the other two swam around and, obsidian blades thrust forward, came at him.

Three against one would have been no difficult combat for Doc Savage on dry land but, here underwater, a foe could slip up from any direction. Possessing no blade, the bronze man decided that discretion was the better part of courage.

Releasing his foe, Doc kicked away, and dived deeper into the crater pool.

Out came the device that expelled a chemical possessing the properties of octopus ink, along with a few other noxious ingredients. Doc directed a spray upward.

This disturbing cloud rolled and spread in the direction of the three mermen and they reacted as if a barracuda was arrowing toward them, intent upon taking off an arm or a leg.

Swimming madly, they retreated to the surface, leaving Doc Savage to explore their underwater lair unchallenged.

Chapter XXVII

THE MERMEN

DOC SAVAGE PLUNGED for the large underwater cave entrance. He moved with incredible speed, even burdened as he was by his diving helmet and equipment belt.

The bronze giant had his powerful flashlight out, and was using it to spray intense illumination ahead of him.

All caution seemed to have departed. Doc slipped into the cave, sweeping the flashlight's penetrating beam all around, noticing that the natural formation was largely hardened lava, interspersed with colorful coral formations that might have belonged to another world. This did not surprise him, for a great number of these Caribbean islands were composed of coral built up over the centuries.

Pushing along with rapid kicks of his bare feet, Doc gave special attention to the roof of the tunnel. Twisting about, he maneuvered himself until he was swimming upside down, the better to play his flash ray on the tunnel roof.

Doc Savage proceeded along in this fashion. His light disclosed a cleft in the roof, evidently excavated by hand. A faint light shone down. It had not the fresh quality of sunlight, but was dull and dingy looking.

Doc kicked upward, and began exploring this phenomenon.

Before long, his head broke the surface of an underground grotto in which a steady artificial illumination predominated.

The light came from bare light bulbs strung along the cavern wall. This revealed a rocky ledge which showed signs of having been smoothed by stone-working tools. A great deal of effort had been invested in the task, Doc saw.

There were strange designs carved into the rear wall. They depicted a civilization that was remindful of the Mayan race, with whom Doc Savage had long acquaintance. But there were differences, too, in the style of clothing and architecture. The latter resembled the ruin of a temple sitting broken and forgotten in the mangrove swamp not very far from this queer spot. It was abundantly clear to the bronze man that this chamber had been excavated for ceremonial purposes very long ago. This despite the profusion of swastikas carved into the design.

Doc directed his attention toward the solitary inhabitant of this grotto, which was wide but not very deep.

Seated on the floor of the ledge was one of the mermen. He presented a remarkable sight, inasmuch as he was crouched before what appeared to be a radio transmitting set, with a pair of fully modern headphones clamped over his finny ears.

The grotesque creature was so intent upon listening to what was coming from the cans that he failed to notice Doc Savage ease out of the water and distribute himself on the ledge unseen.

Doc paused for several moments in a prone position, listening. The metallic helmet of hair capping his head began drying, a quality that it possessed.

The merman did not speak once. Instead, he listened intently. His reddish-green skin, speckled by silvery scales, was very slick from a recent immersion.

Carefully, Doc got to his feet and padded up behind the creature, whose sharp-finned back faced him.

No matter how stealthy a man might be, he has no certain defense against being seen. This was especially true for Doc Savage, who stood well over six feet tall—closer to seven with the addition of the transparent diving helmet encasing his head.

Suddenly, the merman jerked its hideous face around and, sweeping off the headphones, leaped to his splayed feet.

There was a huge monkey wrench nearby and the creature

picked it up in both finny paws.

Charging, he came at Doc full force, his webbed feet making strange flopping sounds against the smooth stone floor.

Doc Savage moved in to intercept the raised weapon. Blocking the downward sweep with one wrist, the bronze giant seized one of the creature's forearms and attempted to yank the wrench out of its grip.

Instead, an awful ripping sound was heard—*and the entire hand and forearm peeled off the merman!*

The wrench came along with it. Doc snapped fingers around the handle, and flung it backward into the water, where it was no longer a threat. The ease with which the metallic giant handled the heavy tool spoke volumes of his prodigious strength.

He examined the reddish-green hide that he had inadvertently harvested.

A glance told that it was very thick, the inner side coated with an insulating substance resembling blubber. Doc had no more time for study, however.

Strange guttural sounds came from the merman's distended jaws. It was apparently startled. Its thick, blubbery lips disclosed a horrible basket of pointed teeth.

These teeth began snapping like thin bone needles. The mouth lunged for Doc's arms.

Doc Savage applied a set of bronze knuckles to the scaly jaw. A satisfying crunch of a noise resulted, and the merman went flailing backwards.

Lunging in, Doc reached down and seized the frilly set of gills that ran along the jawline of the strange being. The result was astonishing.

The ugly green head came away, disclosing that it was composed of some substance resembling formed rubber.

Doc Savage found himself looking down at a perfectly human head atop the grotesque reddish-green physique. Ordinary gray eyes glared hate. The man began cursing at him in a guttural foreign language.

Doc shot back sharp words in the same tongue, with the result that the man in the elaborate merman suit lost all composure.

Hot words were spat. But before the bronze man could press for information, out from the shadows stepped another individual.

Doc turned—discovered himself facing no less than the aristocratic Count Runo von Elmz once more. The debonair one had emerged from a separate chamber, which had been concealed by the deep shadows of a cleft in the natural stone.

The courtly aristocrat was attired in his usual splendid fashion, right down to the Tyrolean hat and snappy sword stick cane which was carved so that a spiral groove ran from cap to ferrule.

The Count directed the tip of this cane at the bronze man and remarked, "You seem to get around, my good fellow."

Doc Savage touched a stud on the breastplate of his diving helmet. This permitted him to speak and be heard through a miniature microphone and reproducer imbedded in the contrivance.

"You have shaved your beard, but it is clear that you are Count Runo von Elmz."

The Count bowed, saying, "At your service. How do you like my lair? It appears as if the ancient race who once inhabited this place is smiling upon my cause."

Doc ignored the obvious reference to the carved swastikas, said levelly, "Such an elaborate subterfuge must mask a powerful purpose."

"Ah," returned the Count. "No doubt you are referring to the Great Objective."

"Objective?"

"I see you have met one of my U-Men," remarked the Count, changing the subject. "They are very handy fellows, especially for scaring away interlopers and eavesdroppers."

Doc said, "Is that what you are doing here? Eavesdropping?"

Count von Elmz inclined his head. "Yes, this is a listening

post. All that was said during your island respite was overheard, you see. It was necessary to learn how much you knew of our plan. It appears, however, that you know very little."

"That is why we were conveyed here and allowed to live," suggested Doc, golden gaze growing animated.

The Count smiled gallantly. "Very astute of you. But you do have the reputation of an *übermencsh*, no? *Der Mann aus Bronze.* A modern Sherlock Holmes. Yet more physically formidable than Tarzan of the Apes. Yes, we could have killed you, but we needed to know what you knew. Murder is messy and time-consuming. This method was much more efficient, not to mention considerably less bloody."

Doc Savage began advancing on the man.

Up came the Count's tricky sword stick. Before he could press the trigger and squirt a dose of vapor, he stopped. Frowned. The nobleman hesitated. It was obvious that the transparent diving helmet made the bronze man impervious to any gas.

Lowering the cane, Count von Elmz extracted a double-barreled derringer pistol from his immaculate jacket, and snapped off a quick shot.

Doc dodged to one side, causing the round to go wide. The bullet, however, managed to graze the side of his clear diving helmet.

Doc Savage's head was knocked sideways. The helmet did not shatter. It was all but bulletproof. But the bronze man was momentarily staggered.

Recovering, Doc resumed his advance.

Redirecting his aim, Count von Elmz attempted to place his remaining bullet in the bronze man's unprotected chest.

Bronze fingers dipped into his equipment belt, and produced a device that flew in the other man's direction.

This proved to be a flash bomb, which exploded harmlessly in midair. This device produced no shrapnel or gas, but instead made a blinding glare. It stunned the Count's optic nerves. Doc swept in and harvested the small pistol from his hand.

Flinging the derringer away, Doc next stripped the helpless man of his cane. The bronze man studied the thing for a moment while the Count made mewling sounds and pawed at his paralyzed eyes.

Finding the lever that released the gas, Doc pointed the cane nozzle at the Count's face and pressed it once.

The spurt of whitish vapor enveloped the man's head. He immediately began laughing, and then laughing much more heartily, as if his entire body were being shaken by an irresistible hilarity.

Doc watched with interest as Count Runo von Elmz rolled dark eyes up in his head and collapsed into his waiting arms.

The bronze man laid the insensate aristocrat across his Atlas-like shoulders. In the act of attempting to carry the man away, the metallic giant was suddenly confronted by three frilly-finned reddish-green heads bursting above the waterline beside the ledge.

Grasping the ledge's rough lip with their outlandish talons, the three mermen started scrambling up, emitting angry sounds.

It was the aquatic trio that Doc had earlier discouraged with his chemical repellent.

Setting the limp nobleman on the ground, Doc raced to the stony edge, and met the first of the oncoming foes.

Taking the man by the top of his head, Doc made a fist, lifted, ripping off the artificial mask.

A metallic fist collided with the exposed jaw, knocking him out.

One of the other dripping mermen rushed in to keep his comrade from sinking underwater and drowning. This occupied him while Doc went after the third of the trio, who had not emerged from the pool.

Plunging into the water, Doc began pursuing the man until he caught him by his slippery fishtail. Strong fingers clamped.

The other reacted in a natural and understandable manner. He began to panic.

Doc hauled the salmon-red tail closer to him, grabbed a

flailing wrist, and soon had his hands around the merman's rubbery neck. Wrenching off the artificial head, the bronze man found the sensitive nerves at the base of the spine, and began manipulating them.

The flopping merman immediately lost all animation.

Doc wrapped an arm around the hapless horror's waist, and began swimming away.

Reaching the blue hole, the bronze giant made for the shimmering sunlight above, broke the surface, and held the man's head above water, so that he could breathe.

The erstwhile merman proved to be no true amphibian. He was choking and gurgling in the manner of a man who had taken water into his lungs.

Doc performed some quick artificial respiration, until greenish fluid began streaming out of the other's mouth and nose.

When the merman's distress finally abated, Doc swam toward the sheer wall of the blue hole, and pulled him up onto a lava rock shelf.

Packing his captive across one shoulder, Doc scaled upwards until he reached the volcano rim. Stepping over, the bronze giant strode down to flat ground. He made excellent time, even encumbered by a full-grown man as he was.

DOC SAVAGE was still wearing his transparent helmet when he rejoined Monk, Ham and the others. There had been no opportunity to remove it; leaving it in place was the simplest way of toting the cumbersome contraption.

The hairy chemist gave out a lusty whoop. "Doc! Where did you come from?"

Doc replied calmly, "Investigating the blue hole."

Ham Brooks rushed up to examine the merman as Doc laid the latter out on the hot ivory sand.

"The very devil!" he exclaimed. "That beggar is actually human."

Doc nodded. "A man in a free-diving suit, designed to look

like a fanciful denizen of the deep. But he is nothing more than a common sailor of a foreign navy."

Long Tom knelt to examine the costume and pronounced it to be, in his words, "just painted rubber."

"Good job, though," said Monk, examining the material with the eye of an industrial chemist.

The puny electric wizard grunted, "So there are no mermen after all."

"Nor mermaids," replied Doc Savage.

Long Tom stood up and made a belligerent jaw. "So what did I see last night that looked like Hornetta Hale?"

Before Doc Savage could reply, the woman in question began stirring. All eyes went to her.

"What happened?" she demanded. Her eyes were very strange. Her voice had lost its tough edge.

"You experienced a misadventure," implied Doc Savage calmly.

The green-haired girl struggled to her feet murmuring, "The last I recall I was laughing…."

"There is nothing funny about your predicament," Doc Savage advised her.

"Don't you mean *our* predicament?" returned the girl. "I am just as much a prisoner as you are."

Doc Savage eyed her without emotion. "There is no further need for pretending. You are Honoria Hale."

"Nonsense!" the girl snapped.

Doc elaborated, "Your hair is cut in a slightly different style. The fact that it is wet cannot disguise that fact. Your skin has been treated with an astringent solution to give it a reddish cast, but you are manifestly not suffering from sunburn. There is no peeling. Furthermore, your attempt to mimic your sister's speech and manners was not entirely successful. You kept slipping back into your normal self."

Honoria Hale turned very pale. She sealed her lips in a determined mouth.

"Where is your sister, and my cousin Pat?" demanded the bronze man. There were golden sparks igniting in the depths of his eyes.

Honoria made an abrupt move for the water's edge.

Doc Savage rushed in and overhauled her. Taking Honoria by one arm, he arrested the woman's headlong flight. She attempted to struggle, but the obdurate strength of the bronze giant's metallic digits convinced her escape was all but impossible.

"Where is the submarine?" demanded Doc.

Honoria's mouth flew open.

"How did you—?"

"Common sense. You were anxious to hire our submarine. This strongly suggested that you were hunting another underseas craft. Something had to tow our cruiser to this spot, and that blue hole and its tunnel passageway form a natural and very sheltered cove for secret anchorage. A phantom lagoon, if you wish to call it that."

"For the love of little fishes!" exploded Monk. "You mean we've been sittin' next to the mystery lagoon all along?"

Doc nodded grimly.

"What is this all about?"

"The Great Objective," said Doc steadily, looking at Honoria Hale.

Honoria Hale's hand flew to her open mouth. "You know more than we dreamed," she gasped.

Doc Savage regarded the green-haired girl without expression. The compelling power of his flake-gold eyes bored into her. She seemed to wilt.

"Let me ask you again," he said firmly. "Where are Hornetta Hale and Patricia Savage?"

Before the woman could form a response, a new sound came to their ears.

It was a familiar drone. They had heard it before—always out on the open Atlantic.

Long Tom snapped, "Sounds like that foreign warplane!"

"Yeah," muttered Monk. "Comin' back for another crack at us."

Honoria Hale became extremely alarmed. She tried to pull away from Doc Savage, but the bronze man's grip was unbreakable.

He pulled her into the scant shelter of a sprinkling of silver-sided royal palm trees.

Handing her off to Monk Mayfair, Doc said, "Hold on to her." And the bronze man shinnied up the palm tree, poking his head out of its leafy crown.

He spied the bent-winged warplane, coming out of the east. It was flying low, and approaching fast like a gray daylight bat. Obviously, its wing fuel tanks had been patched.

Doc Savage slid down to the ground so fast he lost some skin.

"Get down!" he rapped. "Stay down. Do not move a muscle!"

The unmarked warplane overshot the tiny island, and circled back around. It dropped lower.

Banking, the pilot seemed to be attempting to seek them out amid the overgrowth.

He made two more passes, and then threw back the greenhouse-style canopy of his cockpit. A gloved fist was raised.

Something glinted in that hand.

Doc Savage saw it and warned, "Bomb!"

Monk, Ham and Long Tom immediately stuck fingers in their ears. Doc Savage tightened his helmet. They had experience being dive-bombed in the past, and were protecting their ears from concussion.

Seeing this action, Honoria Hale copied it.

When the bomb came, it landed not with an explosion, but a glassy crash.

They heard it only faintly, but when no blast disturbed the tropical atmosphere, they unplugged their ears.

Off about one hundred yards, where the glassy crash had sounded, a whitish cloud arose like a creeping ghost.

Monk bellowed, "It's that laughin' hoodoo!"

Everyone pinched their nostrils shut and sealed mouths, knowing that the measure could be a temporary protection at best.

"Wonder where we'll end up this time?" moaned Long Tom.

"I do not wish to contemplate the prospect," wailed Ham.

But the prospect appeared to be inescapable. Inexorably, the spreading monster of white rolled toward them with its questing tendril-like ghost fingers.

Chapter XXVIII

PHANTASMAGORIA

DOC SAVAGE DISTRIBUTED oxygen tablets to everyone, saying, "Do not inhale or exhale after taking these."

Honoria Hale refused hers, not understanding what they were, and perhaps fearing some trick.

As a result, she was the first one to be affected by the creeping exhalation.

Rolling closer, the whitish spume assumed a more sinister hue, becoming rather purplish at the edges.

They had naturally retreated to higher ground, but there was a vast cloud of the crawling miasma spreading in all directions, and not many places in which to hide.

The stuff got into Honoria's nostrils. The green-haired woman immediately began screaming, not laughing as they expected.

Suddenly, her screams turned to ripping words.

"I'm on fire!" she wailed, slapping at her bare arms and legs.

"Mustard gas!" Ham yelled.

Doc Savage seized her by the wrists. Honoria struggled. Golden eyes stark, the bronze man searched her forearms for signs of blistering.

But there was nothing, only goose bumps.

"What is happening to you?" Doc demanded, shaking her.

Her face twisted. "My arms are on fire! Can't you see that?"

But they could not. There was no sign of any chemical reaction on her skin.

Neither Doc nor the others experienced any such horrific sensation. They were holding up their arms, seeking signs of the kind of hideous blistering produced by mustard gas or Lewisite, but finding none.

While they were puzzling over this, Habeas Corpus suddenly began chasing Ham Brooks.

The scrawny porker commenced by baring his tusks, and narrowing beady eyes in the dapper lawyer's direction. A strange snuffling sound began issuing from his long, inquisitive snout.

Abruptly, fangs gleaming, the shoat charged for Ham's ankles.

With a cry of shock, Ham attempted to fend off the snarling pig with his cane. But Habeas had become enraged, snapped at Ham's shoes like a dog, forcing the bewildered lawyer into ignominious retreat.

This would normally cause Monk Mayfair to double over with laughter, but instead Monk was pointing a finger in the direction of the merman Doc had captured and laid out on the beach.

"*Ye-o-w!*" the hairy chemist called out. "Watch out! He's comin' out of it."

Doc Savage looked toward the beach, and then eyed the apish chemist.

"What do you mean?"

"What do you mean, what do I mean?" howled Monk. "He's gettin' away!"

Doc Savage watched the recumbent half-human form, and saw that the erstwhile merman simply lay there, unmoving.

"Monk," Doc said calmly. "He is doing nothing of the sort."

But the hairy chemist would not hear of it. He was jumping up and down like a frustrated bull gorilla.

"Lookit! Now he's growin' a new head to replace the old fishy one. It's kinda like a seahorse, but with a mane of yellow hair...."

At that point, Doc released Honoria Hale, who went charging down to the beach, and threw herself in the water, splashing madly about in a desperate attempt to put out the imaginary flames that tormented her.

Doc Savage's trilling began to issue from the helmet reproducer. It had an ethereal quality of wonder in it.

The bronze man looked around for Long Tom, and received a shock.

Long Tom was in the act of climbing a mist-shrouded coconut palm and, upon reaching the leafy crown, began throwing coconuts down upon something at the base which could not be seen.

Doc Savage called up, "Long Tom. What is the matter?"

"Sea serpent! Don't you see it? It's winding its way around the trunk!"

There was no sea serpent winding its way around the coconut trunk.

"Now it's breathing fire at me!" howled Long Tom, ducking and dropping another drupe on his imaginary foe.

After Long Tom had exhausted his cache of coconut husks, the puny electrician scooted up to the very top of the crown, and began wildly yanking loose big fronds, waving them and flinging down fragments in a desperate attempt to ward off the creeping sea serpent that only he could see. The expression on his pale features was distraught.

ALONE among them all, Doc Savage was unaffected by the outbreak of bizarre hallucinations. He looked into the sky, and saw that the gray warplane was scooting away, making a moaning noise that diminished with each passing moment. It appeared to have lost interest in them.

The bronze man shifted his attention to the top of the volcanic crater, and decided that there was nothing he could do for his men, who were unlikely to injure themselves while under the spell of the weird gas. So he moved in that direction.

It might have been a kind of prescience that impelled the bronze man to do so. Or perhaps the sudden departure of the mysterious warplane gave him the idea.

Doc moved up to high ground, and found the craggy lip of the crater.

First, he looked downward, but saw nothing of interest.

Then his uncanny eyes began searching the surrounding seas.

They came to rest on something far to the southeast. From one belt pocket, Doc removed an optical tube that could be converted from a pocket microscope to a serviceable telescope and other devices.

He employed the thing as a telescope. It was not very large, but had a good deal of range in a narrow focus.

Against the blue horizon, Doc saw what he soon realized was a pair of Coast Guard cutters, moving in the general direction of this lonely isle. This alone was unusual, for they were not in American waters.

Keeping his spyglass trained upon the two cutters, Doc was surprised to spy a small destroyer taking up the rear. Even from this distance, he could see that it was a United States Navy destroyer.

Shifting the glass around, Doc Savage attempted to discern the purpose of the unusual nautical formation. Coast Guard cutters and Naval destroyers did not normally travel together.

It was after a considerable visual search that the bronze man spotted the yacht.

The yacht was of modest size compared to the destroyer, of course, but it rivaled the Coast Guard cutters. It had not been immediately recognizable in the aquamarine water because it was a dull mahogany color, and the cutters were a bone white.

Doc studied the yacht for a very long time.

That he had in some manner recognized it became evident when his trilling began to flavor the tropical air, so low that it was a phenomenon more felt rather than distinctly heard. Tuneless, it was somehow melodic, as if the sound belonged to some higher realm of reality.

Doc's trilling had the unusual property of carrying in its melody the essence of the bronze man's repressed feelings. The emotions that flowed forth at this point began as a kind of curious wonder and swiftly escalated to a genuine alarm.

Doc was so focused on what he was witnessing that he lost much of his habitual presence of mind.

So it was that he was unaware of the pair of mermen crawling up, snakelike, along the inner wall of the crater, intent upon ambushing him.

They were marvelously quiet, given that they were climbing with webbed hands and feet. They almost reached the bronze man undetected.

But Doc Savage had been training since childhood in many disciplines, and all of his senses had been sharpened to a degree that verged upon the superhuman.

He did not hear them at first, but the unnatural smell of the rubber free-diving suits wafted up to his sensitive nostrils, for he had removed his helmet in order to employ his telescope. Doc took the eyepiece from one orb, and looked downward.

The reddish-green forms were very close. Their flat eyes shone in the light like new coins.

Doc wasted no time with them. Restoring his helmet, he leapt over their heads, went into a long dive that slammed him into the crater pool's surface.

Silvery eyes blank, the two mermen rotated their heads and peered downward.

There, churning waters painted the spot where the bronze man had disappeared into the algae-choked waters below.

Swapping fishy expressions, the mermen reached a mutual decision, and pushed outward with muscular forearms, twisting like grotesque dolphins as they followed the bronze man down.

In their fanged mouths were two of the shell-handled obsidian knives whose bite was more vicious than that of a shark. They grasped them, pulled the weapons free.

Their intent was clear—to eviscerate the bronze man the way a fish is gutted and cleaned.

Chapter XXIX

THE BOTTOM

DOC SAVAGE STRUCK the water with an immense splash.

Under dangerous circumstances, the bronze giant would normally have taken care to cleave the water more cleanly, in order to make the minimum noise. But something momentous was impelling him to move at the greatest possible speed, at the expense of stealth and caution.

Doc's plunge had brought him once more into the seaweedydepths of the emerald pool. He pulled out his spring-generator flashlight and thumbed it on. With this, the bronze giant found his way to the mermen's ancient grotto, where the radio set had been in use.

Doc traveled with powerful muscular strokes, feet kicking furiously, until he reached the ledge himself.

There was no sign of Count von Elmz now, other than drag marks that showed that the sleeping nobleman had been removed from the scene.

But there was a solitary merman. At the sound of Doc's head breaking the surface of the grotto pool, he turned, fixing reflective eyes on the bronze giant.

The latter rasped, *"Der Mann aus Bronze!"*

Doc Savage disposed of him with a careless toss of an anesthetic bomb. The glass capsule landed before the oversized green feet, releasing an invisible odorless vapor which swiftly overcame the shambling monstrosity.

Doc pulled himself onto the ledge while the merman fell with a wet, rubbery smack. He lay still, a grotesque form edged in frilly fins.

Doc himself did not have to hold his breath for the requisite minute or so, due to his protective helmet, of course. Going to the radio set, he began manipulating dials until he found the frequency on the 600-meter band employed by the Coast Guard at sea.

"Doc Savage to Coast Guard naval escort in Caribbean Sea," he called into the microphone. "Doc Savage to Coast Guard escort."

There was no answer. Doc repeated his request. His voice was extremely urgent.

"Doc Savage calling Coast Guard escort in the Caribbean Sea, operating in the Lesser Antilles."

After several minutes of this, an angry voice yelled back, *"Whoever you are, this is an official frequency. Cease transmitting at once!"*

Doc attempted to push through the official obstinacy.

"This is Doc Savage, calling from an uninhabited island in the Caribbean. I can see your formation from my position. It consists of two cutters and a U.S. Navy destroyer escorting a yacht."

"I say again, stop interfering with this frequency," snapped the Coast Guard radio operator.

The bronze man spun the tuning dial, shifted over to the Naval frequency.

"This is Doc Savage, transmitting from an uncharted island in the Caribbean Sea. It is urgent that the yacht being escorted by the Coast Guard and U.S. naval destroyer turn around as soon as possible. There is grave danger to the yacht. Repeat, this is Doc Savage transmitting an emergency declaration."

This call was met with complete silence.

Doc Savage seldom showed emotion, and even more rarely did he display anger. But his face flushed, his skin darkened, and he hauled back and kicked the radio set. This uncharacteristic outburst was an unmistakable physical expression of the bronze giant's inner turmoil.

Doc went in search of the Count. There was not much to the grotto, but he found a crawlspace and examined it closely, employing his torch. It led upward at a shallow angle. Consulting his wrist compass, he determined that the escape tunnel—for that was what it was—went in the general direction of the old temple ruin in the mangrove swamp.

Worse still, it was too narrow to admit his broad shoulders. He could not use it to reach the surface of the cay.

Clapping his helmet back into place, the bronze man leapt off the ledge, and slipped back into the water.

He had not progressed very far when the two mermen who had been trailing him came at him with their vicious black blades.

They swept in, intending to rip him to shreds.

Doc Savage slapped one against the side of his rubber-coated head, and the man's skull smashed into the tunnel wall. An eruption of bubbles from his needle-pointed maw showed that he was out of the fight for good.

The other reached for a hank of Doc's hair, intending to snap back the bronze man's head, the better to slice into his throat.

Doc blocked the sweeping blade with one massive forearm, and kicked clear. He drove a bone-hard fist into that awful basket of teeth, thus smashing in the rubbery mouth, driving the artificial fangs into the man's natural face. Billows of crimson began leaking from the ruin, followed by dribbling air bubbles. The merman lost all interest in the struggle.

Doc left them behind to battle their way to the ledge and oxygen.

Swimming back out into the hidden lagoon, the bronze man located the natural tunnel that led out into the warmer waters of the open sea. He made remarkable speed, causing tropical fish and the odd wild-eyed seahorse to scurry out of his way. His head soon broke the surface beyond the lonely cay itself.

Searching the horizon with his strange golden eyes, Doc saw that the two Coast Guard cutters and the destroyer were steaming closer. He had his telescope out again, and commenced searching the surrounding waters for something else.

It was very difficult work, because the thing he was searching for could hardly be visible any closer than one hundred yards, if that.

But the bronze man had a stroke of luck. Sunlight glanced off something metallic jutting up from the water's surface. At first, Doc could hardly discern it from the sparkle of sunlight on exquisitely blue water. The glint was of a different character. The other glints twinkled with the wave action. This whitish blob stood very still, making it stand out in the dance of tropical sunlight on waves.

Pocketing his telescope, Doc Savage struck out for the strange object.

An Olympian swimmer would have been impressed with his performance. Doc Savage cleaved the waters with choppy motions of his arms. It was if he were hacking his way toward his objective.

The Herculean bronze man ate up a tremendous amount of distance at a speed that scientists would have said was unsurpassable by anything except a fleet porpoise. As he swam, Doc shrugged off his diving helmet and shoulder piece, lest it slow him down. The intensity of his determination was incredible. Doc Savage focused on one thing alone—reaching the stationary thing sticking up out of the water.

As he neared it, Doc saw the approaching ships creeping ever closer, unwittingly driving in the direction of the lurking thing in the water.

Doc reached his objective. It appeared to be an upright pipe, painted dull blue. He wrapped one hand around it, capping its unwinking glass eye.

For it was the periscope of a submarine. Its lens was pointing in the direction of the approaching ships.

But now it was blind. The bronze man's large palm lay flat against the lens, blocking out all light.

Maneuvering in the water, Doc immersed his face and gazed downward.

THERE he spied a vague cigar shape, painted an aquamarine hue so that it was all but invisible in the blue water. Its shape was strange, for it flared out at either side into what might have been the fins of a small whale. But it was no whale.

It was one of the smallest submarines Doc Savage had ever beheld. It was a runt, but no less deadly for its small size. And it struck Doc with great force that he had seen it before. It was the indistinct blue shape he had spied in the water after Hornetta Hale had been dragged under the waves by something that could not be clearly seen except for its blue-gray back fin—really a truncated conning tower.

It was now obvious that one of the shark-finned merman had pulled the blonde adventuress from sight and had dragged her into this waiting submersible.

Pivoting, Doc clamped his muscular legs around the periscope, and took hold of the upper portion directly under the bend in the tube beneath the lens with both strong hands. Flexible fingers clamped tightly.

With a tremendous effort, the bronze man exerted himself. Tendons popping out on his neck and arms, he wrenched the periscope inexorably backward. It commenced complaining with metallic squeaks as the metal began distorting, acquiring a joint that grew more and more pronounced as Doc applied unbelievable pressure…until the glass eye was pointing up in the clear blue sky—useless.

That accomplished, Doc began shimmying down the narrow tube until he reached the flat deck of the submersible.

From one pocket of his equipment belt, he extracted a pair of special grenades.

Easing to the stern of the U-boat, Doc made his way to

where the propeller screw should lie. His intention was to disable the screw, but not damage the submarine, because he was all but certain that Pat Savage and Hornetta Hale were prisoners inside the strangely-shaped submersible.

The grenades were magnetic, so it was possible to place them where they could do the most damage, and not fall away into the water.

However, once he reached the tail—it was actually shaped like the fluked tail of a killer whale—Doc Savage discovered that the U-boat lacked regulation screws.

Instead, there was an open maw, very much resembling a torpedo tube.

Curiosity compelled Doc to investigate.

Swimming head downward, he shone a light into the opening. It was smooth and there was no sign of any propulsion mechanism.

Had the bronze man not been underwater and so constrained, he might have emitted his distinctive trilling sound. As it was, a stream of bubbles dribbled from his parted lips, and the gold flakes in his eyes whirled with a light of understanding.

It seemed inescapably clear that the weird fishlike underseas craft was propelled by compressed air, hence it was virtually noiseless when submerged. It also explained the discouragingly powerful jet of water that had forced the bronze man to abandon the chase when he first encountered the weird vessel the previous time.

Grimly, Doc Savage set the timer mechanism on the magnetic grenades and inserted them into the propulsion vent.

Returning to the deck, Doc moved forward to the bow side of the small conning tower that was shaped to suggest a flat fin.

It was then that the bronze giant began wishing he had his helmet, for he knew that the coming underwater concussion would be punishing to his eardrums. He inserted fingers in his ears, closed his eyes and waited.

The detonations came only seconds apart, and they threw the submersible about the way a helpless fish switches its tail when gigged.

Doc shot toward the surface, and found himself bobbing in the water, with the Coast Guard cutters bearing down upon his position. He cupped his hands over his mouth and called out, "Ahoy! U.S. Coast Guard cutters! Turn back! Danger! U-boat!"

If anyone heard him, there was no sign, no alteration in the course of the approaching ships. They continued steaming ahead.

Then, to Doc Savage's great alarm, the twisted periscope began lifting out of the water, which meant that the submarine was breaking toward the surface.

Doc flung himself to one side, and soon the truncated conning tower popped into view, spilling water off its sides, the fiery sun making its smooth blue hull blaze.

The bronze man swam for the deck, clambered aboard, and stood up.

Facing the oncoming cutters, he again megaphoned hands and mouth and yelled out a sharp warning.

"Turn back! Hostile U-boat!"

This time there was a response.

Coast Guardsmen appeared on the bows of the approaching cutters. They saw the bronze man standing atop the weird floating shape that resembled a small blue whale and immediately lifted rifles. They began shooting in his direction.

That was when the thing Doc Savage had been fighting to avoid happened.

The U-boat unleashed its torpedo!

Chapter XXX
WHEN THE HATCH POPPED

THE TORPEDO SWISHED out of its tube and tunneled along until it broke the surface, then it began charging the Coast Guard cutters with the foaming ferocity of a mad dog.

The shot had been blind, of course. The U-boat captain could no longer aim by sight, thanks to the mangled periscope. Still, the torpedo drove hard in the direction of the small flotilla.

The sight of the dreaded "tin fish" coming in their direction caused the sharpshooting Coast Guardsmen to suddenly scramble to battle stations, calling out an alarm.

That gave Doc a momentary respite. He dived into the water to avoid any more sniping bullets.

One grazed him on his left shoulder. The bronze giant jerked, but failed to take notice that he had been wounded. His concentration was that fierce.

Risky as it was, Doc swam toward the oncoming cutters.

Presence of mind is something Doc Savage always strove to maintain, even in the heat of battle. Even as he arrowed toward the cutters, the bronze man realized that there was a fair chance the torpedo would hit home.

It did. The tin fish caught one of the cutters square in its fast-veering prow. It detonated with an awful roar. Klaxon horns began caterwauling on both cutters, adding to the general pandemonium.

This made the sharpshooters of the other cutter even more

determined to shoot back and hit something.

Doc dived underwater, and swam the rest of the way unseen. Here and there, bullets chopped into the drink, their energy spent by the stopping power of the water.

It was only then he discovered that he had been grazed in the shoulder. Salt water was making the blood-filled groove sting. Reaching into a pocket of his gadget belt, the bronze man clapped a self-adhering bandage over the spot, which was impregnated with cauterizing chemicals.

Doc grasped the lower rungs of an accommodation ladder on one side of the undamaged cutter and climbed up with alacrity.

When he reached the deck, a dozen rifles suddenly pointed in his direction.

Throwing up his hands, Doc Savage said as calmly as he could, "I am Doc Savage."

"You are our prisoner!" a seaman said sharply. "One wrong move, and we will riddle you."

Doc Savage did not move a muscle. The crew looked very grave of countenance.

Their well-tanned faces had the bloodless quality of exposed bone.

The cutter captain came rushing out, red in the face, figurative blood in his eye.

He at once recognized the Man of Bronze. He did not seem very impressed.

"What the hell is going on?" he roared.

"Foreign raider, attempting to torpedo the yacht you are escorting," Doc told him.

That sunk in very swiftly, for the skipper growled, "We'll blow that sea wolf out of the water, just watch us." He turned to bark orders to his men.

Doc Savage called after him, "There are innocent prisoners aboard that sub."

"Too bad for them. But we have to sink that thing. I'll tell you why later."

"No need," said Doc, lowering his hands. "I know the nature of the vessel you are escorting."

"You do? Well, then you understand."

Dully, Doc Savage said, "Yes. I understand." His eyes were very bleak.

Over on the other cutter, they were putting on life jackets and preparing to abandon ship. Coast Guardsmen are all experienced seamen, so they needed no help. The immediate concern was a second torpedo.

Before long, it appeared.

The sight of a new blunt-nosed monster skimming along the wave tops produced considerable consternation. It distracted everyone.

The Coast Guard gunnery officer manning the 20 millimeter autocannon mounted on the forward deck trained it on the churning wake. He opened up, and quickly the stuttering mechanism chewed through its bulky box of belt ammunition. To no avail.

Frantic crewmen hustled to get a second ammo box mounted. No one doubted for a moment that it was too late for that. Too late for them all.

DOC SAVAGE seized a rifle from an unwary man's grip, rushed to the rail, and began shooting.

He fired three shots, and from the sounds of the detonation, it appeared that his second shot had successfully exploded the warhead.

A water spout appeared, which became a genie of smoke that started off very black but began thinning to an ugly gray haze. The cutter rocked in a weird fashion, but that was all.

The cutter captain whistled in admiration. He gave Doc the O.K. sign. "I would never have believed that could be done. Congratulations."

Doc Savage did not reply. He stood by the rail, rifle at the ready, prepared to repeat the performance that so impressed the Coast Guard skipper.

That was when the destroyer started maneuvering into position to take the U-boat apart with its powerful deck guns.

Doc Savage's golden eyes went from the sub wallowing in the water to the maneuvering destroyer, and something akin to helplessness came into his eyes.

From the tension of his amazing muscles, it could be seen that the bronze giant was restraining himself, but that every nerve fiber wanted to jump into the water, to intervene.

All eyes watched this sparkling stretch of Caribbean water lying between the menacing U-boat and oncoming flotilla.

No third torpedo appeared.

His self-control strained to the utmost, Doc Savage turned and spoke rapid words.

"Captain, that vessel may not carry more than two torpedoes."

"Could be," the skipper said doubtfully.

"Radio the destroyer to stand off. Permit me time to try something."

"I don't have any authority over the Navy," protested the Captain.

"I have a naval commission. Tell the other skipper that the request comes from Doc Savage."

"It may not work. This is serious business."

"Try," rapped Doc. Then he flung himself over the rail.

Swimming hard, the bronze man reached the submarine, and gained the wet deck drying in the sun.

Making for the conning tower, he began going through his belt pockets, looking for something that might serve to breach the hatch.

While Doc was taking inventory, the hatch popped open, and a familiar face lifted into view.

Pat Savage smiled. Her shirt was on its way to becoming a

rag. She sported a black eye, split lip, and some of her coppery wealth of hair appeared to have been yanked out of her head.

Taken aback, Doc blurted, "Pat?"

"Who else?" beamed Pat. In her bronzy right fist was one of the supermachine pistols that had gone missing from the *Stormalong*. Two more were jammed into the waistband of her slacks—which now qualified as shorts—along with her old single-action frontier revolver.

Not for the first time in his dealings with his thrill-seeking cousin, Doc Savage was struck speechless.

Pat Savage said cheerfully, "Well, don't just stand there gawking. Help haul out our prisoners!"

"Our?"

"After you mangled this tub, the hull started springing leaks everywhere. The crew kind of lost interest in us. Hornetta and I jumped them, and whaled these sorry sailors to within an inch of their lives. Now get down there and pitch in. This time," she added, waving a tanned finger in Doc's face, "I really pulled your fat out of the fire—and don't think you'll ever hear the end of it."

Chapter XXXI

THE MOP-UP

IN VERY SHORT order, the crew of the whale-like U-boat was brought up from the vessel's innards.

Hornetta Hale did the prodding from below. She was the last to emerge, wielding the sub commander's spike-snouted automatic. She looked as though she had been in a fight, and enjoyed every minute of it. When she grinned at Doc, a gap showed in her front teeth that would have delighted a dentist.

The crew numbered less than a dozen. They looked frightened and dejected. Being bested by a pair of female former captives probably did not add to their present dispositions.

The U-boat captain was not eager to identify himself. Predictably, he gave his name as Schmidt. No one believed him.

Doc Savage strode up and scrutinized the officer's square features briefly, and commented. "*Kapitan* Carl Brock, if I am not mistaken. You are very far from your home base in Lorient."

The sea captain's square face grew very long in the cheeks.

By this time, the surviving Coast Guard cutter had come alongside, and a picked boarding party were descending into the subseas boat to check for any stragglers.

They soon emerged topside to report that there were none.

The prisoners were taken aboard the cutter at gunpoint. There was an argument over whether they should be placed aboard the Naval destroyer, but since the cutter had reached the scene first, its skipper asserted the privilege of taking the prisoners into Coast Guard custody.

The crewmen were pretty rough in their treatment of the prisoners, seemed to find it necessary to use the hard buttstocks of their rifles to prod them along. By this time, the torpedoed cutter had sunk, but all hands had been plucked from the water. This was small consolation to the wounded pride of the Coast Guard.

Once everyone was safely aboard the cutter, the strange submersible was sent to the bottom by a thorough sieving of steel-jacketed lead. The rescued Guardsmen were permitted this honor. They riddled the vessel's blue hull so completely that, if ever raised from the deep, the mystery U-boat could never again be made seaworthy.

The captured crew was made to watch. The significance of this action was not lost on them. The incident was not going to make the newspapers, and they were unlikely to see their homeland again.

That operation concluded, Doc Savage and the Coast Guard commander held a conference.

"This is not over yet," stated Doc Savage firmly.

The Captain nodded tensely. "I imagine they have a base close by."

Doc directed the skipper's attention to the nearby volcanic cone. "My men were stranded on that small island yonder, along with the apparent ringleader of this plot, an individual calling himself Count Runo von Elmz."

The skipper grinned tightly. "Then let's go mop them up. I think my men would enjoy the exercise."

As the cutter got underway, Pat Savage and Hornetta Hale joined Doc Savage, who was keeping an eye on the prisoners. They had been made to kneel on the afterdeck, their hands clapped over their heads. They looked miserable. Or, as Pat Savage wryly put it, "green around the gills."

"What's going on now?" Pat demanded.

"We are going to bring this matter to a satisfactory conclusion," advised Doc.

Pat put her hands on her hips, cocked her head to one side and asked, "Just exactly what is this all about? I still don't have it straight in my head."

"Miss Hale did not inform you?"

Pat grinned crookedly, and dabbed at her bloody lip.

"We were too busy clobbering these goose-steppers."

Before Doc Savage could say anything, Hornetta Hale barged into the conversation, demanding, "Where is my wayward big sister?"

"At last report, safe on that island," Doc told her.

Hornetta made apoplectic faces at Doc Savage, and asked, "What do you mean—at last report?"

Doc replied, "We are investigating the situation on the island. There may be more trouble ahead."

Pat's grin got wider. She pulled a brace of superfirers from her belt. "Wonderful! My blood is up. Just lead the way."

"You have done your share," Doc Savage said firmly, relieving her of the weapons. "We will discuss this later."

Pat went in search of a Coast Guardsman susceptible to feminine charms. She swiftly found a suitable specimen and talked him out of his Garand rifle. It was nimble tongue-work, to be sure.

As they were approaching the volcanic island, the crooked-winged warplane that had earlier disappeared came droning back.

The gray aircraft overflew the island, then the flotilla, and apparently spotted the blue submarine wallowing on the ocean bottom, for it circled the weird U-boat's location twice. The crystal clarity of the Caribbean permitted it to be seen from a height.

The pilot, evidently recognizing that the jig was up, swiftly turned tail. He did not get far.

On the destroyer, an order was given and antiaircraft guns were brought to bear. They commenced firing, multiple barrels working mechanically. Quite a rolling racket resulted.

A punishing barrage began painting noisy black clouds in the blue sky all around the fleeing warplane. The pilot banked, sought higher altitude, then rolled in the opposite direction. He was quite an acrobat. But it did him no good.

The bursting Archie shells tore the gray aircraft apart in midair.

The place where the warplane had last been seen became indistinguishable from the Archie detonations. Then pieces of the aircraft began falling out of the sky. They watched, waiting for any sign of a parachute. There was none.

Doc Savage informed the cutter commander, "The airstrip for that warplane must be on another island in the vicinity."

The Captain nodded. "I will radio the destroyer. No doubt an official request of the British government will lead to a vigorous search for that spot, and appropriate punishment meted out."

The cutter circled around the island without drawing fire, and dropped anchor at a spot not far from the *Stormalong*, which rocked in the sand-lapping waves rolling in.

DOC SAVAGE was the first one off the cutter. He simply leapt into the water and began swimming. He lost no time getting to the white sandy beach.

The bronze man arrived in time to discover Ham Brooks and Count Runo von Elmz engaged in an unusual duel just up from the immaculate beach where the great ground-traveling roots of the charred and blackened Philodendron groped in every direction like questing tentacles.

The Count evidently shrugged off the effects of the brief whiff of gas that had overcome him. He was, as always, immaculately dressed, his clothes as dry as if they had come off the washing line.

Ham was contending with his debonair foeman in a manner that defied all the proper rules of sword fencing. He was using the barrel of his cane, instead of the blade, which remained sheathed.

The Count was beating back with his own cane, so it was a combat of brute force, not blade wizardry.

The Count was somewhat taller, which seemed to give him a slight advantage. Aristocratic features fierce, he was banging down hard, again and again, attempting to break through Ham's defenses as if wielding a Viking war hammer, not a stout walking stick.

Ham Brooks gave back as good as he received. The two stout barrels clashed and clattered against one another, flashing in the sun, as the two men pounded at each other relentlessly, neither one able to land a blow on his resolute foe.

Seeing that he was getting nowhere, and exertion causing him to tire, the Count decided to change the rules in mid-combat. He depressed the stud that caused the small needle of a blade to spring forth from the cane's tip.

Charging, he attempted to impale Ham Brooks in the center of his chest, with the clear intention of transfixing the heart.

Enraged by this flouting of gentlemanly rules, Ham Brooks swiftly sidestepped. With a flashing series of moves, he suddenly came up behind the Count and laid the barrel of his cane against the back of the man's close-cropped head.

The Count's Tyrolean hat went flying in one direction while the hat's owner stumbled forward and smashed his face into the sand. He did not rise again.

Planting the tip of his stick upon his defeated opponent's unmoving back, Ham Brooks turned to offer Doc Savage a thin smile of triumph.

"Where are the others?" asked Doc.

"Monk and Long Tom are off chasing mermen," Ham said casually, directing the tip of his cane toward the brush-furred crater.

Sounds of fists colliding with substantial portions of human anatomy came rolling down from the volcanic cone. One of

Monk Mayfair's tremendous war whoops could be heard.

Before very long, there was complete silence.

Monk Mayfair came down dragging two mermen by their finny feet, one in each hand. He was grinning to beat the band.

"Hiyah, Doc! I went fishin' and look what I caught! This is the last of 'em."

Lugging another, Long Tom added, "We caught them trying to sneak down on us. But it looks like somebody got to them first. They were in pretty rough shape. Not much starch left in any of them for a good brawl." He sounded disappointed.

Doc replied dryly, "We had an encounter earlier."

Long Tom deposited his defeated merman beside the one that Doc had earlier overcome. That first man was still unconscious. There was no fight left in the other two.

Doc Savage looked around, remarked, "Evidently, the gas which creates hallucinations remains effective for only a short period of time."

Long Tom muttered sheepishly, "I found myself up in a tree when it wore off. Literally. It was very embarrassing."

"No doubt it is extracted from this island, as was the laughing vapor," continued Doc. "Some of it must be seeping out of fumaroles in small quantities, odors masked by the smoky air, which would explain why Monk thought he encountered that eight foot tall Satanic King Neptune and Long Tom believed he saw a mermaid with Hornetta Hale's features."

"If that was a figment of my imagination," Long Tom pondered, "how is it Honoria Hale later turned up with green hair?"

"As you were informed before I departed on my mission," replied Doc, "that was my first clue that we were being eavesdropped upon. The Count and his men were inspired by Long Tom's mermaid hallucination to cut and dye Honoria's hair green, hoping to pass her off as her twin, Hornetta, in order to determine once and for all how much—or how little—we knew of the plot."

Monk grinned. "My jaw almost dropped when you switched

to the Mayan lingo and clued us in." His beetling brow wrinkled. "Did you figure out how that tricky Count slipped on and off our boat without getting wet?"

Doc nodded. "No doubt he passed from the silent U-boat to our diving well wearing a free-diving suit, which he shucked after breaching the cruiser's hull. In his hasty escape, it was a simple matter of taking the suit with him, so as to leave no trace."

"It was unlucky for us that Pat failed to seal the hatch that first time she looked it over," Monk allowed, picking up Habeas Corpus and giving the porker a vigorous scratching.

Ham Brooks inserted waspishly, "It was fortunate for that infernal hog that he shook off the effects of the equally infernal gas. Otherwise I would have been forced to trim strips off his miserable hide to make breakfast bacon. I am utterly famished."

To which Monk growled, "If that ever happened, I would grab hold of your ears, jump on your shoulders, do a somersault, and pull your head off like it was your hat."

There ensued another argument, but Doc Savage had no interest in that. He went searching for Honoria Hale.

A contingent of Coast Guardsmen had waded ashore about this time. The importance of their mission was underlined by the fact that they were being led by no less than the cutter commander.

Doc Savage told him, "Matters appear to be well in hand. All but one of the plotters has been apprehended."

Doc led the Captain over to the peculiar pile of helpless foreign seamen.

The officer studied the half human, half piscatorial profusion, noted their brush haircuts, and took off his cap in order to scratch his head.

"Don't that beat all..." he muttered.

"Free-diving suits," explained Doc Savage. "When donned and secured tightly, they formed a sealed envelope, which contained sufficient air to permit ten to fifteen minutes of underwater swimming before the individual needed to surface for oxygen. Sewn into the webbed fingertips are jaguar claws—very deadly in a fight."

The Captain nodded. "That, and the mystery submarine, go a long ways toward explaining some of the strange reports floating about the Caribbean these last few days."

"The passengers who disappeared off the two liners were spirited off into that waiting U-boat," Doc explained. "Its silent method of operation and camouflaged hull prevented the sub from being detected. All in all, a very elaborate ruse designed to confuse observers, and throw maritime authorities off the track of the true plot."

Ham Brooks was hovering nearby and put forth a question, "Exactly what was their plot? I fail to fathom any of this."

Doc Savage gestured out into the open ocean, toward the handsome yacht that had dropped anchor well away from the isle. They could read the name on the stern. It said:

WISTERIA
MIAMI, FLORIDA

"All of these efforts were aimed at sinking the Presidential yacht with all hands aboard," explained Doc.

"Presidential!" bleated Ham, aghast.

"Blazes!" yelled Monk. "Do you mean the President of the United States is on that hooker over there!"

The cutter commander answered, "This is a state secret, of course. You all know that the President recently gave a speech about dealing harshly with foreign submarine raiders that have been sinking commercial and relief shipping in the Atlantic. Well, he decided he wanted a first-hand look at the Caribbean, where some of these raiders were rumored to be based in secret. That name you see is not the real name of the President's yacht. It was painted over to disguise it—although that did not seem to fool Doc Savage, who recognized it from a distance."

"Sort of a secret fact-findin' mission!" muttered Monk.

"Exactly," said the Captain.

HAM BROOKS twirled his dented and dinged sword cane jauntily and pointed the tip toward Count Runo von Elmz, who was being lugged to a waiting dory like a sack of spoiled potatoes.

"What was the motive for his heinous murder scheme?"

The cutter skipper answered that. "Some of the U-boat crew are already spilling. Seems all the official talk of sinking raiders in the Atlantic has got the head mustache over there worried that America would step in and settle the war. His theory was that if the President were to die, the new chief executive might think differently. Or think twice, unless he wanted to be the next target for assassination."

Ham frowned. "I rather doubt that mad scheme would have worked out the way the Count planned for it to," he drawled.

"An assassination started the last World War, you'll remember," agreed the Captain. "This old planet of ours is a ball of powder right now. And there are a lot of spots where an assassination would be the spark to touch it off. Consequences would be stupendous. A lot is hanging in the balance for America."

At that point, two Coast Guardsmen returned, escorting Honoria Hale. They found her hiding in the mangroves.

The former blonde looked crestfallen, and when Doc Savage asked, "What have you to say for yourself?" she hung her head in shame. She was already in irons.

"Who is this?" demanded the Coast Guard Captain, noticing Honoria's seaweed-hued hair.

"Honoria Hale," said Doc. "The key to the entire plot. She evidently fell in love with one of the plotters. This man used her to obtain confidential information about the President's secret trip, enabling the Count and his men to lay this diabolical trap."

"Is this true?" questioned the skipper.

Honoria Hale, her pale lips trembling, mustered up enough strength to say, "I-I had friends in Washington society. I was in love. He-he got me to draw them out. We learned about the—"

That was all she could manage before words failed her.

The officer regarded her coldly, and said, "Well, you're a traitor to your country, now, and liable to be hung for the offense of high treason."

The effect of this cold declaration on Honoria Hale was stark. Rigidity seemed to wrench all through her.

Seeing this display, the Captain relented slightly. "Inasmuch as you're a woman, and only an accomplice, they will probably give you life imprisonment instead."

"I guess it was all for naught," mused Ham. "Now that she and the Count are prisoners, they can never see one another again."

Hornetta Hale said thinly, "It's worse than that. She wasn't in love with that old warhorse."

Long Tom blinked. "No?"

"It was that guy who was chasing me, Pippel. He called himself Lancelot Lacy. He was the one who marooned me on the little cay in the first place—the skunk. He couldn't bump me off, otherwise my sister might get wise, and then spill the beans. So he stuck me on that island, hoping I'd die of exposure and the papers would write me off as going the way of Amelia Earhart. Only I was too tough for them mugs."

Doc asked, "You knew of the plot all along?"

Hornetta nodded. "Most of it. I needed some money for a venture and against my better judgment, I went to Honoria for some dough. She tried to give me the business, but I could tell sis was worried about something. I got her to cough up, and the next thing I knew I was snatched and stranded by Pippel's Bundist Brown Shirts."

"Which one was Pippel?" asked Ham.

"The one the Count had to blast when he was wounded so bad he couldn't leave Long Island," explained Hornetta. "That cold-blooded blueblood executed him with Honoria right in the next room. He was sore that Pippel had boasted of the plot to Honoria, which is why Pippel was so hot to stop me from reaching Doc Savage in the first place. He knew the penalty if the plan did not come off because of his big mouth. In the end, the louse paid it, anyway."

At that grim reminder, the green-haired girl sank to her knees and buried her face in the immaculate sand. Her shoulders shook convulsively. Strangely, she made no audible sound.

Long Tom tugged at an oversized ear. "What I don't get is why they didn't kill either one of you when they had the chance."

"They were going to," Hornetta said tightly. "Don't doubt that for a minute. But the Count knew if he did away with me, Honoria would go running to the authorities. That's why they marooned me in the first place. When the papers broke the story of my rescue, Honoria put two and two together and took a train to New York to find me before the Count did. But they had a spy shadowing sis and he caught up with her before she reached Doc Savage. Later, after Pippel was plugged, they tried the same gag in reverse in the hope I wouldn't go running to the G-Men. Only this time, their scheme was to pack her off to Brazil. Honoria gave me all this dope when we all ended up in that U-boat together."

Ham frowned. "Why didn't they do away with you both then?"

Pat Savage answered that one. "If their assassination plan had come off the way they figured it, they were going to shove all three of us out the torpedo tubes so that our bodies would be found with the ones who perished in the explosion. They thought it would add a touch of mystery to the grisly proceedings. Incidentally," she added, "remember that ugly merman we all saw leaping out of the water that first night? That was one of the Count's U-Men. They shot him out of a torpedo tube just to impress us, recovering him later. Those reinforced rubber suits are plenty tough."

Her clear golden eyes went to Doc Savage.

"When did you finally figure out that the mermen were not real, cousin?"

"From the beginning," admitted Doc.

"Oh, tell the truth, you know-it-all!"

Doc Savage replied calmly, "It was obvious from the first that the purported merman was not a genuine living creature."

Pat cocked a skeptical eyebrow as the bronze man continued.

"The aquatic apparition displayed the tail of a bony fish, but the cartilage back-fin of a shark. The two are not found together in nature. It is evolutionarily impossible. Therefore, the merman could not be real."

Pat made a flustered face, bit her tongue, and stalked off.

NO ONE had much to say as Honoria Hale was hauled off to a launch and brought back to the surviving cutter to join her co-conspirators.

Hornetta Hale watched her twin depart with white-knuckled fists and a strange pallor creeping over her sunburned features.

"We didn't like each other much," she said hoarsely, "but we were still kin. That makes it kinda tough to take."

That was all the comment she offered.

Doc Savage was explaining to the skipper, "This island is honeycombed with pockets of volcanic gas. Some of them, when disturbed, can cause a man to fall down in fits of laughter and go unconscious for periods up to a day. Other pockets, if disturbed, will produce vivid and apparently surreal hallucinations."

The Captain felt of his smooth jaw. "Sounds like the Navy boys could use this spot for gunnery practice. I'll set that in motion."

"Good idea," said Doc.

They set about evacuating the island, and getting the cruiser *Stormalong* seaworthy once more.

Pat Savage and Hornetta Hale were transferred over to the cruiser as Doc prepared to clear the island. Cans of fuel were conveyed from the cutter to the cruiser, and the *Stormalong's* fuel tanks were replenished. A working radio receiver and transmitter came with them, courtesy of the grateful United States Coast Guard.

It was not long before a message came over the set. Long Tom took it, and called up to Doc Savage, "They want you on the yacht. Pronto."

The bronze man was ferried over to the presidential yacht in a small launch, and spent over an hour in conference with the President of the United States.

WHEN Doc returned, the others gathered around him, asking excited questions.

Pat cut through all of them. "How exciting! What did you two talk about?"

"The future defense of the nation," returned Doc Savage quietly. "With Europe sinking deeper into war, it may be only a matter of time before we are drawn into the conflict."

After that sobering statement, all queries died. It was also manifestly clear that Doc Savage was not going to reveal any more of his private conversation with the chief executive.

The cutter and the *Stormalong* soon cleared the island, sailing northwestward toward the United States.

The sun was setting in riotous Caribbean splendor when a series of detonations commenced erupting to the stern.

Turning, they watched as the forlorn little island began to come to pieces under the destroyer's pounding deck guns. Palms shook their crowns like angry fists before toppling. The caldera was blasted apart, and before long the pool it had contained came rushing out to mix with the sea. Quite a quantity of marine life—from groupers and starfish—came with it. Many floated to the surface, unmoving, eyes staring up at the blue sky in stunned surprise.

"That," said Monk, "is the end of that blasted wart on the Caribbean."

Ham pondered, "Too bad we could not get a better look into that old ruin. Who knows what wonders it might have contained."

This caused Long Tom to ask, "What about those swastikas carved on the temple entrance?"

"Coincidence," explained Doc. "Such signs are found the world over. Aside from that, the crosses we saw cut in stone displayed arms twisting in the opposite direction as a modern swastika. It was not the same thing at all."

All seemed over. Then Hornetta Hale, who had been uncharacteristically silent after her sister was taken away in irons, marched up to Doc Savage and said, "Hold up, golden boy! I wanna talk about your attitude!"

"Attitude!"

Hornetta planted scuffed fists on her curvaceous hips as she pointed her thin nose at the big bronze man. "I tried to hire you to go to town on these rascals, and you refused."

"Which is my right. I do not work for hire."

"Cast your mind back over the last few days, high pockets," Hornetta blazed. "If you had gone along with me, we could have nipped this thing in the bud, before the Presidential yacht was almost torpedoed."

Doc began to object, then Pat Savage interjected, "Hornetta has a point. If you had listened to her, we could have cleaned up on these assassins before it ever got to this point."

A rare ire showed in the bronze man's tone as he replied, "Miss Hale refused to divulge any details. It was impossible to know that anything serious was underfoot, or to determine if her shenanigans were merely some madcap scheme for notoriety."

"Doc's right," added Ham reasonably. "This woman is notorious for seeking publicity for herself."

"Yeah," added Monk. "She's a headline hound."

"No, you rusty gorilla," countered Hornetta. "I'm an adventuress! And I'm just getting started on my career."

Doc advised, "It would be very wise of you to put such thoughts behind you. Adventuring is a highly perilous occupation."

"Well, try and stop me," snapped Hornetta.

"Yes, try and stop us!" added Pat Savage.

Doc Savage stared. "Us!"

"You heard me!" retorted Pat. "Down in that submarine, Hornetta and I discovered we make an unbeatable team. So we buried the hatchet. When we get back to New York, we're hanging out a shingle. Savage & Hale, Troublebusters for Hire. We'll clean up."

"You will not," snapped Doc.

"What's to stop us!" demanded Hornetta. "After this triumph, we'll probably end up in the history books."

Doc Savage seemed at a loss for words. Finally, he said, "Normally, common sense would stop you. Between the two of you, there seems to be a shortage of that commodity."

"Hah!" crowed Pat. "Common sense and what army?"

Studying the two excited amazons, the bronze man decided that probably no army on the face of the earth could dissuade the troublesome team of Patricia Savage and Hornetta Hale from doing exactly what they set their minds to do.

Doc left it to Ham Brooks to break the bad news.

"I am afraid that nothing of what transpired this day will be allowed to reach the newspapers," he told them. "Washington will hush it up."

"Well, they can't hush *us* up," flared Hornetta.

"That's right," snapped Pat. "Savage & Hale are unhushable."

"Make that Hale & Savage," corrected Hornetta.

Ham pointed out the undeniable fact that the United States of America was not presently at war. That if word of this attempted assassination of the President got out, a declaration of war would inevitably follow. They had a solemn duty to their country to keep their own counsel on the matter.

"There are no two ways about it," he concluded firmly. "Why, they would probably clap you both in jail if you so much as whispered the truth of this atrocious international incident."

After this sad state of affairs had sunk in, Pat said defensively, "We don't need publicity. Our names and reputations will make us rich. Why, we'll have so much profitable trouble tramping up to our doorstep, you lads will start begging us for the leftovers!"

"May I make a suggestion?" Doc Savage requested.

"Go ahead," Pat and Hornetta said in unison.

"In the future, leave us out of it," said Doc dryly. "It sounds like more excitement than we normally prefer to handle."

With that, the bronze man walked off to permit the two women to argue over whether the new enterprise should be called Savage & Hale, or Hale & Savage.

"I was off adventuring before you opened up that swanky beauty salon, you glorified shampoo slinger," Hornetta sneered at Pat.

"I like that!" Pat hurled back. "For your information, you bleached blonde lobster, I come from a long line of famous adventurers."

"Coming from ain't the same as practicing. But don't fret, toots. I'll take you under my wing and teach you all the ropes. Stick with me and you'll see trouble the likes of which you heretofore have only dreamed. That is, if you're tough enough to take it."

Pat Savage's mouth fell open. She struggled for a choice phrase with which to verbally skewer the brassy blonde. Nothing immediately came to mind, and Pat felt a growing temptation to sock her new partner in the jaw just for the sheer satisfaction of knocking Hornetta Hale into the drink again.

Monk turned to Ham and spoke out of the corner of his mouth. "This could work out, at that. They're startin' to sound like you and me on a good day."

"You mean a bad day," corrected Ham, giving his cane a snappy spin that sent a fully recovered Habeas Corpus scampering for the safety of the lazaret.

About the Author
LESTER DENT

LESTER DENT SPENT most of his youth in the arid wastes of Wyoming, which was once the bottom of an unknown ocean and whose soil is littered with fossilized prehistoric sea life. Despite having been raised on a ranch, he was more interested in pirates than cowboys. Reading pulp magazines he discovered in the bunkhouse, Lester became fascinated with adventure in distant lands, especially having to do with the seven seas.

When he began writing, Dent's first published story, *Pirate Cay,* was set in the Caribbean. "It was about the sea although I had never seen an ocean," he later admitted.

In March of 1933, less than three months into his Doc Savage writing career, Lester and his wife, Norma, booked passage on the *Mauritania,* which sailed from New York to the West Indies. The cruise ship stopped in Trinidad, Venezuela, the Lesser Antilles, Panama, and Havana, Cuba, Seeing first-hand the haunts of the old Caribbean pirates, Lester vowed to one day return in a boat of his own and hunt for sunken treasure.

Dent purchased the forty-foot auxiliary schooner, *Albatross,* in May, 1934, and spent the rest of the year learning to sail, traveling from City Island, New York to Nova Scotia. But his ultimate goal was to take the *Albatross* to the Caribbean Sea. During the Winter of 1934-35 and again in 1936, Lester lived on the boat, plying the Caribbean, headquartering at the City Yacht Basin in Miami, Florida.

A colleague once described him vividly as he was in those days. "He was like a corsair come to life. He was tall and he was brawny. And he was industrious. He knew mining and navigation." Dent searched for treasure with a diving helmet and magnetic metal detector and crewed several yacht races.

Lester's days living on the *Albatross* lasted only three years. And although he never found any sunken treasure, it was a memorable period in his amazing life.

A few years after he sold the *Albatross*, the ship went aground on a reef off the coast of Haiti and was sunk. The schooner lived on in Lester Dent's fiction, however, from Doc Savage to his famous Oscar Sail stories written for *Black Mask*.

About the Author
WILL MURRAY

DESPITE HAVING GROWN up in two different Massachusetts coastal cities, Will Murray is not much of a sailor. In his youth, he loafed on assorted sail craft and powerboats off the Massachusetts coast and in the Chesapeake Bay. Back in the 1970s, he had an opportunity to crew aboard a sloop sailing to Great Abaco Island in the Bahamas. But he foolishly declined it. Or perhaps not so foolishly, since he's a confirmed landlubber.

But you can't make a career out of writing under the name of Kenneth Robeson without penning your fair share of sea stories. Most of Murray's have, fortunately for him, been posthumous collaborations with expert sailorman Lester Dent, so he had a little bit of help along the way.

He's never been to the Caribbean, but Murray has explored assorted islands off the Florida Gulf Coast, from which experiences he drew some of the descriptions recorded in this novel.

From *The Frightened Fish* to the well-received *Skull Island*, Murray has sent the Man of Bronze around the globe by sea in everything from a submarine to a Chinese junk. *Phantom Lagoon* is only the latest such seafaring venture. He's already planning another, *The Secret of Skeleton Reef.* No doubt more lie beyond the dancing blue horizon….

About the Artist
JOE DeVITO

JOE DeVITO'S COVER for *Phantom Lagoon* has its origins in a lifelong love of fantasy, science fiction, and dinosaurs. As far back as he could remember, Joe has been drawing and sculpting along the lines of both the natural and imaginative worlds.

Born on March 16, 1957 in New York City, DeVito formally pursued his art interests in college, graduating with honors from Parsons School of Design in 1981. He went on to the Art Students League in New York City. With famed anatomist John Zahourek, he continued his anatomical studies, concentrating on biped and quadruped comparative anatomy.

DeVito quickly tapped into some of his favorite subject matter professionally, and has been working with Pop Culture and pulp icons for decades. Over the years he's painted or sculpted a pretty good cross-section of the best of them. These include King Kong, Tarzan, Doc Savage, Superman, Batman, Wonder Woman, Spider-man, and even *MAD* magazine's Alfred E. Neuman. He has illustrated hundreds of book and magazine covers, painted several notable posters and numerous trading cards for the major comic book and gaming houses, and created concept and character design for the film and television industries. His Spectrum poster painting has become the revered international art annual's logo, which led to DeVito being asked to sculpt their annual awards trophy.

Recently Joe sculpted the official 100th Anniversary statue

287

of *Tarzan of the Apes* for the Edgar Rice Burroughs Estate. Previously he had sculpted King Kong for the Merian C. Cooper Estate, Superman, Wonder Woman and Batman for Chronicle Books' Masterpiece Editions, and several other notable Pop and pulp characters. Additional sculpting work ranges from scientifically accurate dinosaurs, a multitude of collectibles for the Bradford Exchange in a variety of genres, to larger-than-life statues.

Joe is also the co-author (with Brad Strickland) of two novels, which he illustrated as well: *KONG: King of Skull Island* (DH Press) was published in 2004, and *Merian C. Cooper's KING KONG* (St. Martin's Griffin), in 2005. 2012 saw the release of Kindle and iBook versions of *KONG: King of Skull Island* that were accompanied by Part 1 of a cutting-edge app version of the book, with the second and final part just completed and due out by the end of 2013. With the property in full development by Festa Entertainment, a *KONG: King of Skull Island* YA series and much, much more are all in the works. Joe is also finishing the screenplay and developing imagery for his newest creation, a faction world of truly epic proportions tentatively titled *The Primordials.*

DeVito has been painting covers for Will Murray's *The Wild Adventures of Doc Savage* since the series' inception. 2013—the 80th anniversary of Doc—has been a banner year, seeing not one but *two* full wraparound covers of monumental scale for the wildly popular Savage books. The cover for *Doc Savage: Skull Island,* the first ever authorized cross-over novel of these two iconic characters, was a classic montage painting that conveyed the Savage/Kong world as only such a composition could. The second wraparound cover painting was for *The Miracle Menace,* effectively an 80th Anniversary Doc Savage image, *Wild Adventures* style. It depicts for the first time Doc's dirigible, his tri-motor aircraft, the Hidalgo Trading Company warehouse and more, all backdropping Doc, Ham and Monk in a dramatically lit composition, complete with cameo appearances for Renny, Long Tom, Johnny and even Habeas Corpus.

Wrapping up the year is *Phantom Lagoon*, reintroducing Pat Savage to the series and even more cool Doc gadgetry. And, of course, a quintessentially aquatic monster (one of DeVito's favorite subjects) that quite literally rounds out the composition. Composed with a green palette, *Phantom Lagoon* is a stark contrast to any Doc Savage cover Joe has yet painted.

www.jdevito.com
www.kongskullisland.com
FB: Joe DeVito-DeVito Artworks

About the Patron
TERRY ALLEN

THE FIRST TIME I saw Doc Savage, he was falling to his apparent death at the hands of a werewolf on the cover to Marvel Comics' *Doc Savage* #8. It was 1973, and my parents (both full-time teachers) had opened up a comic book/used bookstore just after Thanksgiving. It was the beginning of a now 40-year love affair with the Man of Bronze.

I collected all of the Bantam Books paperbacks and then branched out into getting the original pulps. Next, I got foreign editions of all types before buying original comic book and paperback cover art.

In 1990, I discovered an ad for Howard Wright's *Bronze Gazette*. I was very fortunate to discover that we lived only a couple miles apart in Modesto, California. My friendship with Howard would lead to my first opportunity to create a new Doc Savage collectible by producing a bookplate edition of Doc's 60th Anniversary novel, *Flight into Fear*. This bookplate was signed by Joe DeVito and Will Murray and was sold exclusively through the *Gazette*. In 1993, I purchased my first DeVito art of the stunning cover painting to *The Jade Ogre*. In 1996, when my wife and I found out we were expecting our fourth child, I commissioned Joe to do a painting for our birth announcement for Christian Lochlan Savage Allen. The announcement was a replica of a Bantam paperback, 24 pages long with pictures and bios of our entire family, and on the front was Joe's gorgeous rendition of Stork Savage, the Bird of Bronze.

A major turning point in my relationship with Doc came in the summer of 2007 when I was offered a chance to commission a painting by Bob Larkin. I had known Bob's agent Spencer Beck for a number of years. After setting up the initial deal, I communicated directly with Bob on the details of the painting. Bob and I tossed around a few ideas, and then I came up with one of the best ideas I've ever had: doing a painting of Doc and his cousin Pat using my wife, Dawn, as a model for Pat. It was something I was hugely proud of and the illustration was later featured on *The Adventures of Doc Savage* CD collection by Radio Archives.

As fate would have it, Bob and I hit it off on a personal level. Just a few months after Bob completed my commission, his wife Fran, who had already fought a battle against breast cancer, was diagnosed with multiple brain tumors. Determined to help the Larkins, I formed my own business called Fantom Press. Along with Keith "Kez" Wilson, we have been proudly producing collectibles (including many Doc Savage items) exclusively for the benefit of the Larkin family. Fran Larkin lost her battle with cancer on April 21, 2013, but our commitment to Bob remains as he looks forward to restarting his illustration career that he had put on hold while caring for his wife.

The stars aligned once again when I got an email from Joe a few months ago to ask if I was interested in being a patron for a new Doc Savage cover. My youngest daughter, Lily, had asked several times when was she going to be included in a painting, so when Joe reached out to me, the wheels were ready to go into motion. After some discussions with Joe and Will, it turned out that Pat Savage was going to be in *Phantom Lagoon* and could be introduced into their cover concept. The three of us worked out the cover details, reference photos of Lily were supplied, and you see the fantastic results on the front of the book you're holding.

I do believe that I'm one of the luckiest guys around. Who else can claim that they have two generations of the women in their lives that have been the models for the immortal Pat Savage?

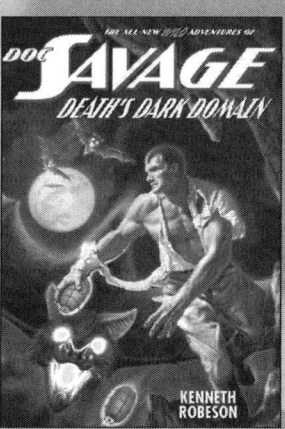

LIMITED EDITION FINE ART PRINTS!

WWW.JDEVITO.COM

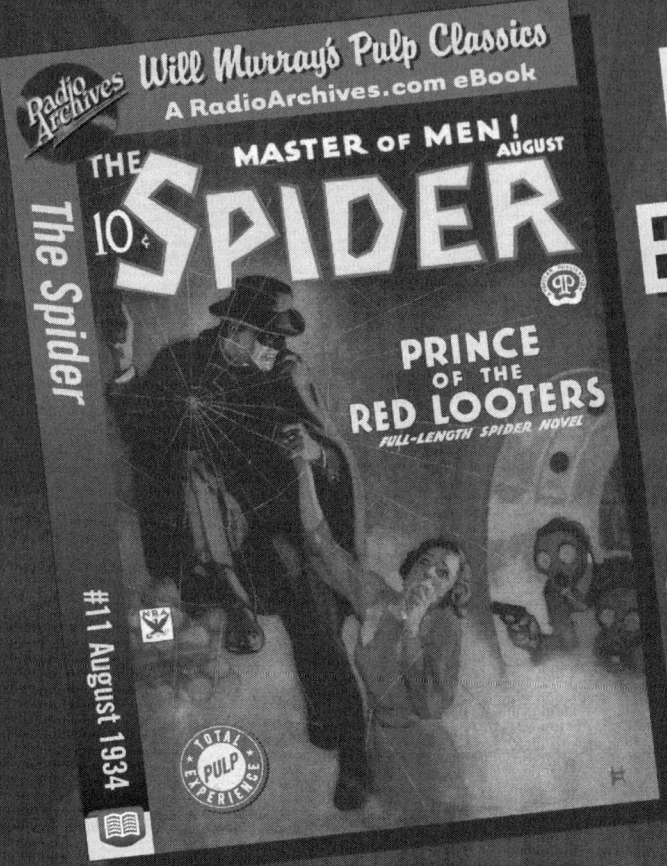

KONG KING OF SKULL ISLAND

A **book app** of gargantuan proportions based on the original illustrated novel by **Joe DeVito** and **Brad Strickland**.

Available now for the iPad through the Apple App store and at www.copyright1957.com

Droid version available soon!

This digital version of the "authorized" sequel takes you back to Skull Island for a dramatic telling of Kong's origins and the civilization that built the wall.

Based on DeVito's 2004 illustrated print edition, abridged text scrolls manually over close-up views of the fantastic paintings and sketches from the original book.

Together, with two latter-day explorers you find the island and view ancient murals and statues, then learn from an old storyteller the tale of island lovers, Kong's parents, and a titanic battle with Gaw, a giant reptile, for island supremacy

A separate gallery of the illustrations and commentary from the original book are also included.

©1957 *It's a pulp-tastic production you'll never forget!*

Customer Reviews:

"Best app I have downloaded yet! Incredible visuals and great story!"

"This is beyond awesome! I probably feel like those who saw the movie for the first time!"

"... this is something I've never seen before ... a completely new way to experience a novel!"

Printed in Great Britain
by Amazon